Praise for *The One-Way Bridge*

"Here's great news for readers: Cathie Pelletier has driven the pickup back to Mattagash, the New England outpost of her wild and fertile imagination, and she's invited us to ride shotgun. Cathie Pelletier is one of my favorite novelists, and she's at the top of her game with *The One-Way Bridge*."

> —*Wally Lamb, author of* She's Come Undone *and* Wishin' and Hopin'

"An ambitious, fearless novelist."

> —Washington Post

"*The One-Way Bridge* is the novel Cathie Pelletier fans have long awaited."

> —*Richard Russo, author of* Empire Falls

"If you liked *Olive Kitteridge*, you'll love *The One-Way Bridge*. Maine writer Cathie Pelletier is a national treasure, her lovely prose filled with grace and humor."

> —*Lee Smith, author of* The Last Girls

"Pelletier's long-awaited addition to the tragicomic annals of fictional Mattagash, Maine, [*The One-Way Bridge* is] a welcome return for the author."

> —Kirkus

Praise for Cathie Pelletier

"Nobody walks the knife-edge of hilarity and heartbreak more confidently than Cathie Pelletier."

—*Richard Russo*

"Cathie Pelletier generates the sort of excitement that only writers working at the very top of their form can provide."

—*Stephen King*

"Imagine a modern-day Jane Austen with a wildly ribald sense of humor."

—*Howard Frank Mosher*

"One of the funniest authors in the country today…"

—*Florence King*

"Cathie Pelletier is a writer of great craft, with a unique ability to be simultaneously sympathetic and wickedly funny."

—Newsday

"Cathie Pelletier accomplishes what every great novelist should. She creates a place, invites you in, walks you around, talks to you, lets you see and feel and hear it, allows you to get to know the people."

—*Fannie Flagg, author of* Fried Green Tomatoes at the Whistle Stop Café

a year after henry

A NOVEL

CATHIE PELLETIER

sourcebooks
landmark

Published by Sourcebooks Landmark, an imprint of Sourcebooks, Inc.
P.O. Box 4410, Naperville, Illinois 60567-4410
(630) 961-3900
Fax: (630) 961-2168
www.sourcebooks.com

Library of Congress Cataloging-in-Publication data is on file with the publisher.

Printed and bound in the United States of America.
VP 10 9 8 7 6 5 4 3 2 1

To those readers who have been with me
from the beginning, those I picked up along
the way, and those I've yet to meet.

· BIXLEY, MAINE ·

SUMMER, 2003

THE SURVIVORS

JEANIE

Henry had been gone a year now, but Jeanie would never forget the moment he died, how the bed became lighter, his soul floating upward like a white balloon. She felt it, as though someone's hand had pressed down on the mattress, indenting, then releasing it again. A guardian angel, maybe. But Henry didn't believe in such stuff. "I believe in the IRS," he liked to say. "And I believe in staying one foot ahead of the bastards." Jeanie knew now that death was faster than the IRS because Henry Munroe had disappeared from the breakfast table, the supper table, the leather recliner, the bathroom, the workshop in the garage. He had disappeared forever.

But that morning he died, maybe the very second it happened, Jeanie had felt a tremor of movement in their bed, a quick shudder. *Henry's heart!* was her first thought. Henry having a heart attack had been a worry for months, ever since the doctor told him his cholesterol was dangerously high. But Henry had refused to change his diet of fast-food burgers and greasy fries. Jeanie could monitor what he ate at home, but each time he walked out the door Henry was a free man, responsible for his own behavior. And this had been his handicap.

They'd been married for twenty-three years, and *that* was Jeanie's next thought. Twenty-three years. She opened her eyes then and saw the thread of dawn uncurling along the windowsill. Without looking, her own heart fluttering, she reached a hand over and touched the side of Henry's face. It was cool, damp almost, and beneath the skin there was a stiffness, as though boards were there holding up the frame of his body, the shell of his life. A fresh stubble of beard had grown during the night, his body still trying in its primitive way to protect his face from the elements. But his body itself had been the enemy, or at least it had *turned into* the enemy, storing all that cholesterol in its arteries. "Henry?" Jeanie had asked. "You okay?" When he didn't answer, didn't move, didn't even breathe, she had reached for the lamp on her nightstand and snapped it on. Then she picked up the phone and quickly dialed 911. "My husband's had a heart attack," Jeanie told the distant voice who answered the call.

And that's when the truth washed over her, her eyes filling quickly with tears. All the time she gave directions to the house, gave her name and then Henry's, she didn't look at him once, there on his side of the bed, as if he might be sleeping in late as he often did on lazy Sundays. Jeanie thought that if she looked at Henry, especially when she said the words, "I think he's dead," that this would make it true. It would seal his fate. And she didn't want to do that if there was still a chance. They could work miracles these days with all that fancy technology.

That's what she kept reminding herself as she waited for the ambulance, as she listened to the kind voice on the other end of the line telling her, *They'll be there soon, Mrs. Munroe. Stay on the phone with me. Try to be calm now.* They could even bring people back from long, winding tunnels, folks who had clinically died. And Henry was young, not yet forty. Maybe they could still save him.

Jeanie had lain back on the bed, phone still to her ear, and put her head on Henry's stiff arm. This was the way they used to sleep in those first, sexy years of marriage. It occurred to her that this might be the last time she would be able to do so. In those minutes before they took Henry Munroe away, she wanted to get all of him that she could. She wanted to imagine that their lives were just beginning, that those seconds left between them were little lifetimes. She tried to think of what Henry would say about this scene, if he could see it, if he were hovering up at the ceiling somewhere, looking down. Just the notion of it would make him laugh: Jeanie, of all people, being appointed by fate to find her dead husband first. Jeanie, who was afraid of spiders, and the dark, and of any suggestion to stray even slightly from the missionary style of lovemaking in all those years of their marriage.

It would take time, Jeanie knew, that morning she lay next to her dead husband, tears running down the sides of her face and onto Henry's cold arm. It would take time. She had given answers to all the questions she was being asked about her husband, questions that seemed so distant from the man himself—*no pulse, no heartbeat*—questions she answered without checking his cold wrist, without putting her ear to the silent drum of his heart. She knew the answers. And as much as she tried to stay there in the present, she couldn't stop her mind from rushing ahead, from giving her a glimpse into the rest of her life. Yes, it would take time to get used to certain words and phrases: *My husband died last month. Widow. My husband has been dead for five years. Beneficiary.* But that's how it was when they'd gotten married, back in 1980, the same year Ronald Reagan became the fortieth president of the United States, and Jimmy Carter took Rosalyn and went back to Georgia. Jeanie had said the new words and phrases then, learning them easily as the years unfolded: *We've been married just a month. Husband. We're celebrating our fifth anniversary. Wife.* The words and phrases of change. And that's when it occurred to her that *she* would have to break the news to the kids. Lisa now lived down in Portland with her new husband. And Chad, poor Chad, was still only fifteen and worshipping every move Henry made.

Jeanie had wanted to tell the woman on the phone other things about Henry Munroe, that morning he died. "He doesn't have a heartbeat, but he's got a sense of humor that won't quit. His favorite food is spaghetti and meatballs. He stills listens to the Beatles, and he loves the Red Sox almost as much as he used to love me." Those were the things you should know about a person before they leave the earth for good, at least as Jeanie saw it. You should know the important things about them, to prepare them for their journey, the way Egyptians put the items a king loved in his pyramid so that he could still enjoy them. If Henry had been an Egyptian king, he probably would've wanted Evie Cooper in his pyramid.

That way, the two of them could row down the Milky Way for all eternity.

It was only after she had heard the wail of the siren in the distance, imagined the ambulance careening past the shade tree on Elm Street, imagined it cutting the corner on Webb Drive, its red light splashing around and around inside the glass dome, as if someone were shaking a jar full of blood, that Jeanie put the phone back on its cradle. She turned her head so she could look once more at her husband's face. Already his skin had begun to turn a grayish blue, and his eyes seemed to be searching for something on the ceiling. They were open and unmoving, the way he stared at baseball players during the World Series, or hockey players in those last seconds of overtime. It was probably how he stared at Evie Cooper's breasts that first night he saw her at Murphy's Tavern, back when the affair started. Jeanie had found the receipt from the Days Inn, room 9, which Henry had forgotten to destroy. Habit did him in, for Henry always kept his receipts for tax purposes. *I believe in the IRS, and I believe in staying one foot ahead of the bastards.* Jeanie had cried then, too, a full week of pans being banged about in the kitchen sink. But all Henry had said was, "Is it that time of the month already?" And for too many nights to count, she sat in front of the TV for an old movie, falling asleep on the sofa rather than next to Henry in their warm bed. But Henry, being a man, had taken the gesture at face value. "You fall asleep again watching movies?" was all he had said the next morning. That's when Jeanie decided not to tell him what she had found, not yet. She would gather her evidence for divorce court, would do her homework, prepare her case. And for weeks, she had done that. She had stockpiled the receipts, even those from the local IGA for bottles of wine and bouquets of precut flowers. She had smelled the perfume in his shirts, had noted the way he always put on clean underwear just to go to Murphy's and watch baseball with Larry. And then, when she was finally ready to lay the deceit at Henry's feet, she had opened her eyes to what would be the last day of her life with him.

It had been twelve long months, and yet it seemed only yesterday that she heard the ambulance shriek into the driveway, excited voices filling the yard. That was when Jeanie Munroe leaned over and kissed her husband's cold lips for the last time, at least in their marriage bed. She wanted to say important things, the things a person hopes to say in times of crisis, she wanted to say, *Sweetie, go to the light. Go to that bright tunnel. Do you see your grandmother waiting for you? Take her hand, Henry honey, it'll be okay.* But that's not what Jeanie had said to her dead husband. When she heard the medics thumping on the front door, anxious to get inside with their marvelous technology, anxious to bring another stray soul back from a warm tunnel of peace and tranquillity, Jeanie had looked over at Henry's blue face and blue lips, his wide-open baby-blue eyes, and she had whispered, "Why did you do it, Henry?" That was when Jeanie Munroe finally admitted the truth, her stomach muscles cramping with tension, her breasts aching, her heart hurting her more than she had ever imagined. *Henry's dead!* And that's when she knew that what she had felt on the mattress, pushing it down gently so that Henry could fly up, up, and away, was guilt, that barnacle that had attached itself to Henry Munroe the very first time he ever opened the door of a motel room and then stood back so that a woman other than his wife could sashay past him.

But now Henry Munroe was free. Guilt had spring-boarded him into eternity.

LARRY

All night long Larry Munroe lay on the bottom bunk with his eyes open, in his parents' house on Hancock Street, in the same room where he and his brother, Henry, had spent their growing-up years. Their mother had bought the bunk beds at Selman's Hardware, back in the summer of 1967, the Summer of Love. Five-year-old Henry, being the younger boy and used to getting his way, had claimed the top bed that day. Other than some nicks and scars embedded in the wood, the bunks had held up well, considering the Munroe brothers were known to be rough-and-tumble boys. Now Larry lay on his old bunk and listened as wind woven with rain tore at a shingle on the roof.

It was the shingle's welfare that kept him awake, and not the violence of the storm. The shingle and the memory of how Henry had been afraid of storms and lightning. And that's when Larry wondered if Jonathan was safe, in his new home in Portland, with Larry's ex-wife and her boyfriend. He decided it was best not to think of Jonathan. And so, with the tunnel of his left eardrum pointed upward to the ceiling, listening, Larry had taken the side of the shingle. This also helped to keep his mind off his father, Bixley's current postmaster.

And the knowledge that his mother would be beating upon his locked door by eight o'clock, demanding that he open it, his father standing behind her with a doomed look on a face born to a legacy of worry. And Larry had not thought about his dead grandfather, Bixley's *previous* postmaster, a stern man with a sterner upper lip. Or his great-grandfather, Bixley's *first* postmaster, a man Larry knew only from the portrait that still hung in the Bixley Post Office, just above the counter where customers addressed letters, licked stamps, and tried to steal the postal pens from off their rickety chains when no one was looking. Larry Munroe came from a long line of mail carriers, men who saw the enemy in hail shaped like golf balls, in sleet twenty feet wide and laced with ice, in snow that crippled plows and capsized towns, in torrents of rain that swept terrified cows and pigs downstream. These were ancestral men who knew well that their reputation lay in a single, haphazard hurricane. Larry Munroe came from a generational army of mailmen, one that stretched from the turn of the previous century until now, to the turn in Larry Munroe's own life. A *long* line, and yet he would be the first to bring disgrace to the honorable profession.

As the storm intensified, and no matter how hard he tried, Larry couldn't keep his thoughts away from his younger brother, one of Bixley's *former* mailmen. At times, when lightning turned the sky and yard a dazzling white, he thought he saw the mattress above him move, as it did in those childhood days when Henry would wake in the midst of the storm. A small foot would dangle over the edge of the upper bunk until it found the ladder. A leg clad in cotton pajamas would be followed by another leg. And then the boy would appear, Henry, climbing down to walk the perimeter of the bedroom, to comfort himself until the cracks of lightning and the booms of thunder had subsided. Sometimes, he would abandon his pride and ask, "Hey, Larry. Can I sleep with you?"

But there was no more Henry. He was dead, a year now.

It was just before daybreak that the shingle lifted loose, free as a raven, and flew away on the wings of the storm. Only then, with pale streaks of dawn on the horizon, did Larry Munroe roll onto his other side, close his eyes, and try to sleep.

At seven thirty, Larry was already awake, before his mother would begin knocking on his locked door, asking if he was ill, if he had taken a sleeping pill too many, if he had forgotten to wind the clock, if he had forgotten to set the clock, if he had forgotten to plug in the clock, if he had forgotten the damn clock altogether. And then, when she had exhausted her supply of possibilities, she would turn to his father, throwing her hands up before her face as though they were doves, the necks broken, useless white things attached to her arms. She would step aside and let the one with the long, worried face give it a try.

Before the knocking would begin, Larry had reached a hand down and felt about on the floor for his mailbag. There it was, the brown leather pouch lying by his bed like a crumpled deer. He lifted the flap and grabbed several letters at random. He placed them carefully on his chest, stacking them in a neat pile before he selected the first one. An electric bill for Tom Peterson, on Mayflower Avenue. Larry tossed it onto the floor and picked up the next. The Howard F. Honig College of Nebraska was replying to Andy Southby's application for admission. Larry smiled at the notion of any sensible establishment accepting Andy into its midst. This must have been the fiftieth letter of application that Andy had mailed out since February, the first ones being addressed to universities that Larry had actually heard of. By June, Andy had begun petitioning any college he could, including the Nashville Diesel Mechanic School. But even they had denied his presence, for Larry had seen the thin-lettered and prompt reply they had sent back. Besides, if Andy had been accepted, Larry and the rest of the regulars at Murphy's Tavern would have heard all about it. Now it looked as if the revered Howard F. Honig College— whatever the hell *that* was—was rejecting the boy as well. At least the letter felt like a one-pager, and one-pagers were all that was needed to say *Dear Sir, Thank you for your interest, sorry to inform you, fuck off.*

Larry threw Andy's letter onto the floor. He wished the Howard F. Honig College *would* accept the pimply-faced youth, get him the hell out of Bixley. He was driving Larry crazy, sitting on a bar stool at Murphy's nightly and talking about his future education when the rest of the regulars were trying to sip their beers and watch their beloved Red Sox on the tiny television set over the bar. With every home run, every base hit, every well-placed pitch, Larry ached for his little brother. But Henry would never again hear a Boston bat crack to deliver a home run. He would never see a well-hit line drive *whap!* itself into a Red Sox glove to deliver the last out of the game. He would never know that his and Jeanie's only son, Chad, was drinking too much beer and driving Henry's old motorbike so fast around the curved roads of Bixley that it was unlikely the boy would see his eighteenth birthday. Henry would never know that Jeanie was now going to a psychologist, too warped with grief to carry on by herself. Henry would never know, nor would he believe, that Larry had taken up the mail sack for him, that Larry Munroe was now delivering letters all over Bixley in Henry's stead, *Larry*, who was to have been a happily married schoolteacher and father for all his earthly days. *Larry*, who was now a single mailman living again with his parents, while his child lived in another house, in another city. And Henry would never know that Evie—ah, Evie with those magnificent breasts—had decided to let his brother, Larry, know what those breasts felt like in his hands. Henry would never know.

EVIE

Ever since she was a child, Evie Cooper has seen the faces of those who have passed on to the other side. Mostly, she watches them filter by in a steady stream, like the line that inches forward at a movie theater. But every now and then, one of those restless souls will stop and turn to look at Evie. They lean forward, as if they're staring into a mirror at their own reflections. Sometimes, they seem confused, as if their eyes are searching through a trunk for an item they've left behind. These are the special people. These are the faces of the dead that Evie Cooper can study well enough to draw. She makes part of her living expenses from spirit noses, and eyes, and mouths shaped like small bows. Evie Cooper makes dollars and cents from sketching angel hair.

Until she was seven years old, Evie thought *everyone* saw the faces of the dead. It was not until Rosemary Ann that she learned the truth. Rosemary had come to her one afternoon when Evie was sitting in the backseat of her father's car. He was driving and her mother sat in the passenger seat. Spring had just arrived in Temple City, Pennsylvania, and all the streets were lined with budding trees. Kids were wheeling about on bicycles and old men sat stiffly on park benches, talking up their pasts. Rosemary Ann must have loved spring, too, the way the hazelnut bushes cascade out over riverbanks, the nesting birds, the hazy clouds drifting across the sky. That's probably why Rosemary Ann visited Evie in the springtime, in her father's Kaiser Manhattan, with the automatic buttons and the plush green seats. But then, the faces of the dead often come to Evie when she's driving. It's as if speed can take her to them, can enable her to catch up to their vaporous heels. Rosemary Ann came to Evie while she and her parents were driving past the Temple City Movie Theater. The movie was *The Alamo*, starring John Wayne as Davy Crockett, a man who fought to his death in the famous Texan battle. There was a poster in the window of the actor, wearing a coonskin cap and holding a rifle over his shoulder. The movie had won the Academy Award because Davy Crockett had really wanted to live. Maybe Rosemary Ann wanted to live, too. Maybe that's why Evie saw her sitting between her parents in the front seat, acting as if she were their only little girl, as if life were something you could put back on once you take it off. As if life might be an old coat.

What Evie felt then was jealousy rising up in her like

a hot liquid, bubbling to get out. Yes, it was jealousy that rescued Evie Cooper from her ignorance. Jealousy set her free, loosed the artist that was hiding in her soul. She sometimes wondered what she would have become in life had it not been for that afternoon, had it not been spring, with life bursting the seams on Temple City. It was such a beautiful day, with brownish dogs floating above the green grass in the park and vendors selling ice cream and newspapers. The sidewalk shops had spilled out into the streets, with sales on towels and dresses and woven baskets. What would have happened to Evie Cooper if they hadn't driven past the theater on that glorious day? Would Rosemary Ann have bothered to come? "What is that little girl doing here?" Evie had asked. When her mother turned to look, Evie knew instantly this was something important. She could see it in her mother's eyes. Even as a child, Evie relied heavily upon the human eye and what it speaks. *What little girl? What little girl? What little girl?* the eyes were asking. "There's a little girl sitting between you and Daddy," Evie said. "Right there." And that's when Rosemary Ann had turned around and looked at Evie. *On the contrary, what are you doing here?* That's what Rosemary Ann's eyes wanted to know. "Make her go away," Evie said. "I don't want her to sit there."

Evie's mother said nothing for a time, but as the Kaiser turned the street at Crescent Drugstore, she leaned across the girl she couldn't see and grabbed the steering wheel. "For Christ's sake, Helen," Evie's father said. "Do you want to kill us all?" Angry, he pulled the Kaiser up to the curb in front of the drugstore. "This isn't going to start again, is it?" But Evie's mother wasn't listening. Instead, she fumbled for her purse and then opened the door. "You can't go in," Evie said. Rosemary Ann had seemed about to follow, one small leg already out of the car. "I don't want you with my mummy." That was when Evie's father swung around in his seat, his eyes glaring like black ice. "Stop it!" he said. "You don't even realize what you're doing." Rosemary Ann, her long brown ringlets trickling down her back, had mimicked him. *You don't even realize what you're doing.* "Shut up!" Evie shouted. Jealousy was on fire inside her heart. Jealousy was eating her alive. "What did you say?" her father asked. And before Evie could explain, he slapped a hand across her mouth. She had never been slapped by anyone in her whole seven years of life. Her eyes filled with tears, but she was too embarrassed to cry, especially in front of such a pretty girl.

And then Evie's mother was back, a notepad in one hand, a pencil in the other. She didn't even notice that Evie was on the verge of tears. And Evie *wanted* her to notice. Evie wanted her to say, *Evelyn, my darling, this day, this invisible girl, this slap across your lovely mouth will not change your life at all. You will remain safe, always. You will never lose the gift of innocence.* Evie wanted her mother to say these things because she could feel safety being wrenched away from her. She could feel it being taken from her possession, as though it were a doll, or a dress. She would soon know some things about life and death that most people never know. And that's how quickly it happened. Her mother put the notepad on Evie's lap. She fit the pencil into Evie's trembling hand. "Draw her," she whispered, her voice lit with pain and excitement. "Draw the little girl you see sitting between Daddy and me."

And that's how Evie learned that not everyone can see the dead, and not everyone can draw a decent picture. But *she* could. She wasn't a Leonardo da Vinci. Or a Rembrandt. But Evie Cooper learned over the years how to capture the true character of eyes, and lips, and noses. She learned to draw a curl so real it looked as if a comb had just passed through it. And maybe that's why those souls who are restless and wandering seek her out. Her hand trembling that day, in the backseat of her parents' car, Evie began to draw. First she sketched Rosemary Ann's oval face and the tightly wound ringlets. She drew the bow-shaped mouth, the eyebrows that curved like thin rainbows over the dark eyes. She even drew the cross Rosemary Ann was wearing around her neck. Then Evie passed the notepad to her mother. Her father was staring out his window, the noise of spring floating through his side glass. He was staring at the life of Temple City, as it buzzed up and down the streets.

Evie's mother took the pad but didn't look right away at what Evie had drawn. "Don't do this to yourself," Evie heard her father say. He was watching Mr. Hanley, the town cop, as he went from parking meter to parking meter. *Don't do this to yourself*, Rosemary Ann mimicked, and then she giggled. Evie's mother lifted the pad and peered down. She said nothing at first. Then, "I'd forgotten about Rosemary Ann's necklace," she whispered. And that's how Evie came to know that the girl's name was Rosemary Ann. Her mother let the pad rest on her lap, carefully, as though it were a masterpiece she held there.

And in a way, it was. It was Evie Cooper's first picture. Crude though it was, it was her first sketch of the faces of the dead that would come to follow her through life. Evie's father started the car and they drove home. Just before they turned the corner of Henderson Street, Evie looked up to see that Rosemary Ann was gone.

When Evie was sixteen, her mother showed her a large framed portrait that was still dusty from being kept in storage in the attic. It was of the little girl with the bow mouth, the girl Evie had drawn that day, the girl sitting with such confidence on the plush seat of the Kaiser. It was a portrait of Rosemary Ann Cooper. Her ringlets were tightly wound and framing the oval face. Her eyebrows were curved like thin rainbows over the dark eyes, which peered up at Evie in defiance, still mimicking. "She was your sister," Evie's mother said. "She died of a ruptured appendix, long before you were born. We put her between us in the car, Daddy and I. We were trying to get her to the hospital, but we didn't make it. It was on Main Street, in front of the movie theater."

After her parents died, Evie Cooper tried to leave the faces of the dead behind her. There was too much sadness in the eyes that appeared on her sketch pads, too much pain on the faces. So she moved from Pennsylvania to the bustle of New York City, hoping to find a certain peace. But the dead followed her. The dead aren't bothered by distance, or road signs, or mountain ranges, or boundaries on maps. The dead pick up and travel. By the time Evie left the city and settled in Bixley, Maine, by the time she met Henry Munroe, she was making good money in tips at Murphy's Tavern as a bartender. But she couldn't live on that income alone. So, she eventually put a sign up on her front lawn: *Evie Cooper, Spiritual Portraitist.* By then, it seemed that she was finally settled down. She was getting her life in shape. She had even told Henry Munroe that their affair was over. It had been a mistake, and was moving on. And she had held to that decision.

It had been twelve long months since the morning Evie heard the news, when Andy Southby stopped by the tavern and announced it to the regular customers, as if it were nothing more than the results of a ball game. Henry Munroe, dead of a heart attack. *This is gonna kill Larry,* that's what Evie thought. And then, the sadness hit her, right in the solar plexus, that spot that picks up the dead so sharp and so fast. Evie assumed Henry would stay close by, turning up behind Larry's shoulder every time his brother came into the bar. But in the twelve months that he'd been gone, Henry never once bothered to peer at Evie through the veil that separates Bixley, Maine, from the other side. Not once. And Evie Cooper knew why. Henry was still mad at her.

2

Jeanie stripped the bed in Chad's room of its sheets, balled them up, and stuffed the wad down into the wooden hamper in the bathroom. She had given in when Henry's mother called that morning and invited herself over for a late lunch. The excuse this time was that she wanted to borrow a book on dried flower arrangements. Didn't Jeanie have such a book? Now Jeanie wished that she had lied. All that Frances wanted to talk about these days was Larry. Larry getting a divorce, Larry being fired from the high school, Larry spending too much time at Murphy's Tavern, Larry not being a good mailman, as Henry had been. Jeanie was tempted now and then, in a fleeting moment, to tell Frances Munroe about those nights Henry himself had spent down at Murphy's. And it wasn't just to watch sports on TV and think a bit, as was the case with Larry. What would Frances say about her precious Henry if she knew about Evie Cooper?

An hour before Frances was due to arrive, Jeanie searched her bedroom closet for the book *How to Dry and Arrange Your Backyard Flowers*. It was while digging past the boxes of Lisa's and Chad's school papers, years of them, that Jeanie accidentally stumbled upon the orange bonnet, Henry's beloved knit hat. She still found things like that, a year later and in the strangest places, items she had forgotten were ever a part of Henry's life. His old orange hunting bonnet. Jeanie held it up to her face, let the harsh wool scratch against her skin. And there it was, his smell, Henry's Old Spice mixed with a splash of natural sweat. Henry Munroe, existing now in photographs in the family album, in an odor here and there, a shard of memory.

It had been a long year, twelve god-awful months that she had had to be firm and steady for the children. First there was Lisa, the baby Jeanie had been carrying the day she and Henry stood before a Bixley judge and tied their lives together. This was just two days after their high school graduation, at a time when they were both still basking in that warm patina of peer idolatry. Henry was a star football player and Jeanie captain of the cheerleaders. How could that golden aura not follow them around forever? But he was eighteen and she was seventeen, and the sweet glow of high school victory began to fade shortly after the bills started arriving, even before Lisa did. Soon their friends found better places to party than in a tiny apartment where someone like Jeanie kept shushing everyone because a baby was sleeping in the other room. It was a fast lesson, that big bounce from one concept to another. Then, just when seven years of marriage rolled around, that risky time that old-timers claim comes with an itch to wander, Chad Henry Munroe had been born. And he had become his father's own pride and joy, just as

Lisa seemed to be Jeanie's. Now Lisa, the baby who had compelled her parents to marry so young, was twenty-two years old and married herself. She was living down in Boston and expecting a baby of her own, what would be Jeanie's first grandchild, a baby Henry would never know about, much less hold in his arms.

It had been a long year, indeed, since that morning Jeanie awakened to find that Henry's heart had finally given up, a *long* year. And yet she still couldn't let go of Evie Cooper, or the fact that she had never confronted Henry about his mistress. A full year that held nights when Jeanie cried from the time she flicked out her bedside light until dawn pushed its way in through the window blinds. A damned year, and still there was anger in her heart, mixed in with the pain of loss.

"Mom?" Chad's voice from the kitchen, followed by the quick slam of a screen door. That boy could enter a room faster than any human should be capable of doing. Jeanie was always telling him to slow down, to take it easy, to *chill*, as the kids said. Truth is, she saw in her son the same nervous energy that had punctuated his father's life. She had often told Henry that stress was his enemy, especially when it came hand in hand with his eating habits. But Henry didn't listen. He loved those steaks on the barbecue grill every Sunday, those beers at Murphy's Tavern, those big plates of nachos with every ball game he watched. He loved betting fifty bucks on a Red Sox game and then jumping from his chair and shouting over every home run, every strike out, every base walked on balls. *Life's too short to worry about stress and cholesterol, Jeanie,* he used to tell her. She wondered if Henry changed his mind in those last seconds. Would he have traded the nachos for a few more years?

"I'm in here, son," Jeanie said. Chad was standing in the bedroom doorway before she had time to add, "Don't forget to wipe your feet." He was already Henry's height, six feet tall and still growing. He looked at the orange wool bonnet.

"Where'd you find it?" he asked.

"In the closet," said Jeanie. She offered it to him. "You want it, Chad?"

He took it from her and looked down at it for a few seconds. Then he did what Jeanie had already done. He lifted it up to his nose and smelled the life still in it.

"Yeah, sure, why not?" he said.

He was gone before Jeanie could offer anything else, perhaps a few words of consolation. She wanted to touch his arm, maybe whisper to him, "It's okay, son. I know. I did it too. You can smell him there, can't you? It's okay to hurt, Chad. It's okay to ache like there's no tomorrow." It had been a long year and yet the boy still wasn't letting his mother be privy to his grief. Jeanie heard the roar of Chad's motorbike in the driveway. It had been Henry's old bike that he had refurbished a few weeks before he died, a new paint job, a new motor, all as a reward for Chad's finally getting his math grade up to a B. Jeanie hadn't approved of this. The way she saw it, Chad should get good grades because it was the thing to do, a move toward his future. She looked out the window in time to see her son pull out of the drive on his bike. Despite what was already turning into a hot day, Chad was wearing his father's orange bonnet.

• • •

Frances Munroe was incapable of visiting without bringing some kind of food, mostly in the shape of casserole
dishes, tuna and noodles, or a three-bean salad. Because of
this, Jeanie had nicknamed her "The Welcome Wagon"
and "Meals on Wheels." In those first years of marriage,
it had bothered her that Henry's mother seemed to think
the only way she could visit her son's house was with food
as an offering. But later, when Jeanie started working part-
time at Fillmore's Drugstore, she had come to appreciate
the warm casseroles, and the meringue pies, and the
rice and vegetable soups. There had even been times
when Jeanie had invited Frances over for a cup of coffee,
knowing she'd bring the pastries to go with it. This meant
that Jeanie wouldn't have to worry about what dessert to
make for Henry's supper. If the Munroe men came from a
long line of postal carriers, the maternal side of the family
came from a long line of women who considered food a
social tool.

"It's raisin squares," said Frances, as Jeanie opened
the front door and accepted the silver baking pan from
her mother-in-law. "Only I used golden raisins instead of
regular. And this macaroni casserole is for Chad."

Jeanie stepped back so Frances could come inside. She
followed her into the kitchen and put the pan of squares
down on the counter. Frances opened the refrigerator and
found space on the upper rack for the casserole.

"Just put it in for twenty minutes at three hundred and
fifty degrees," she said. "Warm it up nice. Chad will love
it, and you won't have to cook."

Jeanie smiled. How could she not? The last thing she felt like doing that warm afternoon, now that the orange bonnet had floated to the surface of her life, was cooking something for supper. Even when Chad did appear at the table, washed and hungry, the two of them barely spoke. Compared to the boisterous suppers the family had known when Henry was alive—talk of sports, fishing, hunting, race cars—Jeanie and Chad now ate almost silently, the *clink clink* of their forks replacing Henry's vivacious conversations with his son. What did Jeanie know about hockey, trout lures, archery, or car engines? Nothing. Not a damn thing. It had become so apparent at suppertime that Henry was missing forever that she and Chad had slowly fallen away from eating together. That's why Jeanie had been pestering Chad lately to bring some of the boys home for supper. She assumed he still kept up with his school friends. *Assumed,* for the truth was that she didn't know much about him anymore. He had grown slowly away from her, and in her own pain over losing Henry, she was too worn out to go look for him. Now, Jeanie thought of her son as a boy standing on the back of a train as it's leaving the station. And there she is, his mother, watching that train roll farther and farther down the track, watching that face she loves so dearly growing more and more indistinct. Disappearing.

"I need to talk to you about the memorial service," Frances said, once she had made coffee and poured them each a cup. She had grown too thin since Henry's death, her face now gaunt beneath the short gray hair, her neat slacks and blouse looking as if they were thrown onto a rack rather than onto a body. Jeanie watched as Frances got two plates from the cupboard and cut two raisin squares from the pan. She didn't mind. Let Frances wax the ceiling if she wanted to. Let her mop the front yard. Dust the roof. Who cared? This is what unexpected death can do to a person. It can surprise them into a long, dark corridor where they will gladly stay forever, unless forcibly pulled out.

"Dad and I have been talking," Frances was saying now. "The postal workers want to do a floral wreath, but they also think a plaque would be nice. You know, one that mentions Henry's years of service. We can insert it in the ground at his grave, a bronze marker, like the kind you see for men who have served in the military."

"Do whatever you want," said Jeanie. "It's fine with me." She picked up the fork Frances put in front of her and took a bite of the raisin square. Funny how everything tasted the same in the year since Henry had died. Golden raisins. Regular raisins. Apricots. Plums. It all went into her mouth and she swallowed it. Mashed potatoes, baked potatoes, scalloped potatoes, hash brown potatoes. Rice soup. Chicken soup. Onion soup. Unless she had reason to pay attention, as she did now, what with Frances hovering over her, all food was colorless and tasteless. It did what nature intended it to do: it sustained her body, provided fuel, got her through another day of hell.

"Well?" asked Frances. She waited. Jeanie saw that her mother-in-law's eyes were puffy. Sometimes, she even hated Henry for what he did to them all, for those plates of French fries loaded with cheese, those thick steaks, those cigarettes she knew he smoked down at the tavern even though he always swore he had kept his 1987 New Year's promise never to smoke again, the year that Chad was born.

"It's delicious," said Jeanie. "What a difference from regular raisins." Frances smiled. It wasn't the old smile Jeanie used to see on her mother-in-law's face. It was the *new smile*, which is to say, it was the *best smile* Frances had left.

"I thought you'd like it," said Frances.

"I'll have to get the recipe," Jeanie told her. How many times in twenty-three years had Jeanie pretended she wanted one of Frances Munroe's recipes? Hundreds of times. And yet not one single recipe had exchanged hands. Now, she wished her mother-in-law could give her a recipe that would tell her how to mix the anger with the grief, how many teaspoons of bitterness with how many teaspoons of sorrow. That's what Jeanie really needed, instructions on how to live again, to taste, smell, touch. Maybe even love.

"Pastor Tyson will give the opening prayer and say a few words about Henry," said Frances, now back to the memorial service. "A couple of his fellow postal workers will talk about him, little jokes from work, that sort of thing. And then, well, we'll put flowers and the plaque on the resting site."

Jeanie could only nod. For a year now, Frances had been unable to refer to Henry's grave as anything but a *resting site*, as if maybe her younger son were merely asleep, taking a power nap before walking in her front door again, a cold beer in one hand, a fishing pole in the other.

"What about Larry?" Jeanie asked. She liked Larry. He

had always made her laugh at family functions when the conversations grew stale. And Larry always treated her like she was an individual, and not just his brother's wife. Frances frowned.

"Larry can insert the plaque," she said.

"But he and Henry were so close," said Jeanie. "Are you sure Larry doesn't want to say a few words?"

"Larry can't even speak for himself these days," Frances said. She pushed her plate away, the untouched raisin square still on it.

"Whatever you think best," said Jeanie. All she wanted was for that day of the memorial to be over. It wasn't her idea anyway, but something brainstormed by the Bixley Post Office, with Henry's own parents most likely at the vanguard. "Let them do whatever makes them feel good," Jeanie had told Lisa on the phone, when word of a memorial service for Henry began to circulate among family and friends. "No, you don't have to go if you don't want to," she had told Chad when he'd staged a protest at the thought of sharing his sorrow with near strangers, and in public.

"Are you sure Lisa can't make it?" Frances asked now. She was pouring herself another cup of coffee and Jeanie had yet to take a sip from her own cup. Jeanie shook her head.

"Lisa's having irregular bleeding as it is," she said. "She's afraid such a long trip and such an emotional day might be too much. And then Patrick is working around the clock just to pay the bills. Lisa has to think of the baby first. After all, Henry is..."

Jeanie stopped. A patch of silence fell between them.

How could it be so difficult, this many days and weeks and months later, to even say that word? Frances poured some milk into her coffee and stirred it.

"Lisa has to think of the baby now," said Jeanie. From somewhere down the street, the music of the ice-cream truck rang out. It had always reminded Jeanie of church bells over the years of hearing it, years when Lisa and Chad would grab her purse and pester her to *Hurry, Mom, it's coming up the street, it's at the Petersons' already, gimme some money, Mom, please!*

"I had some problems when Larry was born," Frances said then. "Some irregular bleeding, as you call it. But Henry, when he came along, it was an easy birth. I almost didn't know I was pregnant until Lawrence drove me to the hospital." She smiled, a smile that belonged to another time and place. Would they ever be happy again? That's all that Jeanie wanted to know.

"How *is* Larry?" she asked, wondering if it would be wise. She knew immediately by her mother-in-law's face that it wasn't a good question.

"He's acting the fool, is what he's doing," said Frances. "I told him right at the start not to marry that vain girl. But Larry never listened to a word of advice from me. Now, if he doesn't snap out of it, he'll be fired from the post office. Lawrence says there are only so many strings a human being can pull. If only Larry had been just a bit more like Henry. Henry was as dependable as they come."

Jeanie watched as Frances reached for the plate with her raisin square and pulled it back in front of her on the table, the yellow raisins spilling away from the crust in a tiny avalanche of filling.

"Frances, there's something I think you should know," said Jeanie. Frances took a bite of the raisin square as she looked at Jeanie's face.

"Oh, this *is* good," Frances said. Then she quickly put her fork down on the table and hid her face in her hands. The sobs seemed longer and more uncontrollable than they did on her last visit. Within seconds, the wave of grief had passed and Frances picked up her napkin, wiped her eyes quickly. "It comes out of nowhere," she said, and Jeanie nodded, recognizing a truth in that statement. "I'll be fine one minute, talking about rosebushes with Ellen Barnes, and the next I'm crying like a baby."

Jeanie went around the table to her mother-in-law's chair. She put her arms around the older woman's thin shoulders and the two rocked back and forth, their pain flowing like a hot liquid from one body to the other. Were women meant to do this? Was this in their genes? If they couldn't sit side by side on bar stools at Murphy's Tavern, saying nothing the entire time, did they rock instead, remembering the babies they had held and nursed and soothed in those same arms?

"I'm sorry," said Frances finally. "I'm fine now, Jeanie. Really I am. What was it you wanted to tell me?"

Jeanie kept the older woman in her arms, not ready to let go. The warm current flowing into her from another body felt good, like a stream of sunlight. With Henry not there anymore to give her a hug now and then, with Chad vanishing into his own cloud of sorrow, what Jeanie noticed most was not being touched.

"It was nothing," Jeanie said. "Don't forget to bring me that recipe."

• • •

It was just coming twilight when Jeanie pulled her car up to the curb across from Evie Cooper's house and turned off the engine. She sat staring at the sign in the front yard, *Evie Cooper, Spiritual Portraitist,* and at the candlelight that flickered from behind the white lace curtains. This was the time of day Evie did her sessions. Jeanie knew this from the ad she had seen in the *Bixley Courier.* It was one of the cheaper ads, sure to be missed except by the most desperate and sincere scholars of the unknown. *Spiritual Portraitist,* it said, and below the words was the silhouette drawing of a woman standing beneath a huge star, like the one that had guided the three wise men to baby Jesus. *Let me break down the veil that separates you from your departed loved ones. Twenty years of experience. Fifty dollars per session. Call now for appointment.* It wasn't as if Jeanie believed that the dead could be dialed up, paged, summoned forth for a chat. She didn't believe it. But at the same time, she did believe in God and an afterlife. What if there *was* a way to poke a hole in that so-called veil? All she knew for certain was that something like a morbid curiosity had finally drawn her to Evie Cooper's street, some kind of indefinable link. She was more curious about the mistress now, a year after Henry died, than in those months when he was actually having the affair.

Jeanie reached into the paper sack on the seat beside her and found the pack of cigarettes she'd bought at the 7-Eleven. Henry never knew that she had taken up smoking, that same day she found the receipt to room 9 at the

Days Inn. Jeanie had lit that first cigarette out of spite, no doubt about it, coughing the harsh smoke back up from her lungs and wondering how on earth any sane person could do that every day without quitting forever. But now, all these months later, she liked the taste of tobacco and the calmness that smoking a cigarette brought with it. Maybe she was even addicted to nicotine. It didn't really matter *why* she smoked. She just did.

Jeanie reached into the same sack and pulled out a margarita wine cooler from the four-pack carrying case. The bottle had perspired in the heat and now the paper sack from the 7-Eleven was damp with humidity. She spun the silver cap around until it broke from the aluminum binding and came free in her hand. She tossed the cap onto the floor on the passenger side, then put her window down a bit to let the smoke leak out. She took a sip of the cold wine cooler and lit her first cigarette of the evening. Birds sang out from the bushes along the street and the muted sounds of traffic floated down from the four-way stop at Foster and Elm. Two women were out power walking, their white fists punching the air in unison as they strode past Jeanie's car. They hadn't noticed her there behind the wheel. Maybe she, too, was disappearing and just didn't know it yet. She exhaled slowly and watched as the smoke left her lips and spiraled up toward the window crack, set free on the night air.

What bothered Jeanie most, what still hurt, what stopped her from finding what the talk shows call *closure*, is that she wasn't sure but what Henry Munroe was still visiting Evie Cooper, in those dark hours of the night when things go bump. Jeanie Munroe wasn't sure but what her dead husband, so attached to the mistress he had unexpectedly left behind, had broken down that *veil* Evie's newspaper ad talked about. Maybe he had forced his way back to the world of the living just so he could touch the life in her again. One thing was certain. Henry's spirit sure wasn't hanging out at Jeanie's house. Not unless you count the leftover smell of Old Spice in an orange hunting bonnet. Jeanie was tempted to walk up to Evie's door and knock on it *bam! bam! bam!* When Evie answered, she would say to her, *I'm getting the number 9. Does that mean anything to you? Yes, he's showing me a nine and a receipt for the Days Inn. What do you think that means?*

By the time Evie Cooper's first client of the evening arrived, Jeanie had already finished off the first wine cooler and opened another.

3

When Larry heard the kitchen door open and close downstairs, he waited another minute until he was certain his mother would be in the garden. Then he unlocked his door and stepped out into the narrow hallway. Sunshine flooded the house, turning it the color of ripe wheat. Motes of dust spiraled up from the rug on the stairs, a universe disturbed, and he wondered if his mother had just crept up to his door again, to listen. The soles of his bare feet slapped on the wooden floorboards as he made his way to the bathroom. With a great sigh of relief, he emptied a bladder that had been pestering him since he woke to the sound of his father's Toyota truck backing out of the drive and whining off up the street. Then he washed his face and brushed his teeth, keeping tabs through the window on his mother in the garden below, her gray hair floating over the cucumber beds like a soft cloud.

In the kitchen, Larry opened the refrigerator door and found a half gallon of milk. He poured a tall glass and drank it as he stood there. He had even dreamed of milk during the night, so thirsty had he been. He dreamed of walking down the aisles of the local IGA, asking clerk after clerk, "Where do you keep the milk?" That's when the IGA had turned into a huge field of talking cows. "Here's where we keep the milk, asshole," one of them said. Larry had knelt by this talking cow and reached for the teats, hoping to milk her and quench his thirst. Only it wasn't leathery teats hanging from the cow's udder. What he held in his hands, and was still holding when he woke seconds later, was the leather mail pouch. Thinking of this now, in the bright sun of day, Larry smiled as he finished the milk. He rinsed his glass and left it in the sink, not caring that his mother would find it and know he'd been there. An empty plastic sack lay on the table, the kind that came full of groceries from the IGA. Larry opened it and stood before his mother's slide-out pantry. A jar of crunchy peanut butter was the first item into the bag, along with a box of saltine crackers, a jar of pickles, and two cans of tuna fish. He glanced out the kitchen window and saw his mother just leaving the cucumber beds and heading for the sweet peas.

In the silverware drawer, Larry found a can opener, a fork, a spoon, and a knife. They clinked against the cans in the bottom of the sack. From a plate on the counter, he grabbed a chocolate doughnut and bit into it, leaving it in his mouth while he opened the cupboard door where the gallons of water were stored. He pulled one out. On the way back through the kitchen, he grabbed two apples out of the fruit bowl. He had never been a Boy Scout, had never possessed the kind of "group mentality" he felt it took to join such an organization. Henry was more the

Boy Scout type and had excelled, his earned merit badges often discussed at the dinner table while Larry scooted a few peas around with his fork, waiting for praise of Henry to subside. It had never really bothered him that Henry seemed cut from a better cloth than he was. He loved his younger brother too much, and love can cushion anything, even jealousy.

Back in his room, Larry made himself a breakfast of peanut butter and crackers and ate it while sitting on his bed, his back propped against the wall. He would save the tuna fish and pickles for lunch. He drank water from the throat of the plastic jug and then selected the larger of the two apples. It oozed a sweet juice the moment his teeth broke through the red skin. He finished the apple in a few quick bites and then reached into the leather mail pouch to select another letter, this one personal. The envelope was yellow and smelled of lilacs. Why did some people odorize and perfume their mail? There were days when Larry's pouch smelled like the perfume counter at Fillmore's Drugstore. He gave a cursory glance at the return address in the upper left corner: *Sheila Dewberry, 1013 Cedar Grove Court, Sioux City, Iowa*. It had been sent to a *Miss Stella Peabody*, the town librarian whose beige nut of a house sat catty-corner on Thorncliffe Street, next to the future site of Bixley's second McDonald's.

Larry took the knife he'd found in his mother's silverware drawer and inserted it beneath the sealed flap of the envelope. He cut his way slowly and neatly along the glued line until the letter was opened. He took it out of its envelope and lay back on the bed, head on his pillow and sheet pulled up to his waist. His own father never opened an envelope without his silver-plated letter opener, a knifelike apparatus that was inscribed with the initials LSM, *Lawrence Simon Munroe*, which had been given to the first Lawrence Munroe ever to be entrusted with the government's mail, upon the event of his retirement in 1928. "This will be yours one day, Larry," his father liked to remind him as he held the silver-plated letter opener up to catch the light. This had been going on from the time Larry was five years old, ever since he could first remember being able to grasp the concept of *letter*. Just as some boys watched their own fathers cut into the silver bellies of freshly caught trout, Larry had watched his father make incisions in the bellies of envelopes, slicing them open with a quick movement of the wrist. He was twelve years old when he knew for certain that he did not want the damn letter-opening thing. And he was eighteen when he told his father outright that he didn't want to be a goddamned postman. He was ready for college, and older, horny women, and *Playboys* all over the coffee table any time of the night or day without fear of retribution. "Maybe another time, another place," he had gone on apologetically, trying to ignore the fact that his father's face was growing like a long, tanned squash, a sad vegetable elongating, searching out a place for the sadness to take root. Maybe in the old days of postal service Larry would've taken up the call. Those were the days of Pony Express riders, when that dangerous route from St. Joseph to Sacramento was waiting to be ridden, to be broken in. Larry had read about it in history class. Maybe *then*, if he'd had a fast horse, a little excitement, maybe *then* he would have saddled up, grabbed the mailbag, and turned his collar up against those outlaws and bandits and dangerous holes in the black road ahead. In those days, mailmen were heroes. Those Pony Express riders must have gotten all the best, loose women, like modern rock stars and athletes. Trembling virgins probably waited on the edges of towns to lift their dresses at the first sound of hoofbeats. And while it would make sense that a good-looking, modern-day mailman would have all the lonely, bored housewives to himself, what small-town, teenaged boy would want to bed down the mothers of his best friends? "I'm sorry, Dad, but the answer is no," Larry had said. A month later, he was enrolled at the University of Maine.

By the time things settled down, Larry Munroe had a BA in history and was teaching at his old high school. And he might have persevered, too, might have made it to the old gold watch and a retirement plan, had he not met Katherine Grigsby. May his ex-wife rot in hell for turning him, in his later years—a time when the gray was just coming to his thinning sideburns enough that it might appear to some student that Mr. Munroe actually *knew* what he was talking about—into a fucking mailman! But that's what had happened after he lost his teaching job at the only high school in town, the problem being that little fistfight in the classroom. He had then put on a decent suit and gone out on one job interview after another, holding in his hand the résumé that spoke of a man aged forty-three with no other visible experience beyond teaching history. After four weeks of what might be considered self-inflicted humiliation, Larry had to face facts. The only establishment sincerely interested in hiring a middle-aged ex-schoolteacher was the Bixley Post Office, where his own father presided over the business of deliveries, stamps, money orders, dog bites, customer complaints, and other sundries. They had lost a good postman when Henry Munroe's heart exploded in his chest, so now the Bixley Post Office and Lawrence Simon Munroe III had thrown open those ancestral doors to Lawrence Simon Munroe IV. May Katherine Grigsby rot in Hades.

There were facts to be faced, and Larry faced them. He was struggling to keep up with his child support payments. He was struggling to pay rent on a one-bedroom apartment now that the house had been sold. He was no match for the twentysomething young men who were fresh out of college and snapping up all the good jobs. What choice did he have but to take up the leather gauntlet of his forefathers? What choice did he have but to move back home with his parents? So he had stuffed his pouch with letters and gone up and down the sidewalks of Bixley, for six days out of every week, bringing people good news, bringing them bad news, bringing them Ed McMahon and the chance at millions in the Publishers Clearing House contest, bringing them foreclosures from the Bixley bank, bringing them the world right at their fingertips, whether they wanted the world or not. For seven full, agonizing months he had done this, wishing every day, every step he took up a customer's brick walk, that Katherine Grigsby would burn in hell's most horrible inferno. But she hadn't burned, or rotted, or even smoldered anywhere, at least not yet. Instead, she was now living with Ricky Santino, who had coached basketball at the same high school where Larry taught history. Nice and messy. Leave it to Katherine, who never forgave him for getting her pregnant and forcing her to choose between ballet and motherhood. He hadn't even realized until Katherine left him that those ballet lessons she'd been taking were so important to her. Larry always thought it was her way of getting exercise and attention at the same time. That fluffy pink tutu, those silky shoes the size of rose petals. She had always reminded him of Tinker Bell, pirouetting through the house as if it were some stage. "She's too young for you, Larry" was all his mother had said when she met Katherine for the first time. Larry hadn't seen it that way. What was ten years, after all? He had always wondered if the frequent pirouetting was what caused Katherine to miscarry that first baby, and then a second baby two years later. Jonathan, coming late as he did, had been such a precious gift, at least for Larry.

The truth was that Katherine Grigsby had as much chance back in her early years to become a professional ballet dancer as had Zelda Fitzgerald. And Larry had told her that, the day he came home from giving his quarterly exam on the Roman Empire to find her packed and waiting for him by the door, Ricky Santino's new green Jeep idling at the curb. This was shortly after the Big Italian Renaissance Fight, at least that's what Larry had come to call it. He should've killed the fucking little WOP while he had him pinned to the radiator. That was the day that Larry Munroe's marriage fell down faster than Rome. The worst thing about it, the worst fucking thing that could happen to a high school history teacher in a small town, whose ancestral family he had already failed for refusing to pick up a century-old mail pouch that smelled of sweat and grime, a man whose stomach was beginning to resemble the spare tire clamped on the back of Ricky's idling Jeep, the worst fucking thing that Katherine had done was that she had taken Jonathan, their son. *His* son.

Jonathan. This was a name Larry had wanted for himself as a child, a chance to be different, a prayer to be unique. But they had called him Lawrence. As a boy he would stand in front of his bedroom dresser, look into the mirror with a grave dignity, and say, "Hello, I'm Jonathan Munroe. Good day, Jonathan Munroe here, Jonathan Munroe calling, Jonathan, Jonathan Munroe." He had envied Henry for possessing his own independent name, this was true. Envious because Henry had not been promised the silver letter-opening knife with LSM inscribed on the handle. And maybe that's why Henry had so willingly taken up the family profession. He had the freedom to choose. But that's why Larry had given his only child, a sweet boy, the very name he'd wanted for himself, *Jonathan*, a name signifying freedom. Larry had given it to his son without consideration of his ancestors because he saw the future every time he looked at Jonathan. He saw the future and not the past. Lawrence Munroe IV had named his own son Jonathan, and he had kept him from letters and postal cards and fliers and *Current Occupant* catalogs as long as he could. And then, when life without the boy seemed unbearable, Katherine had taken Jonathan Munroe and she had driven away from their home, the only house on Pilcher Street that didn't sport a mailbox. Thinking back on that house now, months after he'd sold it to a fellow teacher, Larry had come to see it as a kind of box in itself. All throughout the fifteen years of his marriage to Katherine, they had bounced from room to room in that small, two-story Cape, pirouetted, like particles of dust trapped in sunlight.

The lilac-smelling letter from Sioux City, from Miss Sheila Dewberry to Miss Stella Peabody, was a love letter. *My own darling,* it began. *How I have missed the soft velvet of your sweet mouth, the silk of your nape, the tender arch of your back, the hills of your snow-white breasts, which my lips have climbed so many times in the past.* It was the last image, of breasts rising up white as snow to someone's lips, *anyone's* lips, even an old maid's, that prompted Larry to reach under the blanket and search for his genitals. They were still there. That Katherine hadn't managed to take them with her was a miracle, since she even took the andirons in front of the fireplace, andirons inscribed LSM and passed down from the first LSM. Maybe Larry should thank Ricky Santino for that, macho guy that he was. *Leave Larry his balls,* he could hear Ricky advising Katherine. *It's all the guy has left, and a man needs his testicles in a small town when his wife has run off with one of his fellow teachers.* But Katherine had taken Jonathan. Larry had watched from the porch as Jonathan walked to the green Jeep, his school jacket slung over one shoulder like a limp arm, his face streaked from crying, his cowlick bouncing in all directions, like a confused periscope trying to determine place, heading, bearing. Not yet ten years old and already with a big mission.

Katherine Grigsby had left Larry his balls, but she had taken his heart. That had been seven months ago and there was nothing he could do about it. At one time, he'd have phoned up Henry. "Let's go get a beer," he'd suggest, and Henry would be there, sitting on a stool at Murphy's Tavern by the time Larry even arrived. They would sit side by side at the bar, Larry trying not to look at Evie's ass if she was working, knowing all about Henry and Evie but pretending that he didn't. He and Henry would toss back a few beers, catch whatever ball game was on the tiny TV dangling from the ceiling behind the bar. And when it came time to go home, Larry would feel better, as if he'd actually *talked* to someone about his problems. Henry's physical body sitting there on the bar stool next to him was word enough, a paragraph, a whole book. *I'm here for you, buddy*, Henry was saying. Now, Henry was dead. Larry had lost a brother, but he had gained a court order restricting him from intruding upon Ricky Santino's classroom, upon Ricky Santino's life, upon Ricky Santino period. He now had to stay fifty yards from Ricky Santino, who had stolen his wife and child away from him.

Larry knew that he shouldn't have barged into Ricky's classroom as he did that day when he first found out about the affair. Katherine had been in the teacher's room, smoking another one of her three cigarettes a day, no more, no less. And Larry had come in during study period to find her there. "I think we should take Jonathan to Washington, DC, this summer," he had said, thinking his son, their son, was now old enough to take a deep interest in the nation's capital. But instead of agreeing or even disagreeing, Katherine had prematurely stubbed one of those three daily cigarettes in the ashtray, straightened her skirt, and said, "I need to get back to class." And she had walked out past him, as uncaring as though he were a coat rack. At least that's how he felt then, but he had flattered himself, because no coat rack would ever be given a restraining order. What Larry Munroe didn't know, as he stood there wondering what he had done to warrant the present cold shoulder of Katherine Grigsby, his wife, who had refused all offers of the Munroe name herself, was that he was only days away from losing Jonathan. Or that his life was about to go to hell in a mail sack, the proverbial handbasket being reserved for coat racks. That's when Maurice Finney had come into the teacher's room, his aging hippie look barely contained in his corduroy jacket with the brown patches on the elbows, and the matching corduroy slacks. "Jesus, man," Maurice had said, giving Larry a gentle slap on the back. "I just heard about you and Katherine breaking up. Fucking bummer, man. How are you taking it, buddy? You cool? How's Jonathan taking it? I wouldn't be this together, man, if it was me. I mean, if this was still the sixties, different story. You could pretend it was a bad case of Karma. But these days? Well, this kind of shit really hurts in the new millennium." Then Maurice found the book he had come looking for and was gone again, down the lime-green hallways of Bixley High School.

Larry had stood there for a time, staring at the cigarette butt still smoking in the ashtray, doing the math on what he'd just heard, adding in Katherine's mood minutes before, adding up the weeks and months—my God, it had been months!—that she had turned away from him in bed, had been sullen and withdrawn at the breakfast table. And she never complained anymore that he spent his Saturdays fishing or golfing. It had been since that previous spring that he even remembered her caring where he was going when he left the house. Two plus two equals four. Even a history teacher knew that. So Larry had left the teacher's room and strode on down to Katherine's own room. Before he knocked, he stood at the door and peered through the glass window. She was talking about some poem, most likely, her eyes on fire with meter and rhyme. Maybe even love. He remembered her this way when they first met and later married. They had passion to burn back then, especially Katherine, who was only eighteen and a freshman in college. At twenty-eight and already teaching history, Larry probably appeared mature and worldly to her. But then Katherine got older too, and that's when she found Larry Munroe out. Maybe he hadn't been mature and worldly after all. Maybe he had just been *older*.

So Larry had knocked on her classroom door that day. When Katherine looked over at him, she knew. He could see it in her face. *She* knew *he* knew. She came to the door, stepped outside, and closed it behind her. He was about to ask her who it was, but in a second he realized. How had he been such a fool? How could he have been so stupid, so blind? "You and Ricky Santino," was all he said to her. "You and Ricky." She looked like she might give him an A for answering the test question correctly. "I was about to tell you, a long time ago," she said, "and then, well, Henry died. I thought it best to wait. But now you know." And she had backed away from him, receded into her classroom where he heard her distant voice rising again with the rhythm of the poem.

Lawrence Munroe the Fourth didn't stand outside the

door and peer through the window at Ricky Santino, when he finally reached room 16. That's when he realized he had run all the way from Katherine's room in the English wing, up to the main hall, down the main hall, and over to the left wing. What if Mr. Wilcox, the principal, had caught one of his teachers running in the hall? Larry didn't look at Ricky through the window at all. Instead, he had tossed open the door and barged in. Ricky, his fellow history teacher and Bixley High's respected basketball coach now that the team had actually won a game or two, must have been discussing Italy—the Italian Renaissance maybe—because Larry remembered the shape of a boot on the map hanging from the wall as he lunged across the room, taking Ricky down in front of twenty-some screaming students. Talk about visual aids. They should have made him Teacher of the Year for finding a way to get students to pay attention. Damn Katherine for turning him into a mailman.

Do you remember, oh my precious girl, that little cottage we rented at the beach? I shall never forget those nights of firelight, and moonlight, and the gentle probing of your tongue. Please don't keep me from you, nor you from me, for too much longer. My heart, no, my body, needs you and needs you now. I am all fire as I write.

Larry heard the whine of the Toyota truck again as it pulled into the yard. Its door opened and closed. The front door of the house opened and closed. Five minutes passed.

"Larry!" His mother's voice. Her second assault of the day had arrived right on time. Larry brought his hand quickly away from his genitals—yes, so what if it was one old spinster writing a letter to another one?

Who cares as long as the words are pure and genuine? What healthy man who still possessed his balls could turn away from the *swell of white breasts*, that *gentle, probing tongue*?

"Jesus," Larry said, and flung the blanket aside. He was forty-three years old and he'd just been interrupted while masturbating in his old bedroom, in his mother's house, by his mom herself. Once, she had even caught him in the act, the summer he was eleven years old and Davey Pryor had given him the aging stack of Mr. Pryor's dog-eared *Playboys*—God bless Hugh Hefner, one of America's most unsung sociologists, for having the foresight, if maybe not the foreskin, to publish through snow, through rain, through sleet and hail, a monthly issue of breasts rising up like soft white mountains. God bless that man! And it didn't matter that the magazines were old, as it would with *Newsweek*, or *Time*, or *TV Guide*. Tits never age, at least not on the page. Nightly, beneath his blanket, Larry had hovered over issue after issue, burning up a hundred flashlight batteries after Henry had fallen asleep and only snores wafted down from the top bunk, reveling in the wonder of a naked woman and touching himself for the first *real* time, and knowing that life was going to be good, oh, life was going to kick some ass if this feeling was any indication. But then his mother had appeared—what does a kid who's just discovered the mechanics of his penis know about the value of a locked door?—his mother had materialized by his bed. And how could Larry hear her coming, what with the blood rushing to his penis, to his heart, flooding his ears, the blood rushing to his very soul? She had appeared with an armful of his laundry, clean, pure, pristine shorts and T-shirts and folded jeans, a stack of laundry in her arms, she herself smelling like June Cleaver. She had lifted the blanket and there he was. If the damn thing hadn't been in his hands, if he hadn't been gripping it so sincerely, as though it were a microphone and he was singing "Mister Sandman" into it, maybe he could have come up with an excuse. "What's *that* doing here?" he might've asked. But he couldn't, and although he hadn't bothered to struggle with the fine print, he could almost bet as he looked up into his mother's horrified face that nowhere in that printed material had Hef offered any advice on what to do if your mom catches you with your prick in your hand. On the cusp of a nervous breakdown, his mother had ordered him to burn the issues, along with colored piles of autumn leaves, in a rusty steel drum in the backyard. Early that next morning, young Larry Munroe had stood and watched tender nipples turn browner than a nipple could ever imagine before they crumbled and disappeared in orange tongues and licks of fire. He had seen breasts white as goose down grow black and cindery in the mouth of the flames, and then fly like feathers up to heaven. Tits rising on wisps of smoke as though they had wings. Slender, tender thighs turning to ash. And he had known right then, his two feet planted wildly on each side of the steel drum, that maybe life wasn't going to be so good after all. Maybe it wasn't.

But Larry had no idea how bad it would get, just thirty-one short years later, when his brother Henry would die early of a heart attack, having inherited his ancestors' penchant to deliver the mail but not their longevity. Henry was the only one Larry wanted to talk to about Katherine and Ricky Santino. And it wouldn't be with words. It would be with the closeness of two brothers sitting in a canoe, fishing, saying absolutely nothing about anything but fish and beer and the Red Sox.

"Open the door, Larry," his mother said now. He could hear the veiled anger behind her words. "Your father is home for lunch and is standing behind me, listening to this," she added.

"I'm standing behind your mother," he heard his father say. "I'm listening to this." Larry smiled. Do couples who have lived together longer than they've lived apart not realize that, at the last of it, they become vaudeville acts? Aging, dazed parrots? Had he and Katherine been saved from this same fate?

"Two days of not delivering the mail is one thing," his mother now said. "But this is three days, Larry, and unless you're ill, it's quite enough."

"It's been three days, son," his father said.

"What's worse," his mother continued, "is that Gil thinks you have some undelivered mail. For crying out loud, that's a federal offense. You're lucky your father is listening to this and can do something about it."

"Where's the mail, son?" he heard his father ask, and Larry knew that the long face must be almost reaching the kneecaps by now. The first time Larry ever saw a rerun of Car 54, Where Are You? was the only time he had seen another human face as long as his own father's, when Fred Gwynne had appeared, wearing a policeman's uniform and not a mailman's, but with a face so long it was almost impossible for it to ever appear happy. What must his father's face think about a mailman breaking postal regulations, not to mention committing the most vile offense of all, which was purloining the mail.

"I don't have any mail," Larry told the voices outside his door, as he pushed the mail pouch under his bed. He quickly grabbed up the letters on the floor and shoved them under the edge of his mattress. He got out of bed and picked up the torn envelopes he'd tossed on the floor. These he hid under the top mattress that had been Henry's bunk, back in those glorious growing-up years. Henry wouldn't care. Henry hadn't wanted to be a mailman either. He had admitted this to Larry, one night at Murphy's during a commercial break in the Super Bowl. "But hey," Henry had added. "There's no other job where a pretty woman will invite you in for a coffee while she's still in her nightgown." Larry would never tell anyone that Henry admired him for walking away from a heritage of registered letters, and money orders, and fountain pens that were chained like helpless dogs to the post office counter. May email destroy the American postal service forever. May it put the sucker out of business.

The letters well hidden, Larry crossed the room and, quietly as possible, he unlocked the door. Then he hurried back to his bottom bunk where he covered himself with the sheet. His mother knocked again.

"How much more do you expect your parents to bear?" she was now wondering aloud. "First, you get into a bar-room brawl at school, at *school*, mind you, in a *classroom*.

And Dad is good enough to hire you at the post office, *good enough*, where you should have been working in the first place, like your brother. And now this? How much more should we bear, Larry?"

"I'm listening to this," his father reminded him.

"The door is open," Larry said, the sheet now pulled up to his chin.

"No it isn't," said his mother.

"It isn't, son," said his father.

"Yes, it is," said Larry.

And then they were both standing in his room, his mother looking older than sixty-seven, her face flushed with anger, the same anger as the day of the *Playboys*, his father's face longer than the day when his son told him he wanted to teach history and not receive the silver letter opener after all. Longer than the day when Larry Munroe had walked into his parents' kitchen and told them that their younger boy, Henry, was dead. Would they ever forgive him for being the harbinger of such bad news? Should he have written a kindly letter instead, put it in a yellow envelope scented with lilac, given it a few days to flutter its way to their street, to the pretty mailbox with the bluebird painted on its front, bringing the horrible word. *Henry's had a heart attack. Jeanie found him dead this morning. He died in his sleep. Please don't forget to use your zip code.*

"Why, son?" was all his father really wanted to know.

"Because," Larry answered. How could he explain to his father that there was something in his soul, in his goddamned DNA that said, *no more letters, no more letters, no more.*

"This is a fine shape for you to be in," his mother noted, "what with Henry's memorial service only a week away."

"I don't have any letters," said Larry. "Gil made a mistake."

"Good, son," said his father, his face now like the faces Larry remembered from the House of Mirrors, that summer he and Henry together won eleven teddy bears at the carnival.

"Oh," he heard his mother say, a soft, broken cry, to go with those broken white hands that were still clinging to her arms. She was looking at a picture on the wall, of her two sons in their high school football uniforms, Larry the captain and Henry the best damn quarterback the Bixley Bandits had ever seen pass through their ranks. Larry and Henry, their arms around each other's necks, the numbers on their chests like big bold answers to life's questions. Henry got laid for the first time that night, right after the big game with Montgomery High, when he had thrown seven touchdown passes to Larry, his brother, who had been there to catch them. This was the picture that had been in the newspaper, the fabulous Munroe brothers in victory, and that was the night that Jeanie McPherson, the prettiest cheerleader on the field, had privately told Henry *yes, yes, yes*, something much warmer and finer than *Playboy*.

"Oh," Larry heard his mother say again, a broken word from her broken throat. "My boys," she said, her chin bobbing erratically at the photograph, as if she hadn't really seen it in years, hadn't dusted it a thousand times since the day it was taken. "I've lost both my boys."

Larry turned on his side, covered his head with the sheet. He heard her broken footsteps on the loose board in the hallway, his father's voice floating after her. The Trail of Tears.

"I'll send you a sympathy card," Larry said from beneath his sheet. "As soon as I get my hands on a fucking stamp."

4

E vie handed the finished sketch to her client, and
when she did, she felt again that warm rush, as if
something with wings had flown out of her chest. She
had her own term for the feeling. *Spirit departure*. Simple
as that.

"Take a few seconds and look at it," Evie said. She
could see the surprise on Charlotte Davis's face. Surprise,
followed by that eternal sadness. "Remember, they come
out of love. They come to bring you peace."

Evie always allowed each client, especially the skeptics, some time to come to terms with what they saw
on the paper before them, to digest what they are never
ready for: the faces of someone they find life unbearable
without, someone they miss, even someone they had
almost forgotten. The faces of the dead. It takes time, Evie
knew. As Charlotte Davis stared down at the artwork
before her, Evie turned toward the window and parted
the lace curtains. There was the car again, parked on
the other side of the street. A dark blue Buick LeSabre.
Henry's car. It was his wife behind the wheel, most likely,

although the evening light was such that Evie couldn't see who it was. The headlights flicked on just then and the Buick pulled away from the curb and roared off down the street. The driver must have seen her, peering out into the blossoming night.

"It's my father," Charlotte said now, her voice breaking. Evie turned away from the window and let the lace curtains float back into place. She watched as Charlotte touched a finger to the face drawn on the paper. She stroked the full head of hair, the narrow lips, the thick eyebrows that Evie had taken pains to shade in fully. It was a face that cared about Charlotte, a face that knew her well, the eyes holding memories of many years. Evie smiled the sympathetic smile she always brought out at times like that.

"I figured it must be someone very close to you," she said. "He came through so strong, insisting that I draw him from all the others."

"Others?" Charlotte asked. "There were more?" Evie nodded, and as she did, she looked beyond Charlotte's left shoulder.

"There were several," she said, "both men and women. One is still here with us. A young girl, maybe sixteen years old. Long blond hair."

"Phoebe," said Charlotte, and again her voice broke with longing. "Phoebe was my best friend until she—"

Charlotte looked back down at the sketched face of the man who had once been her earthly father, a face now shaped with pencil lead. She tried to say something, but couldn't. Evie put a hand on her shoulder.

"It's okay," she said. "I already know. Phoebe died in a car accident."

Charlotte began to weep, and now Evie had to do what took almost as much strength and energy as channeling the dead. She had to comfort the living.

"Honey, listen to me," Evie said. She dropped to her knees in front of Charlotte and took the woman's hands into her own. Tears ran from the corners of Charlotte's eyes but she made no sound. Evie knew this was the kind of crying that really hurts. This was the kind that stabs deepest. "Why do you think they bother to come? It's to tell you to find peace. They have pity for us, Charlotte. They wish we were as free as they now are."

Charlotte found her purse where she'd left it when the session started, on the floor beside her chair. She opened it and pulled out a check. She put it on the table, next to the crystal lamp and the small container of burning incense. She looked at Evie.

"I think I'm gonna be okay now," she said. "Just knowing those two are with me. They're the ones I miss most." This was when Evie knew she had done her job well. And she knew that this is all the dead want, too. They don't want to tell us what horse will win the race, what lottery numbers to pick, where the lost ring is hiding. The dead want peace, just like the living.

"Do I owe you any more than fifty?" asked Charlotte. "You know, for telling me about Phoebe?"

"Not a penny," Evie said. She put the sketch of Charlotte's father inside one of the brown envelopes she had ordered specifically for her work. Charlotte accepted the envelope, then held it as if it were something newly born and fragile.

"I know for a fact that you've never seen a picture

of my father," she said. "So how *could* you know, you, a woman from out of state and all? Jerry says I'm crazy for coming here. But I know the truth, Evie. How would you know about that scar on his cheek if you didn't see him?" Evie had been in this battle with the skeptics all her life, people who couldn't see the same things she could. But there was a time when man never believed he'd fly, let alone at the speed of sound. That he would walk on that bright and distant moon. When he didn't know about electricity, or cameras, or computers and such things. What would Neanderthal man have thought about a Zippo lighter? The great discoveries were all ghosts that had to be invented to be believed.

"Go home now and sleep," said Evie. She opened the door and let Charlotte pass. "Sleep like you've never slept in all the years you've mourned them."

Evie watched through the curtains, waiting until Charlotte got into her car and drove off, before she lit her second joint of the day. Then she pushed open the door to the warm summer evening and went out to the porch swing that she had installed just before Henry died. She kicked off her sandals and undid her bra beneath her blouse. A swing, Evie knew, can be like a mother's arms, a cradle that takes you in and rocks you gently when you really need it. And she needed it, as she always did after any session. Her spiritual portraits were doing so well for her now that she had finally cut back nights at the tavern, promising Dan Murphy she would fill in for emergencies. That night was one since Gail Ferguson, the other bartender, had to attend the wedding of a relative down in New Hampshire. But Evie still had an hour to kill before she changed her jeans and her makeup and got herself situated behind the bar, listening to tales of woe and bullshit from the customers.

She took another long draw off the joint and let the smoke out slowly, savoring the warm tingle it brought to her muscles. There was always a soreness in her chest after a session, as if invisible fists had beat themselves against her. Nothing helped ease it better than a little homegrown pot. She finally looked out at the street, to where the Buick LeSabre had been parked. What did Henry's wife want with her now? That's what Evie would like to know. And where had Larry been for the past two nights that he didn't, like a steady heartbeat, turn up on his favorite stool at the tavern, the one with the best view of the overhead television?

Evie closed her eyes and leaned her head back on the swing, eased the strain on her neck. The sessions were getting harder on her as she got older. Maybe it was true what people told her, that she didn't look a day over forty, but in two more months she would be fifty years old. One day, she figured, her own heart would explode with the pressure of channeling and she'd end up being the face some other spiritualist was sketching. But for whom? Was there anyone left on earth, now that her parents were dead, who would want Evie Cooper hovering over their shoulder, looking out for them? Larry Munroe? Well, how could anything important develop between her and Larry if he couldn't get over his guilt and let it happen? She had heard a couple of the regulars talking the night before, saying that Larry hadn't turned up for work at the post office. He had apparently come down with some flu.

Funny, Evie thought, but Larry didn't have any signs of flu three nights earlier, when the two of them had made love in her bed upstairs, in the room with the hanging strands of beads.

It wasn't the flu that was dragging Larry down, and Evie knew it. It was the knowledge of Henry's upcoming memorial service just when it seemed that after a long hurtful year, Larry might heal. Now, Henry was being brought back by his parents in some kind of command performance so that Larry would be forced once more to hear how wonderful his brother had been. And then, for the first time, Larry had finally confessed to Evie that he wondered if Henry knew, somewhere out there in the gauzy film of the afterlife, that the two of them were together, lovers in the wake of his death. *You're feeling guilt, sweetheart,* Evie had told him, that last night in her bed, his head on her pillow, her head against his chest. *I love you with all my heart, but you're just not used to someone loving you more than they love Henry.* And that's when Evie could hear Larry's own heart begin to beat so irregularly and so loudly that she feared he, too, would die of a heart attack. But he didn't. He got up, put on his pants, and left without kissing her good-bye.

There was something about Larry that his younger brother didn't have, and it was the one thing he and Evie shared in common. It was the one trait that made her think maybe, after all these years, Lawrence Munroe IV was the one for her. It was sadness. Pure, undiluted sadness. But when you know that kind of sadness, it frees you to know joy. And she had tried to tell Henry that, mere days before he died. *You're married, Henry. I've been telling you for weeks now that it's over. Larry and I have been talking a lot, nights he's at the bar and you're home with Jeanie. I like him, Henry. And I think he likes me too. I wish we could, well, I wish we could see if there's anything there. I want your blessings, Henry.* What Henry had given her instead was an argument. *Are you crazy? How dare you get the hots for my big brother? Besides, Larry wouldn't give you the time of day, Evie. He knows I'm hoping you and me will start up again, just like we used to be.*

Evie put the last of her joint in the ashtray she kept by the porch swing. It was half-filled with the stubs of other joints. Later, she would roll a fresh one from all those remainders. She had even smoked a joint out at Henry's grave, many times in the year that he'd been dead. She talked to him then, better than she had ever been able to talk to him when he was alive. The trouble with Henry was plain to Evie shortly after their affair began. He was a lot of good things, no doubt about it, but he was also spoiled. If things weren't mostly about Henry they weren't important things. Larry was the sensitive one. The only thing Evie never told Henry, those nights she walked out to the cemetery at the edge of town and leaned against his headstone, so late at night no one would catch her there, was that not only was his big brother giving her the time of day, he was giving her most of the night, too.

• • •

When Evie clocked in at Murphy's Tavern, it was just past eight and the bar was already packed and explosive.

It was Ladies' Night, and that always brought out the sad and the wretched, the forlorn and the loveless, both male and female. The women drank for half price, which meant they were drunker and easier come closing time. It was Evie's least favorite night to work. A bar full of giggling and irrational women, and horny and irrational men, was how she viewed Ladies' Night. She worked her way down the bar, picking up dead soldiers, flipping empty beer glasses into the basin of soapy water behind the bar, and dumping ashtrays. Andy Southby was there, as usual, and already hard at work annoying the other customers.

"Hey, Evie with the light brown hair," Andy said, as she took away his empty beer bottle and wiped the bar in front of him.

"How's it goin', Andy?" Evie hoped he wouldn't tell her. But she had to at least ask. He *was* a customer.

"Good, good," said Andy, that smugness Evie had come to dislike spread across his face. "I've been accepted at four colleges already, but I dunno. The way I'm looking at it now, I might go into business with my uncle. I think college is a waste of time when there's money out there just waitin' to be made."

Evie wiped out his ashtray, made it shine with a wet cloth.

"It will be academia's loss," she said, and moved on down the bar before Andy could respond. That he wanted to talk was obvious. He liked to use Evie as his sounding board, someone he could tell his large stories to since she was trapped behind the bar and he was a patron. But his bragging was meant for the men and women seated around him and Evie knew it.

By the time she got to the boy in the orange wool bonnet, Evie was already feeling the beads of sweat run down the back of her neck. Dan Murphy needed a new air-conditioning system for the place but, like most bar owners she'd worked for, he was too cheap to buy one.

"What can I get you?" Evie asked.

"Beer," said Chad. "A Bud." He looked up at Evie, who looked straight back at him, not flinching.

"Got any ID?" she asked. Chad produced one for her. Evie took the square of plastic and peered down at it.

"Bruce Paulson, from Boston, Massachusetts," she read. "Born December 18, 1986."

"That's me all right," Chad said. Evie threw the card down on the bar in front of him.

"Where do you find these things, Chad?" she asked.

"The Internet," he said, as he took the ID and put it back in his pocket. "You can find pigs that fly on there, if you know how to surf."

"Yeah, well," said Evie, "I don't need a flying pig. Wait until your Uncle Larry finds out about this." Chad shrugged. He waited as Evie opened a Coke and put it in front of him, next to a glass of ice.

"Uncle Larry won't come out of his bedroom," said Chad. "Grandma thinks he's having a nervous break-down. I heard her telling Mom."

Evie said nothing. At first, she hadn't liked the idea of Chad coming into the tavern. But Murphy's served food, and underage clients were allowed inside as long as they didn't drink alcohol. The first day Chad stopped by had been a few weeks earlier, and he was looking for his uncle. The two of them sat side by side on their bar stools and said absolutely nothing, as Henry and Larry liked to do. Wordless, and yet you could tell they were saying all that was important and necessary. It was obvious that the boy needed his uncle. Anyone could see that Henry's son was in deep pain and maybe even headed for trouble. Larry had promised her he'd look out for Chad while he was at Murphy's. Now, here the boy was and Larry was locked in his room, if rumors were to be believed.

"Nice hat," said Evie. "Where'd you get it?"

"Birthday gift," said Chad. He put a dollar down so that Evie would give him quarters for the pinball machine.

"Isn't it kind of warm for a woolen hat?" She put the four quarters on his open palm.

"When you're as cool as I am," said Chad, "you need a woolen hat or you'll freeze to death." He flipped one quarter up into the air and caught it on its way down. He smiled at Evie, that same smile she'd seen a million times on Henry Munroe's face. And this was the thing that was so hard at first, the fact that looking at Chad was like looking at a young Henry. Larry had mentioned it, too. *It's like my brother is back, only it's the Henry I knew when we were boys. Henry is young again, and still in high school, and I'm just old.*

"Well, Mr. Cool, I'd be careful if I were you," said Evie. "It's Ladies' Night and I'm already out of patience. I catch you sneaking beers again, you're out the door for good. Got it?" But Chad was already headed for the pinball machine.

. . .

By the time Evie got home, she was too tired to shower or even eat. She rolled her last joint of the day and took it with her up the stairs. Lying back on her bed, pillows propping her head at the angle she liked, one that would help release the tension in her neck muscles, she watched the light from the street flicker across her ceiling. It always reminded her of the northern lights she saw as an eight-year-old child, that Christmas her parents had rented a small cabin in northern Vermont. A full, cold week of lights cutting up the night sky as she and her father stood outside, bundled in thick coats, noses cold at the tips, watching. She had been so overcome with emotion that it was difficult for her to put it into words. But she knew then, even so young, that she would always be a kind of replacement for Rosemary Ann, that little girl with the dark and perfect ringlets, the one who had been sitting on the plush seat of the Kaiser Manhattan just a year earlier. Evie had already figured it out. That week in Vermont had been like the week in Nova Scotia, just another attempt to make Evie happy, to pretend there was nothing missing from their lives but the seashells they might find along the beach. In fact, her mother had spent both of those weeks, and all the many other vacations over the years, inside whatever house or camp or cottage they had rented, in the shadows, as if Rosemary Ann might visit her there instead of in bright sunshine. Finally, just Evie's father kept up the charade of being a parent. That wintry night in Vermont, with strings of blue and white lights zigzagging the sky like lightning, Evie had stood close to him, grateful as a child is for any kindness from the adult world. She wanted desperately to tell him that she understood his grief, that it was all right if he couldn't give himself completely to her. It was okay if a good part of him, a big piece of his heart, would always belong to Rosemary Ann. But she couldn't. Instead, she had whispered, "I love you," into the cold night. She had watched the warm puff of breath form in the chilly air and then drift away, taking those three words with it, taking them away from her father's ears. Over the years she had even wondered if the puff had come to earth somewhere. Perhaps it had floated out to sea. Maybe it was still drifting, waiting for someone to burst it with a pin so that ears could hear the frozen words. *I love you.* One thing was sure. Evie never spoke those words again until she finally said them to Larry Munroe, that night he got up out of her bed, put on his pants in a hurry, and left. *I love you.* Funny, but they are such tender, sweet words, bringing with them such promise. And yet, they can cause so much damage. Or, in Larry's case, fear.

Evie released her breath and let the last of the joint out in a thin stream of smoke. She put the small butt into the bowl she kept up by her bed, next to the other roaches that were already there. The Roach Garden, she called it. She sat up and took off her blouse, then threw it onto a chair by the side of her bed. She unhooked her bra but left it on. She wanted to loosen the thing so that her breasts could fall free. "My breasts need to breathe," she liked to say. If it weren't for the looks she was always getting at the tavern, she would never wear a bra to work. On impulse, which was now part of her life, she turned to look at herself in the mirror. But all she saw was what she always saw: an older woman who looked like the young woman she knew herself to still be. An older Evie with thick brown hair trickling down her back. An Evie tired from a long day and a long night's work. Tired of wondering where it was that Larry Munroe had gone. Where, and *why*. That's all she saw, a woman almost fifty and still pretty enough to turn a head here and there, now and then. But there was no kind father peering over her shoulder, no mother, no sister, no old friend from school days, no distant cousin, no loving grandmother. And there was certainly no Henry Munroe. The truth was that Evie was gifted enough to see the faces of everyone else's dead, but she could never see her own, not since that first and last visit from Rosemary Ann. This was why, from the time she woke in the morning until she smoked her last joint of the night, Evie Cooper knew with certainty that she lived her life alone.

· 5 ·

Jeanie sat before the psychologist as she had been doing for two months now, each woman waiting, Jeanie for the hour to pass, the psychologist for Jeanie to say something. This had been her friend Mona's idea, when the grief counseling sessions Jeanie had been to hadn't seemed to help. "It's been ten months," Mona had said, "and you've not moved ahead as you should have." Apparently, there was some schedule tacked up on some giant bulletin board that told people how long they had to mend themselves after losing a loved one, and Jeanie Munroe was way behind. A clock ticked somewhere—at least Jeanie thought she heard one. Maybe it was *time* she could now hear, ticking away, second by second, reminding her that life was passing by while she was still floating in some dark cloud. Life was leaking away from her, in drips and drops, while she kept herself at a safe distance. Her biggest thought these days had been for the children, for Lisa delivering a healthy new baby, for Chad living one full day in which all he did was smile, as he used to. For Jeanie herself to get through the hours to that four-pack of margarita wine coolers.

"Do you sleep well?" the psychologist asked. There was a ring of impatience in her voice.

"Not really," said Jeanie. "Do you?"

The psychologist said nothing. More time passed.

"Well, that's all for this week," she announced, a quick glance at the tiny box clock on her desk. "Maybe next week you'll feel more like talking."

"Maybe," said Jeanie. She smiled at the woman, the smile she had manufactured for occasions such as this, the one she shuffled out on cue. She reached for her purse on a chair by the door and left without looking back. She heard the soft *click* behind her, the door's latch catching, and that's when she finally felt free. She had come to think of this sound as a soothing lullaby. When she felt it was necessary to visit Frances and Lawrence, she did so, still being the dutiful daughter-in-law. But when she heard that soft *click* at the end of an hour, signifying she was free again and could now be on her way home, she knew she'd just gotten past another hurdle and had lived to tell of it. The *click* at the library, when she returned all those books on *How to Grieve*. The *click* at the drugstore, each time she refilled her sleeping pill prescription. The *click* at Mona's house, after she said good-bye, was a sweet sound because it meant that Jeanie could finally be alone, could nurse her sorrow in the way she saw fit. She had grown to yearn for the last *click* of the day, the sound of her bedroom door closing, locking out the world, locking out Chad's sad face that had disappeared down the hallway to his own room, allowing Jeanie to fall into the pieces she had held together all day.

Out in the parking lot Jeanie could hear children at

play in the Bixley pool across the street. She stood for some time and listened, remembering the aboveground pool Henry had bought for the kids one summer when they were little. It was blue and not the sturdiest thing in town. Showing off for the kids, he had dive-bombed into it, cracking the plastic of one side and releasing all the water they had fed it with the garden hose. A full day's work, and now the pool was busted and unusable. The children, however, had thought it was the funniest thing they'd ever seen. They had clapped their hands and sang out, "Daddy broke the pool! Daddy broke the pool!" And so Henry had packed them all into the tan Buick he owned back then and drove them over to the new community pool, one he couldn't break for it was made of concrete. Afterward, red-faced with sun and tired from swimming, the whole family had gone to the town's new McDonald's for burgers and vanilla shakes.

Jeanie got into her car and cracked the windows, letting out the heat of the day. She drove toward home at first and then, at the last second, turned down Market Avenue and cruised by the Days Inn. She had done this so many times in the past that it was more a habit now than a deliberate decision. Several cars sat in the parking lot, many of them with out-of-state plates, most likely tourists and salespeople. Jeanie used to do this when Henry was still alive and his Jeep would be parked around at the back, hidden, or so he thought, behind the Dempsey dumpster and a thick hedge of box elders. These were the nights he claimed to be at Murphy's Tavern with Larry, watching sports on TV and drinking a couple beers. Jeanie knew why Henry would ask for room 9. It was the number

Ted Williams had on his uniform before the Boston Red Sox retired it for good. Nine had become Henry's lucky number. But it hadn't been so lucky for Jeanie, for in another parking space she always saw the blue Mazda that Evie Cooper still drove to this day, the fenders rattling a bit and a thin crack in the windshield. Then, for weeks, it had been just Henry's black Jeep back there. She had found the Mazda parked out behind Murphy's Tavern, so she assumed Evie had left it there and ridden to the Days Inn in Henry's Jeep. So why hadn't Jeanie parked next to the Jeep, marched over to the door with the number 9 glued to it, and banged her fist like a crazy woman? For one thing, what if Henry hadn't been able to get number 9 that night? What if someone else had rented it first? This would mean that he was in one of five other rooms, but it was a crapshoot as to which one. He could be in number 8, which was Carl Yastrzemski's number before they retired it. Or in number 1, or number 27, or even number 4, which were the retired numbers for Bobby Doerr, Carlton Fisk, and Joe Cronin. But if he wasn't in any of those rooms, then chances were he was in number 42, since that was Jackie Robinson's number, which had long been retired by Major League Baseball. Jeanie knew all six of Henry's lucky numbers since he played them in the lottery every Wednesday and Saturday for years. He was always telling folks his lucky numbers and why they were so. But the real truth was larger than numbers and much more indefinable. There was some kind of power in collecting this evidence against Henry Munroe. Nights when Jeanie had driven home to lie awake on the sofa, watching David Letterman and waiting for Henry to shuffle in, she would plan the day of the Big Showdown. She would imagine Henry's face when the time came to shovel out the receipts, to mention where he always parked the Jeep, the color of Evie's car. She would imagine the shock on his face, especially when she told him she wanted a divorce. She'd triumph, is what she'd do. And she was right on the cusp of shouting, "Aha!" when Henry died. And now, it had been a year since the parking spaces at the Days Inn had seen either the black Jeep or the blue Mazda.

At the end of Market Avenue, Jeanie turned right onto Hayes Drive, and again onto Ezell Street, which she followed down until she saw the sign in the front yard: *Spiritual Portraitist.* She pulled the car up to the curb and sat there, waiting, until the lacy curtain in the downstairs window moved, ghostlike, as if a wind had rippled through it. She knew then that Evie was home, peering out at the Buick. The woman didn't need to be a spiritual psychic to know that this was the Munroe family car. Henry had sometimes driven the LeSabre down to Murphy's Tavern on those nights when Chad had run off with the Jeep. And Evie Cooper didn't have to be a rocket scientist to know that it wasn't Henry behind the wheel but his wife. Jeanie wanted to make her presence known, that's all. She wanted to make that stand she'd been preparing to make just before Henry died. She wanted to *haunt* Evie Cooper, a ghost from among the living that had a few things to say for itself.

When the curtains fell back into place, Jeanie put the car in gear. Now, as on all the other occasions, she would be able to drive home. As she was about to turn the corner of Oakwood and Hurley, Jeanie slowed the car. Something had caught her attention at the local 7-Eleven: an orange wool bonnet. It was Chad all right, leaning up against the building, one leg kicked back behind him as he rested his foot on the wall. He was looking down the street to where construction men were tarring the road and didn't see the Buick pull in and park behind a U-Haul truck with Texas plates. Jeanie sat waiting and watching until, finally, a boy older than Chad left the store, carrying a brown sack. Chad saw him coming and straightened, a smile on his face, Henry's old smile that caused pain in Jeanie's heart every time she saw it. Now, seeing it again, she realized that perhaps Chad wasn't smiling in her presence for that very reason. Perhaps he saw the pain it brought to his mother's face. But he was smiling now as he accepted the six-pack of beer from the older boy, a boy Jeanie knew very well to be Milos Baxter. As she watched, Chad passed a couple bills to Milos, who quickly bunched them up and shoved them into his pocket. Milos went then to his car, got in, and spun it out of the parking lot. Chad took the six-pack over to his bike and fitted it into the saddlebag on the side. Then he jumped behind the wheel, kick-started the thing, and in seconds was gone. Jeanie had to wonder if she saw this scene unwind or had imagined it, so quickly had the film of it run. She sat there in the heat of the parking lot for another ten minutes thinking of Chad, of that sweet boy who wanted to be a professional bass fisherman when he grew up. Jeanie sat there at the 7-Eleven and thought about her old life that was now gone.

• • •

Dear Marshall,

I think you know by now that this is the end, and I mean it this time. If you bother me again I'll get a court order, so help me god. And I don't want you bugging Timmy at school like he says you been doing. Please respect my wishes this time around. If not, I'll have to take some action. So help me.

Paula Lynn Thompson

Larry folded the white sheet of typing paper in the same places Paula had used when she freshly creased it, put it into the envelope, and mailed it to Marshall Thompson, her ex-husband. The handwriting was in a purple ink and stood out nicely against the white, as if trying its best to be bold. Larry could almost smell food—eggs and bacon, maybe—wafting up from the fiber of the paper. He wondered if Paula had written it during her break at the diner, just after the breakfast crowd of truckers, farmers, and local businesspeople had paid their checks, taken the free toothpick, and left until lunchtime. They had places to go and things to do, but Larry always lingered over his cup of coffee. This was during those after-teaching and before-delivering-the-mail mornings when, jobless and having passed out all his résumés that day, he had nowhere else to be, what with Murphy's Tavern not yet open. This was before he came to realize that he had no choice but to accept his father's offer of a job at the post office. But until then, Larry had watched Paula watch those last customers out the door. That's when she had taken a few minutes to herself before preparing the cold luncheon plates, her own time to sit and smoke a quick cigarette, drink a small Coke with ice. As Larry read her letter to Marshall, he could almost see Paula in that booth by the window, head bent over the sheet of paper, curls on the nape of her neck in soft, damp spirals, the smoke from her cigarette corkscrewing up from the ashtray, her thin lips moving softly as she wrote each word. *If you bother me again I'll get a court order, so help me god.* Larry had also seen the soft blue bruises, growing like grapes on Paula's arms. Once, he had seen a bruise on her cheek, an inch-wide scrape, as though perhaps the smooth skin had been pulled across something harsh. The floor carpet maybe. He had even considered asking Paula out on a date, but hesitated, knowing Marshall Thompson from the old high school football days, knowing the streak of violence that ran below his surface. Paula had a son, a boy about Jonathan's age, and Larry wondered if maybe it was missing Jonathan as he did that was pushing him to find another family, one ready-made. A take-out family, if you will. And why not? Everything seemed fast these days. Fast foods, fast deliveries, fast marriages, fast divorces.

Hearing a quick knock on his bedroom door, Larry scooped up the loose letters lying on his chest and shoved them back into the mailbag beneath his bed. He knew who it was. Who else but Frances Munroe, his mother.

"Larry, I want you to open this door," she said. There was silence as Larry waited. He assumed that soon, very soon, his parents would find a screwdriver and take the door off its hinges. Like Gestapo they would storm in, wearing tall black-leather boots, helmets, leather jackets. They would take the mail pouch back by force. All he wanted to know was, "Is today the day?"

"Larry?" he heard Frances say now, and he caught what sounded like a different pain in her voice. This wasn't the Henry pain, but the Larry pain. He knew she loved him and cared about his welfare. She just didn't love him or care about him as much as she did Henry. But then, who could? Henry was that kind of guy, the kind of personality that demands attention when it enters a room.

"Yes?" he said. He couldn't bear to hurt her, not when he heard the Larry pain in her voice.

"I need to talk to you," said Frances. She waited. Larry sat up in bed and let out a long breath of air. It felt good to do this, as if he were letting out sorrow. He went to the door and unlocked it. He saw the knob turn and the door open slowly. There stood Frances in a pink cotton house dress, her perfect gray curls smooth and shiny on her head. He liked the looks of her, it was true, that pure mother look she had. It used to make him feel comfortable, for in those days when Henry was around, there was enough mother in her for Larry, too. Now, it seemed all of them lived only to keep Henry's memory alive. This had become their new occupation while they went doggedly about their day, pretending those other occupations were important. They weren't, and Larry knew this now. Nothing meant anything to them anymore but Henry, that he had once lived, that he had once walked among them. They existed now only to serve his memory, and Larry had had enough of it. He wanted his old life back, the one before Jonathan disappeared, the one in which he taught history. He wanted to turn up at his parents' door and see in their eyes happiness that he was there. Now, as he looked down at his mother's face, all he saw was despair.

"When are you going to stop this?" Frances said. She couldn't contain the disapproval she felt right then. Or was it disgust? Larry could no longer tell. The sadness had mixed their emotions all together, like a kind of primordial soup. Their happiness and joy now comingled with their pain and sorrow, like a thick syrup that was smothering them. Was that ache Larry felt when he awoke over missing Jonathan? Or Henry? Or both? Or was it for the life he thought he would live, back when he was a teenager and catching all those footballs, making all those touchdowns just behind Henry? He had come to realize that it no longer mattered, since an ache was an ache.

"I don't know," Larry said. "I don't know when I'm going to stop this." And he realized for the first time that this was the truth. He didn't know. Maybe he would live in his old bedroom forever. Maybe his parents would die, and then vines and thorny growth would cover the entire house, the town forgetting that he was ever in that upper room where the small yellow light was still burning. Until one night, the light no longer came on. Maybe.

"I want you to go see Dr. Carden," his mother said. "You've got to get a grip, Larry. You've got to pull out of this."

Larry felt an immense love for her then. He wanted to put his arms around her, wanted to weep tears against her neck, to feel her arms around *him* as he did when still a child. But he had gotten too big and too old for her to hug. It made her uncomfortable, and he sensed it. He was a grown man and now, like those Easter chicks that are so fluffy until they grow into clucking hens, he was no longer something to be cuddled.

"I need some time," Larry said. He felt very awkward standing there, one arm against the doorjamb, the other hanging limply at his side. Bare-chested and barefoot, he was wearing only his black sweatpants. But even in a full suit of clothes, tie, cuff links, cummerbund, the whole works, he always felt very boyish in his mother's presence.

"Henry's memorial service is a week away and you're still locked in this room," Frances said. Larry smiled down at her. What else could he do? It wasn't really about him, about his welfare, about his son disappearing down the interstate to another life, about his failed marriage, about his lost job. It wasn't even about the goddamned purloined mail, a government offense if ever there was one. It was still about Henry.

Larry closed the door in his mother's face. Then he locked it.

• • •

Evie dreamed of Henry that night. She had slept with the bedroom window open, the curtain fluttering in the breeze, the ends of it slapping the foot of her bed. Henry was at the Days Inn, holding the door wide open to room 9. Evie was telling him again what she had told him the last time she met him there. She was sitting in the rickety motel chair and Henry was lying on the bed, his head on a pillow and a lit cigarette in his hand as he listened. *No more, Henry. I feel ashamed is what I feel. This can't go on. I've lived in this town long enough to meet your wife at the grocery store, our carts banging together. I hope she never finds out. I want this to end now.*

In the dream, Henry had done just what he'd done when he was alive. He'd jumped from the bed wearing nothing but his white jock shorts. He'd grabbed Evie up off the chair and flung her onto the bed, covered her with the weight of his body. *Are you nuts? You know you're crazy about me.* But Evie had resisted him, had spurned Henry's attempts to pull her back to the magnet of his personality. Henry wasn't used to being rejected in any form, she could tell. He'd grown furious with her. *You'll be back, Evie,* he'd said. *Where you gonna go? Who you gonna go to?* But Evie hadn't gone back. Instead, Henry had taken to getting that same room at the Days Inn, getting into bed with a six-pack of beer, and phoning Evie up, whether she was at home or at the tavern. *I'm in bed at the Days Inn, with a six-pack of cold beer and wearing nothing but a smile,* Henry would call her to say. *I got you a bottle of that French wine you like. Come on over, Evie. There's a pillow next to mine with your name on it.* But Evie had stopped going. Later, Henry told Larry that he'd come to enjoy watching sports on the Days Inn television, no tavern noise to disrupt him, no Chad playing his CDs at top volume, no Jeanie talking loudly on the phone to her friends. It was just Henry, the TV, that six-pack of beer, and a pillow where Evie's head used to be. It might have been true. Or maybe it was Henry's pride talking.

Whatever it was, it was a year old. Now that the Buick was turning up in front of Evie's house, parked at the curb like some kind of spy car, she knew that Jeanie wanted to talk. That's why Evie had finally written Jeanie Munroe a letter. She had mailed it three days earlier, but there had been no response, not yet. It was a mess, that's what it was. Their lives had gotten all mixed up in tangles and briars, so much so that maybe they'd never unravel themselves.

When Evie woke it was still only one a.m. She knew it would be a couple hours before she could fall back asleep. She always had a hard time sleeping in the heart of the night, ever since she began her sketching as a profession. Sometimes, she even heard muffled voices talking to her, as if a group of people were all wrapped up in cobwebs and trying to tell her their secrets. She would sit up in bed to listen, but the voices were always too distant to hear well. She wondered if this was her own family, trying to break through the veil to reach her. If so, they needed to poke harder. They needed to speak up.

"Fuck it," Evie said. She hadn't the concentration to lie there for two hours, waiting for sleep to come back to her, not that morning. And not with so many new variables being tossed about, from Henry to Larry, to even Jeanie and Chad. She got out of bed and found her rumpled jeans where she'd stepped out of them the night before. She pulled them on and grabbed a denim shirt from her closet. She selected one of the joints she'd rolled in case of an emergency and slipped it into the shirt pocket. She put the lime-green plastic lighter into the hip pocket of her jeans.

She didn't bother to lock the door behind her, not in Bixley. The night air was damp, still moist with a brief summer rain that had come and gone earlier in the evening. Evie counted stars as she walked, the big bright ones that manage to shine through haze and light pollution. A ten-minute walk later, and she was at the cast-iron gates of Woodlawn Memorial Cemetery, at the edge of town. She stood there a minute, letting her eyes adjust to the light coming from the pole lamp that had been erected near the cemetery. *I Go To Prepare A Place For You*, said the brass plaque on the front gate, which Evie opened slowly. She heard the creak echo across the tops of the headstones. Twenty stones in, five stones over: *Henry Munroe, b. November 10, 1962—d. July 8, 2002*. At the grave, Evie sat on the ground and took the joint from her shirt pocket. She lit it up, the Bic snapping its own tiny echo out into the night. In the mottled light, she could see that someone had left a new pot of flowers at the base of Henry's stone. She held the Bic's small flame closer to the pot. The flowers appeared to be pink geraniums. The grass had already grown, not as thick and green as the older graves, but thick enough and green enough that the earth was making a statement. The earth was taking Henry's body back into itself, into its mouth, digesting it, taking it home.

One of the few things Evie Cooper remembered about high school was the play her junior class had done, *Our Town*, where the dead in a small cemetery talk to the living who come to visit them. But the living can't hear their words. By the time her class had done the play, Evie already knew the truth, that spirits show themselves to some but not to others. And so she had paid attention for the first time in her school years. She had clung to every word. And maybe that's what brought her to a small New England town. Maybe it was the memory of how she had felt almost safe while the class was reading that play. Feeling safe is what the living want most. But sometimes, only the dead realize it.

Under the large pole lamp at the cemetery entrance, bats and moths swooped and dived beneath the light. Evie watched them as she smoked, taking each draw far down into her lungs and holding it there. She looked back at the headstone that marked Henry's resting place. Dear Henry. He deserved to live. He deserved to fall in love once more with Jeanie, some wild night of wine and an old black-and-white movie. He deserved to see the baby his daughter was carrying. He deserved to see Chad grown into manhood, proud and tall and handsome. As Evie finished the joint, she saw a bat swoop down fast and swift into a circle of moths. And then, just as quick, it was gone again. One less moth in the world. With the pot finally settling in, turning her thoughts pleasant for a change, it all seemed funny now. Bats and moths. Sometimes you win, sometimes you lose. Life was really quite simple, especially when you considered its qualities late at night, in a country cemetery, stoned to the heavens.

Evie lay back on the cool grass, stretched herself out as long and lean as she could, one arm over the mound of earth, as if it were Henry himself. They had slept that way at the Days Inn until guilt, or maybe it was duty, would pull Henry out of a deep sleep, send him scurrying to his pants and shoes, and the jangling keys to his Jeep. Most of the time, Evie would spend the rest of the night there alone, between the cool sheets, hating to waste money spent on a room for just a couple hours. But that was before she told Henry it was over.

"Hey, it's me," she said. Her words sounded hollow, lost among the numerous headstones. She could hear movement in the brush and knew the raccoons and foxes were out searching for food. A few stars were bright enough overhead to break past the light of the pole lamp. They squinted and blinked down at her from their dark sky. "I can't sleep."

"Neither can I." It was a voice that came from out of the shadows. Evie's heart went wild, beating so hard and fast that she could feel it press against her breast, a small fist pounding. Then time slowed down for her again. She sat up.

"Who the hell is it?" she asked. "That's not funny, you know." She heard a rustling from behind the rosebushes that grew along the edge of the cemetery. Footsteps came toward her. She held her hand up to her eyes, trying to make out the shape in the blue-purple glare of the pole lamp. It was a tall man with an easy, halfhearted stride, the way Henry Munroe walked. Her heart began its rapid beating again, a heart thinking for itself since Evie now knew the truth. It wasn't Henry. Under the rays of artificial light, the orange wool bonnet looked almost yellowish.

"Chad," she said. "What the hell are you doing out here?" He squatted at the end of his father's grave, rocking on his haunches, staring at the stone, unable to see the words that Evie knew were written there: *Beloved Father, Husband, Son.* From across the short distance she could smell the thick odor of beer, a smell she knew well from Murphy's Tavern.

"Guess I could ask you the same thing," Chad said. Evie had to think fast.

"I couldn't sleep," she answered. "So I went for a walk and, well, when I ended up here, I figured I'd visit old Mrs. Conley. She died, you know. She used to make such good pies. Conley's Bakery isn't the same without her. And then, well, I remembered your dad was here, and he was always such a good tipper."

In the shadows, she saw Chad nod his head, and she knew this pleased him. It was the kind of legacy Henry had wanted to build for himself, that of the social man, a man who always had a good joke ready to roll and a tendency to buy a round of drinks for the house every time the Sox hit a home run.

"He was something, the old man," Chad said. Evie smiled now, still feeling the sweet stupor of the pot, relishing in the irony of the moment, as only one who is stoned in a cemetery can. What if someone had told Henry before he died that on one star-filled night in the near future Evie Cooper would be sitting out by his grave while his son, Chad, squatted at the end of it?

Chad put his head back and sniffed, wolflike, at the air around him.

"I smell something better than beer," he said.

"I'm all out," said Evie. "And even if I wasn't, I wouldn't give you any."

"I'm not out," said Chad. He reached into his jacket pocket and quickly produced what Evie knew would be a joint. When his lighter burst to flame, she saw it clenched in his fingertips as he lit it. He inhaled and then offered it to her, for she saw the fiery tip coming toward her in the night. She wanted to accept it, knowing the pot would carry her a bit deeper into herself. She trusted Chad, even though he was just a boy. He was a smart boy, the kind of boy the dead might even talk to, when he was ready to listen. He was a boy who seemed to know things only older folks should know, a knowledge of the outer world that some folks are born with and others can't learn, not even at the best university. Evie almost reached for the joint.

"I can't, Chad," she said. "You're not of age, and besides, you're Larry's nephew. He'd have a fit if he knew you were out here right now. And doing this." She heard Chad inhale again, long and deep. The smell of the pot was laced with that *other* smell, what smelled like a *library* to Evie, a smell that took her places, carried her into other realms, toward new ideas and poetic adventures, the same things a good book is supposed to do.

"I told you," said Chad. "Uncle Larry is hiding out in his old bedroom, afraid the bedbugs will bite."

A night owl gave its low and mournful *hoo hoo hoot* from beyond the crest of trees behind the cemetery. Evie sighed, giving in, giving up, maybe. She knew the boy wanted to talk hard and deep. He was a smart boy, and he was certain she had some kind of connection to his father, some kind of lifeline, a bungee cord, maybe, that Evie Cooper could pull and it would bring Henry Munroe bouncing back to Bixley.

"I know you're hurting, Chad," said Evie. Again, she pushed away his offer of the joint that came toward her in the darkness, its orange glow so tempting. "I can see your pain every time you come into the tavern."

For a long time Chad said nothing. Instead, he rocked in that same way, down on his haunches, as if maybe he was about to learn something that would make him want to spring up and run for his life. As Evie waited for him to respond, more bats swooped down under the pole light. More moths disappeared into their bellies. A car passed the cemetery, loud music booming from its radio, the glassed-in sound of laughter beating around inside the interior. Teenagers, coming home from some late party, no doubt. Chad reached into his jacket pocket. She heard a tinny *pop!* as the tab of a beer can was pulled off. She saw him tilt the thing and drink.

"Sometimes," said Chad, his voice so low Evie almost couldn't hear him, "sometimes, I don't think I can get through the day. Other times, I'm so mad at him that I'm glad I got another day to live that he don't."

"It's not easy losing a parent," said Evie. "I know." She wanted to reach out and hold him to her, the son she never had. She wanted to comfort him with the strength she knew came from the circle of her own arms. She had that kind of power over people, the kind they want to sink down into and finally feel safe, the kind of sinking she, herself, would love to do in someone else's arms. But she knew she couldn't. She had made enough of a mess in this boy's life without his even knowing it, at least not yet.

"Does my dad, you know?" Chad stopped. He took the last draw of the roach and then snapped what was left down onto the ground, at the end of Henry's grave. He let the smoke out in a warm stream that soon made its way to Evie on the wind. "Does my father *appear* to you? Do you ever see him around *me*, like when I come into the tavern? Is that how it works? I mean, maybe a ghost don't want to come into a place like Murphy's." He laughed then, a laugh that turned into a giggle. It was the tingle of the pot that had made this seem funny to him, and now Evie was thankful. She was afraid she might say the wrong thing.

"Come on," Evie said, and stood. She reached down one hand until it touched his shoulder. Funny, but he seemed so small beneath that big jacket he liked to wear, even in the summer, so thin and innocent inside it. But a jacket is sometimes a good place to hide, especially if you're right out in the open. A jacket, topped off by an orange bonnet, and a boy could almost disappear, if he wanted to. "Let's walk on back," Evie said. "It's getting late."

6

Dear Jeanie,

I am so very sorry for your sadness. I have seen your car outside my house on many nights. Would you like to come inside and talk sometime? I would then have the chance to apologize to you in person, for I owe you that. I realize we will never be friends, but life is too short for us to be enemies.

Evie Cooper

L arry stared at the letter a long time before he folded it again. He put it in what he was considering the "still to deliver" pile. At least, he put it there until he could decide what he should do with it. All other letters were being tossed into a clothes basket, which he could quickly cover with a towel in case his mother came patrolling. It hurt him to see Evie's name, written in a dark blue ink, a flourish to the capital *E*, as if wind were carrying the fluid that had created it. He missed her. He missed so much about her that now he tried to forget he'd even seen the damn letter. It hadn't said who it was from on the envelope, just that it was for *Ms. Jeanie Munroe*. Larry's territory all lay west of the high school and that was where Jeanie lived, several streets over from Thorncliffe, where Stella Peabody lived, Stella, the sixtysomething librarian with the silver-gray hair and yet no husband in sight. Now, Larry knew why. He had not one but two lilac-scented letters from Sheila Dewberry of Sioux City, Iowa, in the "still to deliver" pile. How could he not deliver them? Love letters were so important to human beings. They were so much more important than pleas to colleges for admittance, such as were Andy Southby's letters. Or the angry letters that Peter Finn was sending to Mack Phillips, who owed him four hundred dollars for a stereo. Or the many credit card bills folks all over town were receiving for the tons of junk they bought themselves, from snowmobiles and six-day cruises to electronic gadgets that Larry didn't know existed. He now felt that he'd accidentally stumbled upon a plan that could revitalize the United States Postal Service at a time when it needed a good attic cleaning, what with email breathing down its neck. How about if a select group of mail carriers were chosen to *read* the mail before it's allowed to be delivered? Letter writers would have to compete with each other in order to get their letter delivered. Therefore, they'd write a letter as letters were meant to be written, wonderful epistles as in those days of yore, with thought and passion and intelligence. Maybe they'd be expected to seal the envelope with a glob of dark red wax, like a huge drop of blood. There should be more to the art than jotting some shit down on paper and quickly licking a stamp with Elvis's face on it. Those letters that weren't chosen, the meaningless bunk, would be tossed into wastebaskets, such as Larry was now doing. And the good stuff, the winners, could even be hand-delivered, adding a personal touch that not even the Internet, with its dumb yellow smiley faces and inserts of flower bouquets, could compete with.

Larry quickly tore open the next letter since he could see it wasn't personal. Jimmy Thompson owed Liman's Hardware almost eighteen hundred dollars for a sofa and a reclining chair. Larry could almost see Jimmy's fat ass sinking down into the cushions, the springs and coils whining beneath the weight of him as he flicked TV channels with the remote control. If there was no such thing as the remote, Jimmy Thompson would probably weigh at least fifty less pounds. Larry tossed the bill into the clothes basket. Jimmy had all those kids, so he didn't need another bill. Debbi Sutton was sending out her wedding invitations. Larry had already found two others. The real purpose behind the wedding invitation, in general, or so Larry had come to believe after his weeks of delivering them, was to ask for a wedding gift.

Nevertheless, Larry put Debbi Sutton's three invitations in the delivery pile. He liked Debbi, had seen her blossom into a fine young lady during the year he taught her history. It seemed as if she'd grown a foot from early September to late May, her breasts getting larger, too, looking more round, like a woman's, rather than those perky, peaked things that teenaged schoolgirls like to point at every boy they meet in the hallways. And

Debbi's personality had changed, too, with her interests becoming a bit more cerebral. She had been talking about universities and careers more and more as the days went by, and less and less about boys. And then, just as she should have been packing up for some good school out in Arizona or Illinois, she and Bruce Finney had decided to get married. Who knows why? A baby on the way, maybe. Time would tell. Larry knew a lot about this phase in a young person's life, this "edge of the cliff" phase where they would either jump or get a plan for themselves. Having taught so many high school kids, he had a ringside seat for watching as nature, with the silent help of estrogen and testosterone, molded these young people, some for the better, some for the worse. Andy Southby being one of the latter. Here was yet another rejection letter for the little bastard, this time from a school in Kansas City that didn't have any interest in teaching Andy how to succeed at Restaurant Chain Management. *Perhaps your services would be put to better use in some other industry.* Larry put the rejection letter on the top of his delivery pile, where already rested the other rejection letter for Andy, from the Howard F. Honig College of Nebraska. Sometimes, it was important for a person to know how much the world didn't want them.

"Larry?"

He froze, his hands still holding the letter he'd just opened, yet another from Sheila to Stella. But what else did two horny old maids, hundreds of miles apart, have to do with their time but write perfume-scented letters? And this one had started with a bang, too.

*Darling, I hope I don't smother you with letters since I
cannot smother you with kisses, but a rainstorm woke
me in the night. Such thunder and lightning! Pussy and
I then lay awake, thinking of you.*

Larry had been trying to decide if Sheila were talking
about an actual house cat, or being metaphorical, when
the knock came.

"Would you open the door, please?" Jeanie asked. "I'd
like to talk to you."

Larry rapidly shoved letters to and fro, under things,
on top of things, between things. He would soon need to
develop a kind of method, something akin to the Dewey
decimal system, whereby he could hide letters quickly,
perhaps in order of their street numbers, since that's how
he'd come to think of the residents of Bixley who lived in
his territory. He thought of them as addresses now, and
not by their last names. When he saw Stella Peabody, for
instance, he immediately thought, *215 Thorncliffe*. If he
had no choice but to see Andy Southby being obnoxious
at Murphy's Tavern, he didn't see Andy. He saw *566 Gray
Lane*. Marshall Thompson wasn't Marshall Thompson,
former football player and ex-husband who was making
Paula Thompson miserable. He had become nothing
more than *45 Oakwood Street*. And now, now, here was
39 Hurley Avenue, banging on his door. *Jeanie*.

Larry had hidden all the letters and pulled on a gray
sweatshirt before he opened the door. Jeanie looked sadder
than he remembered her. Rarely had he seen her when he
was delivering mail to her box, and he preferred it that
way. He knew she did, too. Not that they didn't like each

other. They did. Jeanie had been the sister he never had. She had been the one to sit quietly on the sofa next to him and listen while Henry paced the room, all other eyes upon him, as he told a joke. Henry was one of those men who needed to stand up and use his hands and his whole body when he had a story to tell. Larry knew the truth about such men, and he suspected Jeanie did too. They are men who need to be watched, who ache to be adored. So they stand to tell their jokes or their fishing tales, as if to say to the listeners, "Look, here is all of me standing before you, so please notice and love every inch of me." Instead of resenting Henry's large personality, as he had done now and then back in those high school years, especially where girls were concerned, Larry had come to feel a certain measure of sorrow for his little brother. He often saw a panic in Henry's eyes, as if he were alarmed to find himself the center of attraction, as if Henry were saying, "Look where I am again, Larry, right here in the middle of the fucking ring." Henry was addicted to being onstage, long after the narcotic of it, the *adrenaline*, had worn off.

"Come on in," said Larry. "I'd offer you a drink but my parents have locked their liquor cabinet."

Jeanie smiled at this. This was the side of Larry she had come to love. At all those family functions over the years, it had seemed like the two of them had joined forces, a small army of two. They had watched Henry perform and had loved him in spite of it. They had watched Katherine keep a cold distance from the entire family, as if she were too good to be among them in the first place. They had watched their children play the backyard games of childhood. And then, they had watched Frances and Lawrence watch Henry. That was a job in itself. But through it all, she and Larry had passed a funny notion back and forth, so quietly, so un-Henry-like, that no one ever noticed but them.

"I see you haven't lost your sense of humor," said Jeanie. She sat on the bottom bunk and crossed her legs. Then she looked around the room at all the photos of Larry and Henry in their football uniforms. But Larry could see that there was a vagueness to her eyes, as if a film were over them, as if maybe she had trained herself not to let the memories rush in if they should ever ambush her, catch her off guard. The sight of Henry Munroe in his old football uniform should be one big memory that could knock her down. But Jeanie might as well have been looking at some paintings in a museum.

"I'm not trying to be funny," said Larry. "They really *did* lock the liquor cabinet. I went down to get a bottle of scotch yesterday, when the coast was clear. Someone put a padlock on the door."

Jeanie laughed out loud this time. It surprised her to hear the sound of her own laughter again. But somehow, with the memorial service a few days away, there was a kind of electricity in the air that she could almost feel on her skin. There was now so much tension over the first anniversary of Henry's death that it was having a reverse affect on her. Since she couldn't cry anymore, it was possible that she would start laughing and not be able to stop. The way some people hiccup until they end up in the *Guinness Book of World Records*. She opened her purse and took out a pack of cigarettes. As Larry watched, she went to the window and eased it up. She lit a cigarette and stood smoking it there, letting the gray smoke meet the outside breeze and be carried off, down to the green lawn, and the potted geraniums on the front steps, and the pinkish walkway below.

"When did you start smoking?" Larry asked. Jeanie looked over at him. He was Henry's serious side, that's what she had always said. Larry was who Henry *might* have been had he known how to settle down to a small notion of life. She could see that he'd lost weight, too. They had become, unwittingly, one of those weight-loss plans that large businesses or whole communities set out to accomplish as a team. Jeanie had seen such things on TV. *A few dozen workers at the local mattress factory have decided to lose two thousand pounds in six months.* Or, *the town of Collins, Missouri, has joined President Bush in his fitness awareness campaign by vowing to lose ten thousand pounds in a year.* The Munroe family was doing this, too. They just didn't know it. Jeanie took a deep breath.

"I started smoking when I first found out about Henry and Evie Cooper," she said. This seemed to take some energy out of Larry. He sat down on the chair at his desk, but said nothing. Instead, he kept his eyes on his feet, on the gray slippers he had put on that morning. He didn't know what else to do. This statement ambushed him, the way Henry's old football picture should have caught Jeanie off guard. "It's okay," Jeanie added, when she saw how uncomfortable her words had made him. "I'm used to the idea of it now. Trouble is, I don't know if I'm still hurting over *that*, or if I'm hurting over losing Henry. If I knew what was causing the most pain, then maybe I could finally heal."

Larry heard birds outside the window, their songs clear

and pure now that Jeanie had lifted the paned glass and let the notes inside. He heard the whine of traffic as Bixley went about its day. He knew that in an hour or so, he would hear the school bus coming up Hancock Street. A school bus has its own sounds, unique only to it, big gushes of air as its brakes go on, a *swish* as the door opens, another *swish* as it closes, and then the gushes again as it lurches forward. Sometimes, the two *swishes* are punctuated by a child's laugh. Larry had come to resent the very idea of the school bus for it reminded him of his teaching days and how they were now over. Mostly, it reminded him of Jonathan, who was going to school in some other life.

"How about some lunch?" Larry asked. "The special today is tuna fish and pickles." Jeanie smiled. It seemed to her that it was a real smile, but she wasn't sure anymore, not since she had learned to crank out the fake one at a moment's notice.

"I'd love some lunch," she told him.

Larry opened the top desk drawer and Jeanie saw that it was full of a variety of tinned goods. He took out a can of tuna and closed the drawer. He opened the middle drawer, which was crammed with pastries in sealed packages, a loaf of bread, even condiments. As Jeanie watched, Larry took four slices of bread from the wrapper and then found a jar of mayonnaise. He looked over at her.

"You want any dessert?" he asked. When she shook her head, he closed the drawer and pulled open the bottom one, which held a few utensils and paper plates. He took two plates, a plastic knife, and two plastic forks from the drawer and arranged them on the desktop. He went over to a shelf against the wall. Jeanie saw a tall stack of paper cups towering there in a corner. Larry pulled two cups off the stack and then knelt to lift a liter of Coke out of a blue plastic wastebasket that was filled with melting ice.

Within minutes they were having tuna sandwiches, pickles, and cups of cold Coke on the top of Larry's desk. Jeanie couldn't remember the last time she'd felt so *alive*. Maybe the thing that all adults *really* want is to go back to their youth and try again, to get inside those old bedrooms with posters on the walls of movie stars and athletes, school pennants and class pictures, a place where the future is still locked out, a place where dreams can be tacked up over the bed. A safe place.

"Now I understand the problem of the padlock," Jeanie said. "Coke is good, but wine would be better."

"Did Mom ask you to come?"

Jeanie took another bite of the tuna sandwich before she answered.

"Well, sort of," she said. "She's worried about you."

"You can't blame her," Larry said. "I mean, imagine raising a son and watching him go off into the world, all shiny and new and full of potential. Then one day you open your door to find him back, hairy and potbellied and turning gray, all that potential leaked out of him like air from a balloon."

"You're not potbellied," Jeanie said.

"Of course, if it were Henry," Larry added, "she'd be putting a private bath in this bedroom, buying new blankets and curtains."

Jeanie said nothing. With her fork, she rolled a small pickle around her plate. She looked up at Larry.

"Did it take him dying for us to understand how

much he shaped us?" she asked. "Did it take him disappearing, for Christ's sake, before we realized we were just satellites spinning around him?" Larry nodded. Henry was a tough act to follow. After all, where do planets go when there's no sun? He took the bottle of Coke and twisted off its cap. The carbonation inside let loose a loud *hiss*, as if reminding Larry once more of the school bus, those gushes of Jonathan's life that he was no longer privy to. He filled his paper cup and gestured to Jeanie, offering to pour her more, too. She shook her head.

"Hey, how about dinner Thursday night?" Larry asked. "The senior Munroes have a meeting with my fellow postal workers to put the finishing touches on Henry's memorial service. I cracked my door this morning and heard them talking about it."

Jeanie thought about this.

"What's the dress code?" she asked.

"Something old, something new, something borrowed, something blue," Larry said. "Take your pick."

"You got a date," Jeanie said. "Want me to bring the wine?"

· · ·

At three o'clock Evie Cooper opened the door to her first client, Marilyn Foucher, who seemed almost frightened to step inside. This didn't surprise Evie. Often, it's the skeptics who are most scared, knowing that if they're proven wrong, they will have to rethink their lives.

"Don't worry," said Evie, as she put a hand on Marilyn's

shoulder. "It'll be okay. Come in and let's talk first, make sure this is what you want to do."

Marilyn sat on the settee that Evie had pushed into the front room for her clients. She had redone the fabric on it herself, choosing a flowered pattern, light blues and lavenders, since color sets a tone, creates the atmosphere.

"This is a pretty room," said Marilyn, looking at the crystals jangling from lamp shades, the framed prints of angels keeping watchful eyes on the earth, the hanging Boston ferns, the potted palms. A pretty room, and Evie had thought about its décor for many weeks before she had opened a can of paint or bought a curtain. She wanted it to be a place where the living could feel safe.

"Thank you," Evie said. "I want you to feel comfortable here." She sat in the chair positioned a few feet from Marilyn and let a few seconds pass before she began her talk. "Now, as you may already know from Charlotte Davis, I don't pretend to have any answers to any big questions about life and death. But I believe that when we die, we do not cease to exist. I believe we live again. As a matter of fact, I know it, for I have seen the faces of the dead since I've been a very little girl. The first face I ever saw belonged to my own sister, Rosemary Ann. For some reason, God— or whatever power may be—has seen fit to give me this talent. I wish I could share it with you for free, I really do. But if I can accept a reasonable fee for my services, then I can spend more time with folks like you, and in doing so, I hope I can bring you some measure of peace."

Evie knew this warm-up speech by heart. In the earlier years, she had tried to make it original for each and every client, since she wanted them to know that she was truly sincere. But after a number of years, it became easier to remember the words and then deliver the speech to each new person as if it had just been written.

"I do not ask the dead questions for you," Evie went on. "As a matter of fact, none of them speak to me, not since that day I saw my sister. Instead, I study their faces, their eyes, and in this way, they are able to tell me what is still in their hearts. If you have visitors today, and if I see them clearly enough to sketch them, you'll be able to see this for yourself."

Marilyn began to cry. Evie wished she had some kind of assistant for times like this. As much as she cared about the pain and sorrow that life delivered to her clients, it was getting harder and harder for her to be the sounding board for it. And then, these people were mostly strangers to her. She wanted to say to each of them, *Listen, I know you're hurting, I'm hurting, the whole world is hurting. I know life sucks, but it's still the only game in town. So live with your chin back. And hey, believe it or not, the hardest part for me is to channel them. But you don't know that, do you? You think the spirits come to me as easy as turning on your TV set. Well, they don't. They make me pay for every smile, every nod, every wink. Thank the gods for cannabis, and if you really want to do something to help me channel your loved ones, then cast your vote to make the stuff legal.*

"Sit back now and relax," is what Evie said to Marilyn Foucher. She reached for her sketchbook and placed it on her lap, flat across her legs the way she liked it. She selected one of the lead drawing pencils she had sharpened that morning and left in a vase by her chair. Slowly, delicately, she began to make light circles at the top right corner of the page, her pencil going around and around as if it were thinking for itself. All this time, Evie kept her eyes to the right of Marilyn's shoulder, although sometimes spirits also came in at the left. Other times, they were on both sides, if the sitter's energy were so strong that it pulled many of them at once. And then she saw it forming, the face of an older woman she guessed to be seventy years old, maybe older. The contours of the face came first, shaping themselves as if it were a paint-by-numbers picture, the features appearing, the texture of hair and then the hairdo itself, the ball on the end of the nose, the thick eyebrows, the thin lips, the brown mole above the left eye, the dark eyes that seemed so kind. And then, as always, something to nail it, something to say, *Yes, this is who I think it is!* as if all those other things weren't enough. When Evie's pencil finally stopped, a dark-colored cat was cradled in the woman's arms. This was the part of the drawing that Evie referred to as the *coup de grâce*. What was it her mother had said, that day in the green Kaiser when Rosemary Ann had first appeared? She had stared down at the crude drawing and whispered, "I'd forgotten about Rosemary Ann's necklace." The *coup de grâce*, that's what it was. Evie had seen it work time and again over the years. She could thank the dead for this visual help. It was that one *something* that took away the last shred of doubt for the sitter. Today it was the cat. She gave the finished drawing to Marilyn Foucher, who stared at it for a time before she spoke.

"Mama never did go anywhere without that goddamn cat," Marilyn said.

7

When Jeanie got back from Fillmore's Drugstore it was almost noon and Chad was still in bed. She could knock on his door, the way she often did before Henry died, and say, "Chad, honey, you're missing a beautiful day out there." But this was back when nothing was really wrong. This was in that other life when Chad might oversleep a half hour if he'd been up late the night before, watching some rental movie with a friend. But these days he was sleeping in later and later, rising sometimes as Jeanie was having her lunch, that dazed look on his face that seemed to ask if he'd missed something important.

Jeanie put her keys down in the glass bowl that she kept on the hall table. The house was deathly still, and that was the adjective she had come to prefer when she walked in and stood in the hallway, stunned by the silence that settled around her. What she wished now, knowing that she couldn't undo the dead, was that Lisa were back home again, still growing up, still dating different boys until she found the right one, still talking about the children she might have one day. Jeanie wished this as much for Chad as she did for herself. Lisa had been seven years older than her brother and it seemed as if he was too busy riding his bike, fishing, playing softball with the guys, to fully appreciate his sister's presence in the house, to understand that one day it would be gone. But how does a kid know that? That's what Jeanie often woke to ask herself, those nights when she heard Chad tiptoeing up to his room, thinking she wouldn't hear him and ask again why he was out so late. He had that big, wide upstairs to himself, and had for some time before Henry died. How could she, as his mother, have helped prepare Chad any better than she did? What mistakes did she make that other mothers might have seen coming? Did they possess some rare wisdom that had been denied her? Did they tuck their children in at night, kiss them, and whisper into their ears, *I know you're just a kid, but be careful. Be oh so very careful. Touch each day as if it's made of glass.*

In the kitchen, Jeanie could smell the leftover aromas of her own breakfast that morning, the cup of coffee, the waffle she had taken a single bite from before tossing it out for the birds. The bowl of cereal she had left for Chad was still waiting on the table, covered in clear wrap, next to a glass of orange juice, also covered. She wondered if Chad knew how hard she worked to make it appear that life was going on as usual, that this was just another day, another bowl of cornflakes. She went past the table to the fridge and opened the door. She bent and pulled out one of the plastic bins at the bottom, the one on the right, the one designated to hold Chad's favorite drinks. Two cans of Pepsi were neatly arranged at the top of the bin, along with a package of cheddar cheese and some candy bars.

Jeanie shuffled the Pepsi and cheese and candy aside and counted the cans of beer that lay hidden beneath. *One, two, three, four.* Chad used to share that refrigerator bin with Lisa, years before Jeanie ever imagined he would one day hide beer in there. Instead, it had been his Cherry and Vanilla Cokes that had vied with Lisa's Snapples for space. Now, well, the whole bin was his.

Lisa. While Jeanie had watched from behind a kitchen curtain, watched as Chad horsed around with the neighborhood guys, still only twelve years old, Lisa had been with her girlfriends, up in her lavender bedroom, where they were all growing up too quickly. Boys were so different from girls. Boys seemed to hang on to childhood much longer. Once girls started their periods, once their breasts began to grow into soft mounds beneath their sweaters, it was as if they heard a silent language whispered to them by the wind. They put dolls that were still like new up onto shelves where they were to be looked at and admired, but no longer played with. They packed away the Judy Blume books, knowing one day their daughters might read them. They looked with pride upon the snowy white pads or those thin boxes of slim Tampax that were designed for tiny bodies. They felt suddenly *older,* not knowing the rivers of blood that lay ahead with the years, not even caring about cramps, or back pain, or the whole inconvenience of what a boy would surely consider an alien act upon a human body. Girls got down to the business of growing up. And they did it so much faster than boys. At least, that's what had happened to Jeanie and her friends, and it's what she had seen happen in her own home, to her own daughter. And then Lisa had moved to Portland to take a job at a small advertising firm, and that's where she met Patrick Bailey. The wedding had come and gone so fast, as if the day were made of nothing more than lace and satin. All Jeanie could remember of it was how beautiful Lisa looked as she walked down the aisle on Henry's arm. And then, with Henry gone less than four months, Lisa announced that she was pregnant. "I know it's bad timing, Mom," Lisa's girlish voice had told her, the night she called with the news. "But it was an accident." Hearing this, Jeanie had to smile. Lisa had been an accident too, many long years before, a wonderful accident. Now she would have her own family to watch grow up, to fuss over, to guide wisely. That's when Jeanie knew it was time to turn her only daughter's bedroom into something more useful than storage space for abandoned dolls and Judy Blume books with worn covers. Had Chad come to realize that there were only empty spaces in the house where his sister had been? That her departure was like a little death, too? Now and then, a reminder of Lisa Munroe still turned up when Jeanie least expected it. An old hairbrush. A lost earring that Jeanie found while vacuuming. A blue cotton hair band. It was amazing to her how quickly she had begun referring to Lisa's old bedroom as *the guest room,* all those teenaged leftovers gone into boxes in the attic, as if childhood and adolescence were things that could be boxed up and put away. It had happened so fast that Jeanie didn't know how any human being could ever prepare for it. If a *mother* wasn't ready for it herself, how could she warn her *son?* Besides, Jeanie had come to see lives like one of those Hollywood action movies Chad was forever renting. Sometimes, lives play out while you're in the kitchen getting a snack.

After making sure the beers were still covered, Jeanie pushed the bin back in and closed the fridge door. What had she been telling herself for weeks now, once she was finally able to come out of her own stupor enough to pay more attention to Chad? *Every teenage boy is going to drink a beer once in a while. That's how he impresses the girls, not to mention how he handles peer pressure.* At least, that's how Henry had seen it. So, when Jeanie occasionally smelled alcohol on Chad's breath as he hurriedly kissed her cheek and then went past her, up the stairs and into his room, the closing of his door like the period to a sentence of words he could never speak to her, she had remembered what Henry told her. *He's a boy, he's growing up, he'll be okay, he's our kid, we raised him right.* She had been a fool even before Henry died, and now she was a bigger fool. Now, she had seen with her own eyes as Chad waited outside the 7-Eleven until an older boy could deliver him some beer, in the middle of the day. And so Jeanie had driven home and gone on a search, what the cops call a raid. Where else to keep beer but in the fridge? Had she become so ineffective as a parent that her teenaged son didn't have to go any farther than her own kitchen in order to hide booze from her? What would Henry do? Would he slap Chad on the back and say, "That's my boy, that's my man"? Or would he be furious, red-faced, so angry that his son would know immediately the best thing to do was to give up, give in, as Chad had always done in times of trouble? Those two Ds on his report card. The time he was caught smoking at Sunday school and still only twelve. The time he put the roadkill—apparently a squirrel, since it still had a bushy tail attached to the flattened body—into his science teacher's mailbox. The science teacher happened to also be the football coach. That one had hit Henry too close to home for comfort. "I'm a gee-dee mailman!" he'd screamed at his son until the boy had gone so pale that Jeanie stepped in. "He'll go apologize first thing in the morning," she'd said, calming Henry and reassuring Chad at the same time. She had learned well how to do that, how to wield the double-edged sword in her life that was forever falling between her husband and her son. This was how she discovered that while boys aren't always as anxious to grow up as girls, they use that extra time to demand more of each other. Lisa was Daddy's frilly little girl. Chad was Daddy's chance at finally becoming a professional athlete. Sometimes, or so Jeanie had come to realize, the big themes in life are so small and simple, they're almost laughable.

When the phone rang, it frightened Jeanie at first. Ever since that morning when she had to call the ambulance, she dreaded holding a telephone to her ear. *Symbolic* is what the psychologist called it. Jeanie didn't need to pay her money every hour to learn this. She already knew it. But it was more than the memory of those minutes she lay in bed next to Henry, his body cold, his heart finished, that caused her to panic when a phone rang at her house. The funny thing was, for a year now, she was afraid that when she answered it, she'd hear Henry on the other end of the line. This is how the years can train you, like a dog that jumps to a bell. Every day Henry had phoned her from work. *How's it going, baby? You okay? Listen, what about pork chops for supper? I'm starving.* Later, as the years unwound themselves, his message had begun to change. *Don't worry about supper, honey, I'm stopping for a beer with a couple of the guys. No need to cook. You take the evening off, okay?* At the end, his calls were kind but brief. Sometimes, they were just messages on the answering machine that Jeanie played to an empty house. *Jeanie, it's me. I'll be home about ten. Click.*

It was Fillmore's Drugstore calling. They had received the application she left there earlier, asking for her old job back. It was Mrs. Leona Fillmore herself.

"Jeanie, if we get an opening, you're the first one I'll be phoning," she promised. It was after Jeanie thanked her and agreed that *Yes, the memorial service for Henry will be very nice* and hung up the phone nice and neat, that she broke down and wept.

· · ·

Evie made her way down the bar, picking up empty bottles and dumping the butts from ashtrays, then wiping them clean. Billy Randall was just finishing his Jack and Coke, with his usual beer chaser. Evie didn't ask if he wanted a refill. She knew Billy's habits by now. A Vietnam vet who kept to himself, Billy always left before the bar grew packed and noisy. He nodded good-bye to Evie and slipped out the front door.

At Andy Southby's favorite stool, the one in front of the small poker machine that sat atop the bar, Evie wiped faster, making large round circles, as if the bigger the swipe, the bigger the rush. Pretending to be in a hurry was one way to avoid Andy, but it was early evening and the bar was still too empty to use customers as an excuse. She could always do a quick mop job on the floor behind the bar. Gail had spilled some Pepsi there the day before and the soles of Evie's tennis shoes were still sticking to the tiles every time she walked over the spot. Maybe by the time she was done mopping, Andy would have already lost his usual three dollars into the poker machine and the door would be swinging shut behind him. Before Evie could turn away and head for the mop stick out back, she heard a loud *pop!* She stopped, a small rush of anger coming up from inside, coming quickly, the way anger does when it wants you to say something fast, something you might be sorry for.

"Damn it, Andy," she said to the young man who was perched with his face just inches from the five poker cards. "How many times have I told you not to crack your knuckles in here?" Andy hunched his shoulders, his eyes still on the brightly lit cards.

"It's just acoustics," he said. He punched a couple buttons on the poker machine.

"It's obnoxious, is what it is," said Evie. He shrugged again, another habit of his that was annoying to bar regulars. Evie wished Andy Southby would find another establishment to make his own personal hangout, maybe one filled with people who actually liked him.

"I can't help it," said Andy. This was followed by another loud *pop!* "I heard a doctor talking about it on the radio once. When you pop your knuckles, the change in pressure releases nitrogen into the spaces around the joint, and *that* causes a small release of endorphin. I been doing it for years and now I'm addicted."

"Well, from now on endorphin is illegal in this bar," said Evie. "Unless you want to get busted, stop it."

Evie went for the mop. If only some college would take Andy Southby. There had even been a suggestion one night by another of the regulars that they take up a collection by putting a big glass bottle on the bar. Every time Andy popped his knuckles, or said something obnoxious, or hunched his peaked shoulders, which was often, another dollar or two could go into the Send Andy Southby to College Fund. But there had to be a college that would take him first.

Evie was mopping the last of the sticky Pepsi spots when she saw Chad step into the bar, the orange bonnet pushed back on his sweaty forehead. Again, it caught her unawares. Chad had that easy stride that Henry used to have, as if his legs were thinking for themselves. Evie watched as he walked up to the bar and pulled out a dollar bill.

"One Megabucks ticket," he said. "But not a machine pick. I wanna pick my own." Evie leaned the mop against the bar, wiped her hands, and went to the ticket machine. She waited for Chad to give her the numbers. He did so slowly, as if wanting to be sure there were no mistakes. But after hearing the first two, Evie could have punched them in all on her own. *Nine. Eight. One. Twenty-seven. Four. Forty-two.* Henry's lucky numbers. When the machine spit out the ticket, Evie handed it to the boy.

"Good luck," she said, giving him a quick smile. The truth was that Henry had never won more than an occasional free ticket with those lucky numbers. They had worked a lot better for the Red Sox. Chad took the ticket from her fingers and slipped it into his shirt pocket.

"Thanks," he said. Then, "You seen my uncle?" Evie shook her head. She could see the damp strands of dark hair poking from beneath the woolen bonnet, so wet they were matted to his forehead.

"Why don't you wait until winter to wear that thing?" Evie asked him. This is when Chad cranked out the famous crooked smile.

"I didn't know bartenders cared so much about their customers," he said, just as a loud *pop! pop! pop!* erupted from the poker machine. Andy called these *triple headers*.

"Goddamn it, Andy, don't do that!" Evie said, a hot flush covering her chest and neck, moving up under her hairline and across her face. Her gynecologist had warned her to get ready. *Your estrogen level is dangerously low*, he'd said. *You're headed straight for menopause*. Well, maybe she was. So be it. But she had no intentions of taking Andy Southby with her, and it was a fact that he annoyed her so much these days that she was blaming *him* for each and every hot flash.

"Sorry," said Andy. "Shit, maybe it's time for me to spend my money someplace where I'm wanted." Evie looked at him. The thin, narrow face beneath a shock of brownish hair. He spent three dollars a night in the poker machine, twelve quarters, no more, no less, lining them up on the bar in three neat rows until they all disappeared. That was fifteen dollars a week since he was in every night the bar was open but Monday, and that's because he spent his three dollars that night on a rental movie that he watched with his mother. He never drank more than two beers per evening, sometimes nursing just one all night long while he nursed his quarters at the poker machine. And he never left a tip, not even one of his twelve quarters. He seemed to think that by sitting at the bar, he had outwitted any social demands to tip the bartender. Murphy's Tavern could weather the financial blow if Andy spent his money elsewhere.

"You don't need to leave," Evie said. "Just don't crack your knuckles." It was her job, after all, to keep the customers happy. When she looked back at the other end of the bar, Chad was gone.

Gail Ferguson arrived an hour later to relieve Evie. With her was her new boyfriend, Marshall Thompson, who grabbed a stool at the end of the bar under the television, near the spot where Gail smoked a cigarette if things were quiet. Evie liked Gail, and had from the very first day they met. Gail was tall and thin, with a long mane of thick, dark hair. There had been sadness not just in her own marriage breaking up a couple years earlier, but with a recent and devastating loss when her niece died of leukemia. This was her sister Margie's child. Evie wondered if maybe this loss had been what prompted Gail to take up with Marshall Thompson in the first place. Sometimes, all a person wants is an arm around them at the saddest hours of the night. But now, in less than a month, Gail's eyes already had that dazed, "in love at any cost" desperation about them. It was common knowledge that Marshall was a loose cannon, a man rumored to be roughing up his estranged wife. But Gail didn't see it that way. "He treats Paula like a queen," she had told Evie the first night Marshall turned up on the stool under the television set. As Evie got her purse and sweater, she saw Gail quickly slide a scotch and water in front of Marshall, his first free drink of the night.

Out in the parking lot, Evie had just creaked open

the door on her aging Mazda when she glanced up to see
Chad. He was straddling his motorbike, his eyes staring up
at the sky as if he were trying to find something he'd lost.
She felt a rush of sadness for the boy. He had come looking for Larry since there was no longer any Henry. Larry
had better turn up soon and keep an eye on his nephew. If
he didn't, who knew what might happen. On her way out
of the lot, Evie drove past Chad, but the boy never looked
her way. His gaze was still on something only he could see,
something up in the black sky over Bixley, something out
among the stars.

• • •

On the drive home, Evie kept her window down so that
the breeze would cool the sweat of the tavern that still
clung to her face and neck. The air had a heaviness to
it that comes of July nights, a smell of decay wafting out
from under trees and up from flower beds, an odor of
fertilizer mixed with rich, dark soil. She loved the honest
smell of a summer night, those breezes that came down
from the wooded hills around the town, and the breezes
that came up from the dank and narrow river. Those
were the places where things grow and root in the moist
darkness, away from the lights and traffic of human
lives. Those were the places that churned up that rich
smell of *life*, of things breathing and eating and dying,
all unseen and unnoticed. She imagined bluish crayfish
and spiders that stride atop long legs, slimy snakes and
crickets whose legs can sing, and the small frogs that hop
onto roadways when it rains, giving their lives up to the

night. Those were the midnight creatures that existed in that other, nearby universe, another world that most humans rarely see.

She turned down her own street, shifting the little car into second. It was this kind of thinking, this "a universe is burning next to us and we don't even know it" philosophy that always sent her quickly to that first joint after work. The truth was that a tension grew inside her that she hadn't been able to shake all afternoon, the tension that comes of expectancy. Each time the door at Murphy's Tavern opened, Evie had looked up, hoping to see Larry Munroe step inside the bar, longing to see him slide onto that stool he liked, the one Marshall was now sitting on, drinking free scotch-and-waters. She would lean close enough to smell Larry's cologne as she put a Bud down in front of him. He would say, "Thanks, Evie," and wait patiently for her to find a few spare minutes to sit on her own stool behind the bar, sip at a glass of iced tea, give her swollen feet a rest as Larry told her all the news of the town. *The mayor's in the hospital. They're building a mall out where the old drive-in used to stand. Laura Miller is pregnant. They're having a grand opening for the new nursing home wing. Len and Macy Freeman are moving to Ohio.* Evie had come to realize that mailmen have a pulse on any town, whether they like it or not, and Larry was no exception. "I can't help it," he would say to Evie, his smile not as charming as Henry's, but so genuine that it always made her smile back when she saw it. "People want to talk to their mailman. What can I do but listen?"

But Larry hadn't turned up for the third night in a row. And now, because of it, Evie was on her way home alone, the evening just beginning. She would take a cool shower and then sit with a spinach salad on the porch swing. Afterward, she would think those heavy thoughts of nature and life in between tokes. She had a session scheduled for the next afternoon and it would be a tough one. It was with Gail's sister, Margie Jenkins, whose ten-year-old daughter had just died. Margie and her husband, Phil, used to stop by the bar every Saturday night for a game of pool and a drink, and to say hello to Gail. A year younger than her sister, Margie was also tall, and pretty, with that same long, dark hair. Evie liked Gail's sister, but she had politely refused to do a session when Margie telephoned the week before. "It's too soon, sweetheart," Evie said. It *was* too soon. It hadn't been a month. People need to spend some time missing their loved ones in the very house where their lives used to take place. They need to miss them in the middle of the night. At the breakfast table. They need to find traces of them, still, that strand of brown hair in the hairbrush, that yellow sweater that has fallen, forgotten, behind the sofa, that cassette tape of the last birthday party, the words curled inside like a long, black tongue. "Margie just wants to talk, if that's okay," Gail had said, pleading, and so Evie had agreed. But she knew the meeting would be difficult.

Evie had just reached her driveway and pulled in when she saw the Buick sitting at the curb on the opposite side of the street. She hit the brakes, put the car in park, and jumped out, leaving her door wide open. She managed to get close enough to lay her hand on the Buick's trunk before she heard the gears of the car shift, and then acceleration. Evie stood in the middle of the street and watched the two red taillights cut the corner. She stood there until the sound of the Buick's engine grew so faint it finally disappeared, most likely over on Market Avenue. She stood there in the street and smelled it again, that smell of decay seeping out from under trees, up from flower beds, fertilizer mixed with soil. Then, on the night breeze, came that odor of things like love and laughter, pain and despair, the things that grow under rooftops, that root in the darkness of bedrooms, those things that breathe and eat and die, as if their very existence were lived out in the highest treetops or down by the river. The wind brought with it the stench of human lives that spin like universes, without ever touching.

· · ·

Larry cracked his bedroom door and stood there listening before he stepped out into the hallway. He tiptoed to the banister that ran along the upper side of the hallway, put there years earlier by his father to keep the unruly Munroe boys from plummeting to the first floor. He leaned over, his hands firmly on the rail so that he could hear any activity coming from the rooms below. His parents were just settling down in front of the television set. His mother's talk of what the show would be about that night drifted up to him, followed by his father's brief replies, so short they were almost grunts. It was *Dateline*, one of their favorite programs, and Larry knew it would keep them busy for a time. He made his way silently along the hallway and into the bathroom. He doubted they would hear the shower, not with Diane Sawyer blabbing away about something.

He turned the hot and cold knobs, finding the perfect temperature before he climbed into the tub and closed the curtain. The water felt better than he'd imagined while he lay on his bed and waited for nine o'clock to arrive. The warm strands beat against his chest as he stood, eyes closed, and let it rain. He hadn't had a shower the whole time he'd been holed up in his bedroom. Now, he might never be able to step out of the tub. He'd be there for days, waterlogged and drowned, while everyone else was at Henry's memorial service.

Beneath the lavatory sink, Larry found a disposable razor, still sharp enough to be taken seriously, and a can of shaving foam. He had been intending to pick up some razors and shaving cream just four days earlier, the day he stood staring at the mailbox in front of the two-story Cape on Pilcher Street, the house he and Katherine had moved into shortly after their marriage, the house they had moved out of just eight months earlier, selling it and filing for divorce all on the same day. He had stuffed letters and junk into that mailbox for seven months, knowing a fellow teacher had happily taken up residence inside, knowing it was *his* kids who owned the swing set in the backyard, *their* bikes leaning against the front steps. Who knows why, but on this day Larry had done what he swore he'd never do. He had put the letters into the mailbox—a contraption he himself had refused to erect, no matter how much Katherine had pestered him—and then he had turned and looked up at the top left window of the house. He had done to himself what he promised he would never do. He had torn his own guts out, after seven months, by gazing up at that window, the room that had been Jonathan's bedroom once. Jonathan had been his son then, and he had been Jonathan's father. Once. Who knows why Larry did it? The upcoming memorial? Henry's former mistress fitting so nice and pure into his arms that Larry now felt certain he loved Evie Cooper? The pressure of living as a grown man in his parents' house again, in his old bedroom, without Henry? Maybe it was all of those things. But perhaps, just perhaps—and Larry entertained this answer more than the others—perhaps the moment in time had come when a father could no longer bear to be without his only child. Maybe that was it. Whatever it was, he had clutched the leather mailbag to his chest and walked away, had taken with him all the letters yet to be delivered in his territory beyond Pilcher Street. He had gone straight home, he had gone up the stairs, he had disappeared into his bedroom, and he had closed the fucking door on the world. It had seemed like a damn good plan four days ago. Except that Larry had forgotten to get some new razors and shaving cream.

In five minutes, he was rubbing a hand along his jaw and feeling just smooth skin beneath. He quickly rinsed the razor and put it away. With a towel, he wiped the sink until it shone, something his mother was always nagging her boys to do when they were still growing up in the house. Maybe Larry could start over. Maybe he could be the teenaged son his mother had always wanted. It would be a kind of *reprogramming*, and why not since this was the age of computers? He'd feed his brain a new software. Out in the hallway again, Larry paused, an ear pointed down the stairs. He could still hear the distant sound of the television coming from below. After *Dateline*, his parents would watch the news. Then they would go into their downstairs bedroom, where they would change into pajamas, wash their faces, brush their teeth, and pee until their bladders were empty. Larry had been back in the house long enough to know the routine. His father would then sit on the sofa and do his best to stay awake for David Letterman, as he had always been able to do for Johnny Carson. But just before midnight, Larry could depend on sounds coming up the stairs that would tell the rest of the story. First would come the soft, light snores. Then, his mother's voice from the bedroom, telling her husband to wake up and come to bed. This would be followed by a series of noises, the old man rising from the sofa, confused grunts, as if maybe he'd been dreaming that he dropped an insured package somewhere in the snow or had left letters in a wrong mailbox. He would rise and go to the kitchen for a glass of milk, the refrigerator door *sucking* open and then *sucking* shut, the glass being placed obediently in the sink, and then the last noises of the night as Bixley's most loyal postman flushed the downstairs toilet and stumbled off to bed. Only then could Larry fall asleep, knowing that the house had grown silent for the rest of the night. Knowing that one day there would be no more noises coming from the two people who had given him birth. *Noise* meant *life*.

It wasn't until Henry Munroe disappeared that Larry realized how quiet the world had grown without his little brother there to stir it up.

8

Jeanie waited as Mona Prescott read the day's lunch specials from the menu. This had been their ritual, to meet at the Silver Lady Café once a month. Soup of the day, a nice salad, and a soothing glass of white wine. Every month after Henry died, Mona had faithfully phoned Jeanie up and said, "Well, what about tomorrow? It's probably the last month we can still eat on the outdoor patio before they close it for winter." And Jeanie had said *no, not yet, it's too soon.* But Mona never missed that monthly call. She and Jeanie had been meeting once a month for lunch ever since their senior year at Bixley High. They had been the two most popular cheerleaders and their soon-to-be husbands were the football stars. It doesn't get any sweeter than that in a small town. Through babies, and mortgages, and weight gain, and family crises, they had kept up that promise to get together once a month. Otherwise, they would become old friends who drifted apart. The monthly meetings had moved over to the Silver Lady ten years earlier, when Mom's Diner finally closed its door and the Lady opened with a trendy lunch menu and a nice selection of wines. Over the past year, Mona's messages had changed monthly. "I bet they've got a fire in the fireplace since the cold weather has arrived" had slowly faded into "They must be just opening the outdoor patio again, what with the flowers all in bloom" and then to "We can reserve that table in the back, to get away from the summer heat." Mona would soon be back to "This will be the last month before they close the outdoor patio for winter." So Jeanie had given in. And with the memorial service only days away, maybe it was time.

As they waited for their bowls of soup and salads, they sipped at their white wines and tried to appear casual, as if it had not been a full year since they'd had lunch at the Silver Lady. Jeanie had dropped by Mona's house several times, for those occasions she couldn't avoid and still feel like a best friend. Mona's birthday party was one of them, in October of the previous year, just three months after Henry had died. Henry's own birthday would be coming up again that November, and so Jeanie knew she had to start taking part again. When the tenth of November rolled around the previous year, she did what the grief therapy class had taught her: she changed the routine of Henry's birthday. Instead of baking a cake, as she would have done if Henry had been alive to celebrate, Jeanie had asked Mona to do so instead. *Rule Number One: Break the routine. Don't expect your life and special occasions to be the same as before.* But how could they? Sometimes those therapy sessions were just plain stupid. People had been grieving for thousands of years. They know how to do it. It's like learning to walk, or having sex. It's instinctive. People figure it out as they go, even if they might stumble a few times in the process. But Mona, bless her, had baked the cake. And everyone had gathered and did their best to eat and enjoy it: Chad, Larry, Lawrence, Frances, Jeanie, and Mona. Mona's husband, Paul, wasn't there. He had moved out the month before, deciding that his new secretary with the long legs and Hollywood-style hairdo was the best step he could take now that he was forty years old. In comforting Mona, Jeanie had helped to heal herself a bit. But everywhere she looked these days, she saw people with cracks in them, people hurting, people unable to cope. Why hadn't she seen it before since it was probably always that way? The world had become like the House of Mirrors at the carnival, everyone distorted and only resembling the happy people they'd once been. Or, at least, the happy people their *neighbors* thought them to be. Maybe even the people they thought *themselves* to be.

"High school should last forever," Jeanie said, as Mona ordered a second wine. She was drinking more these days, too, Jeanie had noticed. One glass of wine with lunch had always been more than enough in the old days. "Why didn't we know how lucky we were? Why were we so anxious to grow up?"

"It's nature's fault," said Mona. "Nature doesn't want us women having kids in our forties."

"And you and I sure didn't disappoint nature," Jeanie said.

Mona ran a hand through the short hair she'd turned up with just two weeks earlier. She had decided a new hairdo, something more modern, would be a great idea, a new boost. And she had signed up for Weight Watchers, determined to take off that extra twenty-five pounds. Jeanie was relieved to see the change. For a time it seemed as if losing a husband to his secretary was far worse than losing him to death.

"The Japanese have invented a new watermelon," Mona said. "It's square so that it can sit in the fridge without rolling around."

"That ought to help civilization," said Jeanie.

"There's a drawback," said Mona. "It costs a hundred and twenty-five dollars."

Jeanie shook her head. She had learned long ago not to be surprised by the world. A man came into the café with a young woman walking close to his side. The hostess seated them at a table by the window and gave them each a menu. Jeanie saw that Mona was watching the couple. She wondered if she should try to engage her in some conversation that would make her forget about Paul, some gossip maybe, even if she had to invent it. But she knew that grief has to be confronted the hard way. Grief is a train, meeting all travelers head-on. You stand there and wait for it. She'd learned that herself.

"At least he's not gay," Mona said at last, her eyes still on the couple.

"Who?" Jeanie asked. Mona had three sons, all gone to college.

"Paul," said Mona. "At least the bastard's not gay, which is what I thought for months. I'd catch him primping in the mirror, wearing bikini underwear."

"Paul gay?" said Jeanie, and laughed. "I don't think so."

"Football players can be gay," said Mona. "Hockey

players, too. I saw a race car driver on a talk show who likes to wear his wife's clothes. And she lets him."

"That's where I would draw the line," said Jeanie. "It was bad enough when Lisa wore my clothes."

There was a patch of silence as they ate their salads. Mona kept her eyes on the couple at the other table.

"Lover or daughter?" she asked. Jeanie studied the two. They seemed polite on their opposite sides of the table. Almost distant. She was about to say "daughter" when the man reached over and covered the young woman's hand with his. It wasn't a fatherly squeeze, but a lingering squeeze. Then he ran his forefinger along the side of her hand and up her wrist, sensuously, delicately, as Jeanie and Mona watched.

"Lover," said Jeanie.

"Bastard," said Mona.

• • •

When Jeanie turned into her drive, she saw her mother-in-law waiting for her on the front steps. This time, Frances had a pot of beef stew and a baker sheet of home-made biscuits. Jeanie opened the front door and let the older woman go ahead of her into the cool house. When she had risen that morning, Jeanie decided to keep the window shades closed, knowing the weather report had predicted one of the hottest days of the summer. Now, she could tell by the look on her mother-in-law's face that the cool darkness seemed suspicious, more a state of mind than a logical act. Frances squinted her eyes as she peered toward the kitchen.

"I'll just open these shades," Jeanie said, giving in. "They say it's going to be our hottest day, and I thought—" She stopped. Why was she still trying to please Henry's parents, as if she needed their approval? Who cared anymore? In truth, this need had evaporated years after their marriage. But people fall into habits, as if they are deep, dark pits. Jeanie had always felt in competition with Katherine, her sister-in-law, the smart one who taught English and watched those boring operas and ballets on the educational channel while the rest of the family was having a barbecue in the backyard. Jeanie had been the one to quickly clear away the dishes from the picnic table while the men sat in lawn chairs and smoked, or told a few stories about cars and sports, and waited for the rest of the day to unfurl. Jeanie had been the one to help Frances clean up the kitchen, the greasy pans, the flour on the counter, the mud tracked in upon the floor by grandkids. And Jeanie had liked the way Frances would peer into the living room at Katherine, who was pirouetting and doing whatever ballerinas do, along with the program on television, oblivious to any domestic work taking place in the kitchen. Frances would roll her eyes up to the ceiling, and Jeanie knew what it meant. It meant *us against her*, it meant *you're the perfect daughter-in-law, Jeanie*. How many years had it been that Jeanie quit caring about this? Many, and yet here she was, operating on a kind of automatic pilot, a lifetime of habit.

"Remember how much Henry loved my biscuits?" Frances asked, as she put the baker sheet on the counter. "Be sure to heat this stew on the stove. That's what I always do. I wish they'd never invented the microwave. It just spoils food is what it does." She set the small pot of stew on a back burner of the stove.

Jeanie said nothing as she opened the refrigerator and got out a pitcher of lemonade she'd made that morning. She hadn't really wanted it, but she knew the lemons were in that bin opposite the one Chad was using. This seemed a good reason to go rummaging in the bottom of the fridge. And while she was down there, why not check to see what Chad was up to? The cans of beer were gone.

"Did Lisa find out what the baby's going to be?" Frances asked. Jeanie smiled at the thought of Lisa becoming a mother, of a little baby smelling of talcum powder.

"She called last night," said Jeanie. "It's going to be a girl." Frances smiled, too, and it seemed an honest-to-God smile this time, genuine and pure.

"Do you know what Lawrence said?" she asked. She waited until Jeanie shook her head. "I told him that Lisa had decided to go ahead and find out what the baby was going to be. He said, if it's a girl, she might be the first female Munroe to work for the post office."

"That's a long way in the future," said Jeanie. "But it could happen." Much had been made at family functions of how this particular line of Munroes seemed to produce all male descendants, at least until Lisa came along. It was as if something in the Munroe DNA understood that there was a great need for mailmen.

"My mother was good at telling what a baby would be," said Frances. "She'd take a needle and thread out and dangle it over your wrist. If it went back and forth in a straight line, it was a boy. If it made circles, it was a girl. It worked pretty well, believe it or not."

Jeanie put a glass of lemonade in front of Frances and then sat across the table from her. Sat, and waited. They had been doing this twice a week for the whole year that Henry had been gone. At times, Jeanie knew what prisoners feel like when they get visitors. They sit and stare, incapable of real communication, incapable sometimes of even *touch*. They sit and stare and wait for the visit to be over.

"Well?" Frances asked finally. Jeanie thought about what she was going to say. She wanted to be sure she worded it just so, knowing Frances was capable of reading volumes into a thin sentence.

"I think he's just going through a bad time," said Jeanie. "He didn't say, but I think it's as much about Jonathan as it is about Henry. Have you seen the picture he's got on the dresser? It's of him holding Jon as a baby."

Frances ran a forefinger around the rim of her glass. She dabbed at the beads of sweat on the side of it. Then she turned to watch chickadees as they flitted down to the feeder just outside the window. Finally, she put her gaze on the pot of beef stew sitting on the stove.

"If you're not going to have that until supper," said Frances, "maybe you should stick it in the fridge."

• • •

Larry poured from the plastic bottle of Coke until the paper cup on his desk was filled to the top. He opened the envelope, careful not to spill any of the drink on it. This one was special, too special to treat like ordinary mail.

Dear Aunt Jeanie,

Thank you for the birthday money. Grandma and Grandpa sent me money, too, and so did Dad. I used it to pay for my karate uniform. And I bought Monsters, Inc. *It's my favorite movie. I miss my dad, but my mom says I can go home for Thanksgiving. How is Chad? School is okay if you like school which I don't. I have to go to karate class now.*

Love, Jonathan

Larry put the single sheet of paper up to his nose and smelled it, hoping there was something of his son attached to it, something more than the mere shape of letters and words. He wanted to sense the flesh and blood of the boy. He wanted to hold him again in his arms, feel the small and sturdy bones pressed into his chest, the silky hair touching his face. They had been talking by phone twice a week, and that was good. But it was not enough. Larry had asked several times if he could drive to Portland for even a quick visit, but his request had been denied by Katherine and her team of lawyers—well, maybe she had just *one* lawyer, but he was a *high-powered* divorce lawyer, and from Larry's corner of the ring, Katherine and *any* lawyer would make a formidable team. Especially since Larry was alone in his corner. How could he afford a lawyer? After paying child support and the old bills he and Katherine had accrued in their marriage, and fifty dollars a week rent to his parents—who hadn't wanted it but Larry insisted—he couldn't afford to buy *Monsters, Inc.*, even if it had been his favorite movie too. The few dollars he had to spare went to the beers he drank at Murphy's and the modest tip he left for Evie. Larry considered Murphy's a cheap kind of grief counseling. But the old bills would soon be gone, all paid off, and he'd be able to get his own place again, start over, maybe even ask his parents if he could have permission to use the car. Katherine had gotten the *new* car in the divorce, and since the *old* car had waited for the ink to dry on the settlement papers before it fell apart, Larry had gone without one. But a few months before, Jeanie had surprised him by giving him Henry's black Jeep. "Chad has the motorbike and that's all he needs for now. I've read that Jeeps flip over easy. The bike worries me enough. I know Henry would want you to have his Jeep."

It was good to have something tangible from Henry, and Larry was thankful to Jeanie for that. He felt his brother in the Jeep sometimes, sensed him floating about on the passenger side as Larry breezed down the highways and byways of town. This is how they cruised when they were just brothers, and also sons, but not yet husbands and fathers, and certainly not what they'd become: ex-husband and deceased husband. Some nights, on his way back from Murphy's Tavern, wind in his hair and some old song by the Eagles, or Bob Seger, or Springsteen cutting up the airwaves, Larry would just drive around town, often passing the football stadium, until the light on his gas tank hinted to him that it was time to go home. He talked to Henry on nights like that, reminded him of the old fun they'd had, back in those golden days. *Hey, Henry. Remember the night we didn't know who Ginnie McCowell picked to have sex with until the very last minute, and then I was so surprised it was me she picked, I couldn't do it?* And he could hear Henry laugh from the passenger seat, that quick, large laugh that was big enough for a lot of people to enjoy. How many times had Larry seen some stranger at Murphy's look over from across the room to see where the big laugh was coming from, and then smile to see Henry's beaming face? Henry was like smoke. He could move in a lot of places at once since no place could keep him out. He was wind. Electricity. Even when you weren't with him, you *felt* him. He was that powerful a personality. He was that strong a brother. And that's why, for all these months that Henry was gone, Larry had just seemed to drift. He still felt his brother in the empty places. He just couldn't find him there. He could talk to him, for he already knew what Henry would say to the old memories. *Christ, how could I forget that night? You had to walk home with your dick in your hand since I'd already left with Dad's car. It was almost dawn when you crawled into your bunk. You looked like hell. What a wasted piece of ass that was. If Ginnie had picked me, she and I would still be rolling on the grass out behind the stadium.*

When had Jonathan started karate class?

Larry looked at the envelope again, the boy's easy scrawl spelling out the letters and numbers. Jonathan had kept up on his promise to mail the occasional math or history paper, a school drawing maybe, or just a regular letter since Larry wasn't computerized like so many people were these days. Katherine often referred to him as Larry Luddite, especially in the teacher's room. Maybe it was the weight of the postal service in his blood. Who knows why? But he still liked to open an envelope and see a real letter in it, maybe a small school photo hiding in one corner. It made it more real somehow, more honest. Larry took the envelope over to his bed and tucked it safely under the pillow. He lay down on the bunk, not wanting to think about boys who live without fathers, whose lives are shaped by men who start out as Mr. *Santino the basketball coach*, and end up as a second dad. But when he lay his head on the pillow, it was almost as if he could feel the body of the letter pushing itself up, that single page so buoyant with energy, a boy's life, one filled with the latest movies and the kinds of classes that kids sign up for, and the kind of longing that so many families know well these days: *I miss my dad, but my mom says I can go home for Thanksgiving.*

He had never even heard of *Monsters Inc.*, and yet it was his boy's favorite movie.

The way Larry looked at it, you didn't have to be a high-powered attorney or a grief counselor to understand what a boy wanted in his heart.

My mom says I can go home…

Sometimes, it's as plain as writing on the wall.

• • •

Evie didn't have to be back at Murphy's for four days, and that was a good thing. She needed the rest. Not just from Andy Southby and the sound of his knuckles, but from looking up each time the door opened to see someone other than Larry Munroe walk in. Once her meeting that afternoon with Margie Jenkins was over, Evie intended to take a short and self-imposed vacation, not just from the tavern, but from her sessions. Maybe she'd throw a few things into her car and head out to Portland or Boston. She could return once the memorial was firmly over. *Finis*. Maybe then Larry would be back to his old self. But first, she would have to deal with the visitor she was expecting.

When Margie Jenkins arrived, Evie led her away from the parlor where she held her sessions. Instead, she and Margie sat at the kitchen table where Evie poured them each an iced tea. This would help it seem like a visit and not an appointment. Margie clinked her spoon around in the tall glass, stirring up the sugar again and again until Evie took the spoon from her and placed it on the table.

"You look enough like Gail to be her twin," said Evie, hoping to lighten the heavy mood. Margie smiled at the notion of this. She and Gail were close in spirit, too, always looking out for each other's kids, always scraping together a few dollars if one of them was broke and the rent due. The way sisters should be.

"That's what everyone says."

"Margie, I'm so sorry for your loss," Evie said.

Margie nodded at this, probably having heard it a few hundred times in the month since Annie died. What to do now but nod?

"Sometimes, I think it's harder on Phil," said Margie. "She was Daddy's little girl, you know."

"I know," said Evie. "Gail told me."

The two women sat like bookends, one at each end of the table, holding silence between them. The faint buzzing of the clock over the refrigerator, and the refrigerator itself, filled the small room with its own kind of mantra. Outside, occasional horns tooted. Kids bicycled by, their noise fading at the end of the street, disappearing. Next door, Mrs. Albion's dog barked at each passerby. Seconds came and went as time did its job of passing. When it became apparent that Margie Jenkins had no intention of talking, Evie did instead.

"Come on," Evie said. "I do my sessions in the parlor."

Evie poured the rest of her iced tea down the kitchen sink and then took several deep breaths, preparing herself. She filled the glass with water and sipped at it. She just needed a few minutes alone, the time to put her mind in that place that was necessary, a mental game she had learned. She had taught herself, years before, to block out the faces of the dead until she was ready for them. Otherwise, she'd have burned out long ago, like one of those stars out in the universe that just winks out one night. It was a way to survive in a world filled with pain. Then, as ready as she could be on such short notice, she put the glass in the sink and went to the parlor.

Margie was sitting on the sofa, leaning back into the lavender flowers on the fabric, when Evie saw the little girl. She knew who it was, of course, there could be no doubt. Annie Jenkins. Ten years old and already there was a wisdom in her eyes that Evie knew well. It was the wisdom that comes of letting go, the knowledge that goes hand in hand with the fragility of life. But, still, a child is only a child. With that wisdom Evie could also see confusion, as if the eyes were asking, *Why did I have to know all this now, when I was just starting to learn my earthly body, the small buds of breasts, why when I was so close to being told all those secrets the older girls know? Why now?* And this was why it was too soon for Annie to come. It was too soon. If Evie were to sketch this worried face, it would not bring an ounce of comfort to Margie Jenkins. Instead, it would bring her immeasurable pain.

Evie took her sketch pad and began, as she always did, to make circles in one corner with her drawing pencil. As she did so, she remembered Annie Jenkins the last time the little girl visited Murphy's Tavern. It was before she became ill and Evie never saw her again. It had been the previous December, a couple weeks before Christmas. The place was all colored lights, reds and blues and greens, with strands of bulbs encircling the bar itself and then decorating a lighted fir tree in one corner. Gail was taking her niece home after work since Margie had some shopping to do. So Annie sat on a bar stool and ate the burger and fries that Gail made for her. She had sipped at the glass of soda. Annie, with a thick ponytail, thick and full, and eyes so dark they sparkled with energy. A happy child on her way to living a long and happy life.

Evie drew the shape of the face first, oval and sweet, and then the dark hair and the eyes full of such Christmas excitement, eyes happy to be seeing what they were. She finished the drawing off with the sweater Annie had been wearing that day, with small kittens embroidered on the collar. Maybe it was cheating, and Evie didn't like to cheat. But she could tell as she looked again into the troubled eyes of the child who stood just behind her mother's shoulder that this was the best thing to do. Annie would want this, too. She handed Margie Jenkins the finished sketch. Margie stared at it for some time before she spoke.

"Maybe it *is* a better place," she said to Evie, her voice so low and soft that Evie had to lean forward to hear the words. "When we die, I mean. Maybe it really is a happier place than here." She looked back down at the face of her only daughter, Annie Gail Jenkins, who woke up one morning before Christmas vacation feeling too sick to go to school. And so she never went again, going instead to the doctor who took the tests and delivered the news.

Evie put the sketch pad down.

"Come on," she said. "That little café on the corner of Frederick Street has ice cream. Why we don't we go for a walk, you and me?"

Margie Jenkins rolled the sketch up neatly. She reached for her purse and held it in her arms. When she stood, Evie saw that the back of her blouse had grown wet with sweat, as if Margie's body had become dead weight in just the past month. Margie Jenkins could feel Annie there in the room, Evie was certain of it. She could tell by looking at the woman's face. The ties were still so strong between mother and daughter. Sometimes, Evie had a client tell her what it was like to feel their own child nearby, just beyond human reach, the pure energy of your firstborn, or second born. *It's like being on a roller coaster and you've just crested the very top, and then the car rolls over and down you come, your stomach riding so high inside you that you know you're going to pass out just from the pull of it.*

"I wonder if they have chocolate," said Margie. The ice cream had done the trick. It was a way of surviving, is what it was. A way of grabbing up a simple notion, a nice idea, and hanging on to it like it's a piece of driftwood. "Chocolate was Annie's favorite," she added, as Evie opened the front door. The diamond-shaped crystals hanging from the lamp shade in the parlor rattled as the door closed behind them.

9

His mother was back. Larry heard the soft *squeak*, that same board beneath the carpet at the top of the stairs, the step that had been talking ever since he could remember. All those high school nights that he and Henry had crept into the house just ahead of dawn, they had been careful of that step, not wanting its painful sound to rouse their mother. But it was as if she and the step had an agreement: *Wake me when the boys sneak in so I can scold them in the morning.* Now the step had turned on her. For the past three mornings Larry had heard it, and then the soft movement of a body lurking just outside his door. Or maybe he *felt* her there, in his gut, she being his mother and all. Maybe nature gives humans that ability. But this was the third morning, and Larry couldn't bear it anymore. He knew what she was doing, eavesdropping, her small white ear pressed like a seashell to his door, hoping to catch the ebb and flow of his life, to hear some clue as to what he was up to.

Larry rose from the chair at his desk where he had been writing a letter to Jonathan. *Dear son, Aunt Jeanie got your letter and we're all very happy that you're coming home for Thanksgiving.* He walked to his side of the door and stood there, waiting quietly, wondering if perhaps *this* was the morning she'd come up with a screwdriver in her hand, determined to flush him out. When she arrived like this, midmorning, the time of day that his father was just seeing the last mailman out of the post office, Larry knew she was alone. And that was a good thing. When the old man was with her, she seemed to draw some kind of energy from him, rising up higher on the heels of her feet, straightening her back, turning now and then to catch her husband's eye, to see if he was *listening to this.* The old man was like some kind of ammunition truck that follows the tanks. But soon, Larry knew, they would come for the mail pouch, and when they did, his father would need to be at the vanguard, if for no other purpose than the symbolic. And they would come with a battering ram. But for now, his mother was alone again in the hallway. Larry could almost feel the warmth of her coming through the door, as if her pain were something liquid that could be poured out of her body if she let it. What could he do? What *should* he do? Larry remembered the skink Jonathan had tried to catch the summer before their lives went all to hell. Before Larry had a chance to warn him, the boy had grabbed the bright blue tail of the lizard, hoping to pick the thing up. Instead, he was left with the wiggling tail in his hand, the rest of the skink long gone. *That's its protection, son,* Larry had explained. *The tail is bright blue so that predators will grab it, and not the soft body. Its tail will grow back in time.* Thinking back on this now, Larry wished the same worked for him. Perhaps if he could toss an arm or a leg out into the hallway, something for his mother to hold in her hand, maybe it would buy him some more time. He could slam the door, lock it soundly, and then sit in the dark with the mail pouch on his lap as he waited for the arm to grow back.

More time for *what*? It was a question he still couldn't answer.

On an impulse, Larry unlocked the door and opened it slowly. His mother was standing in the hallway, looking down over the banister at the living room below. He could tell by the way she glanced up at him, the confusion in her eyes, that she had forgotten why she'd come upstairs in the first place. Larry knew this because it often happened to him. Many times, on his way back from the bathroom, he'd stop and look down at the living room as if it were a stage set waiting for a family to enter and do their parts, the two sons rushing in to fight over *TV Guide*, the parents following, the father smiling at his sons, the mother frowning and telling them to take off those muddy shoes now and go wash up for supper. It's when no one rushes onto the stage, and you're still standing there looking down, that's when you get confused. That's when you wonder where the actors are, the director, the audience. And then you realize that the play is long over. He often wondered if this is what the faces of the dead tell Evie Cooper with their eyes. Is this what *they* feel, too, as they peer back at the stage where they once lived out their lives? Maybe the dead are just confused. Maybe all they really want to know is *where the hell* is *everybody*? But Larry didn't believe in the dead. And as far as he could tell, he no longer believed in the living either.

"Mom?" He said it in a soft and caring way, so that his intention could not be mistaken for confrontation. He wanted no argument on that morning. He needed his energy to finish the letter to Jonathan. *We're all very happy that you're coming home.*

"I came up to talk to you," she said, her eyes still on that small world below, the light blue sofa, the tan-shaded lamps, the vase of dried flowers, the heavy oak coffee table her sons had made for her in shop. Larry could tell that the fight had gone out of her. He left the safety of his bedroom and walked over to the banister, wanting to be closer to her, fearing she might even pass out. The truth about life does that to people. Sometimes, it punches them so hard they can't breathe anymore.

"Are you okay?" he asked, and was relieved when she nodded. Not that he believed her. But she was back in some measure of control again.

"Did I tell you that I called Katherine?" No, she hadn't told him. This was his ex-wife. It would have been nice to know about it. "I left a message on her machine. I asked if Jonathan could come for the memorial. We're his family, after all."

"Thanks, Mom," Larry said. Otherwise, he was afraid he would say what he was thinking. *How dare you call my ex-wife, about my son, without telling me first?*

"Do you ever get tired of that same hardwood floor, day after day, year after year?" she asked. She was staring down at the living room floor now, talking more to herself than to him.

"Not really," Larry said, wanting to put her at ease, to let her know that he was close by. In the end, after all was said and done, he was the older son, and the one who felt most protective of his mother, more so than Henry.

"Remember that teal-colored rug I put in the summer my mother died?" she asked then. "Remember how hard you boys were on it all through your growing-up years? Spilled colas, spilled Kool-Aid, spilled God-knows-what. Still, when you put in a hardwood floor, you're stuck with it for life." She turned to look at Larry's face.

"Mom, are you all right?" he asked.

"I came up here for something," she said softly, "but now I just can't remember what it was."

"That's okay," said Larry. "That's been happening to me a lot too. You came to tell me you invited Jonathan."

He stood there beside her as they both looked down on the sofa, the lamps, the heavy coffee table. He had read once that the *living* room started being referred to as such to set it apart from the parlor, which was where the dead were waked in years past. Except for the hardwood floor, not much had changed since he and Henry had made that room their own, the place they often did their homework as they watched television, one lying on his back on the sofa, the other sprawled on his belly on the teal-colored rug, their books or bowls of popcorn and cans of soda covering the oak coffee table. The truth was that *he* had done all of the work on the table, with Henry using shop time to practice his foul shots for basketball. Mr. Harris, the shop teacher, was also the basketball coach and so no one ever knew. Henry's foul shots were so important to winning their games that this seemed like a great idea at the time. It was only years later, when Larry had become a teacher himself, that he saw the folly in this notion. It was as if the whole damn town had been aiding and abetting Henry's whims. But when it came time to present the coffee table to their mother, her gift for Mother's Day, it wasn't Larry who handed her the card. It was Henry: *This table is made of white oak which can grow as tall as a hundred feet. The bark is gray and the leaves turn purple-red each autumn. This table was made by your sons, Henry and Larry Munroe, in Mr. Harris's Woodworking Shop, 1975. Happy Mother's Day.* Larry didn't have a hard time remembering what was written on the card for it was still lying inside the thin drawer that slid out of the table's belly. That drawer alone had taken him a month of classes to make, the groove requiring many hours of painstaking work. He'd read the card several times over the years, especially on Sundays when he'd come to watch the Super Bowl with Henry and the old man. Or those Saturday afternoons when he was there to mow the lawn for his mother. Larry would come in from his workout with the lawn mower to pour a glass of lemonade and then sit on the light blue sofa to drink it. No matter how hard he tried, he couldn't help himself. He always slid open the drawer and found the card in the plastic sheath his mother had bought to protect it. And he would open it and read again. *This table was made by your sons.* Well, Henry did turn up that last week to help with the varnishing. And the Bixley Bandits did win the basketball championship that year.

Larry's mother turned away from him now and walked back to the top of the stairs. The step squeaked, and she was on her way down. Halfway, she stopped and peered up at Larry, who was still standing at the banister, looking down.

"Do you believe in God, son?" she asked.

This caught Larry by surprise. It was supposed to be all about the mail, and the mail pouch, and did he have any letters hidden in his room? Where was this "God" shit coming come? And what to tell her? The best answer, of course, but how to word it? God didn't give him any trouble when he was talking to his fellow teachers, especially the ones in the science wing. "If there was a God, I'd fire him," Larry liked to say. It was true. You'd fire the CEO of any company who had done such a piss-poor job with overall production and employee morale. A God who allowed wars. And then, a good part of the world was starving to death, while another part was overweight. Obesity had become a *disease*, while children died in Africa with flies swarming their malnourished bodies. As Larry saw it, you should fire the bastard behind a company that allowed any of this to happen. Or you should certainly *sue* him. And you should fire the bastard who allowed lives to be shattered and broken, such as Larry's had been in losing Jonathan, the bastard who turned a cold shoulder to the world he supposedly created out of love. Fire the son of a bitch and then bring in some new blood to replace him.

"Of course I believe in God," Larry said. "You always told us we had to, Mom."

Frances was still standing on her step, halfway down the stairs, one white hand holding on to the railing, the other resting against her throat.

"Did I say that?" she asked. Then, "I honestly don't know what to believe anymore."

As Larry watched, she descended the rest of the stairs, her feet hitting the hardwood floor of the living room, her dress brushing against the oak coffee table as she floated by, a ghost of the woman she used to be, the woman she was before Henry died. *This table was made by your sons… white oak can grow as tall as a hundred feet.*

And then Frances Munroe was gone.

• • •

Evie slept until noon, something she hadn't done in a long time. She had nixed the idea of a quick vacation, just she and the little Mazda cruising along Route One to visit the ocean, and the fishing boats, and the rocky shoreline. It all seemed like too much work, especially after her meeting with Margie Jenkins. Evie hadn't intended to do a session. But the little girl, Annie, had pulled so much energy out in just those few minutes she appeared that Evie had slept for hours, all night long, and then all morning, in a stupor of broken dreams and noises filtering in from the street. The cotton top sheet was wrapped about her ankles when she kicked it free and finally sat up in bed. That's when she saw the clock. Almost noon. Why had she let Margie do this? She had only intended to talk to her, drink some iced tea, offer a kind of aloof comfort. But the pain in the woman's eyes had seduced Evie again. She was a sucker for a mother's grief, had always been so. And little Annie Jenkins, dead just a month, was still learning the ropes, still finding her way around in that new dimension that was now her home. There was still too much connection to the old world at that point, too much confusion. When this happens, it's as if both worlds are pulling on the newly departed at once. A tug of war. Coming through as Annie did, with Evie channeling for her mother, took just too much energy. It reminded Evie of what used to happen to the lights in those houses built next to prisons that had electric chairs. It takes a lot of current to kill someone, and so all those lightbulbs over dinner tables, and on bedside stands where Bibles are kept, or on desks where kids did their homework, those bulbs in attics and basements, they had to grow dim just to allow it. The same is true of bringing the dead back. If they aren't standing at the veil peering through on their own, ready to look back at the world again, then you need to draw them, like a nail to a magnet. But in six months, maybe, Annie Jenkins would not only be ready, she'd be a good contender. She had high energy, this kid, and the connection between mother and daughter was sharp and strong. When the time was right, Annie Jenkins would be back.

In the kitchen Evie ground some coffee beans and then found a filter. While the coffee was perking, she rolled a joint, taking a few strong tokes before she snuffed it out again. She left it in the cigarette notch of the ashtray, a treat for later in the day. With a cup of coffee in her hand, she stepped out onto her front porch and opened the lid to the small wrought iron mailbox that hung near her door. Two bills and a flyer ad for some new shop out at the mall. Gil Taylor was the one who delivered mail in Evie's part of town. Evie had planned to be wide awake by the time Gil came whistling up her walk. She would pretend to be taking a morning swing, there in the shade of the porch, just a coincidence. And she would ask Gil, in the most offhand way she could muster, if he'd seen Larry Munroe around work lately.

It was the ringing telephone that brought Evie away from snapping more dead leaves from her porch plants. She put her coffee cup down on the table, near the glass lamp with the lead crystal diamonds hanging from its shade. The crystals chimed their sweet chime as she reached under the shade and grabbed the phone.

"Evie speaking," she said. It was how she liked to answer the phone. Cut to the chase, that was Evie's motto about most things in life. There it was again, the sound that comes when a telephone line is alive, not dead, that sense of a person hovering at the other end but saying nothing. "Hello? This is Evie Cooper. May I help you?"

There was no reply, but Evie knew the sensation that came over her. She was aware of space, and time, and the gut feeling that you are connected to someone, someone you can't see or touch, but someone you *know* is there, hanging on to you for dear life. Evie waited. Nothing.

"I see your car," Evie said then. "I know it's you. And I know it's you calling me like this and hanging up."

Now, she heard breathing at the other end of the line, as if speaking those words had caught the caller unawares. There was a static noise as the phone on the other end moved about, maybe from one ear to the other. Then, that soft sense again of being joined, person to person, connected by an electrical wire. The telephone had always struck Evie as a kind of channeler itself, bringing together two people who cannot see or touch each other. It had taken scientists a long time to discover how sound works, how signals change in volume and pitch over great distances. One day, she was sure, the skeptics would understand that the dead work like telephones, from their own great distance, to contact the living.

And then, Evie said something that made her feel proud for the first time in a long time when it came to Henry's wife. She didn't say what she really wanted to; she didn't shout, "How dare you telephone me and just hang up? Talk to me, damn it, or leave me alone!" Instead, she closed her eyes and breathed deeply.

"If I live to be a hundred," she said, "I'll never be able to apologize enough. I didn't know, didn't know the color of your hair, your face, the way you dress, the children you have, the way you push your cart at the IGA. I'm sorry. I wish I could take it all back. I'm here if you ever want to talk, even if it's to shout at me. So please remember that."

And then the line went dead and the connection was broken.

· · ·

At six o'clock, Jeanie did what Larry had asked. She parked down the street and waited until she saw Frances and Lawrence putter off in the Toyota truck. Only then did she start her car and pull up closer to the house. Still, she parked on the opposite side of the street, under a large elm with branches that cascaded down as a kind of cover. The key to the front door was under the huge, cast-iron pot filled with red geraniums, the same place it had been when Jeanie first started dating Henry. As she pushed it into the lock and opened the front door, she wondered how many geraniums had come and gone over the years in that same cement pot. Lots of them. Enough blossoms to bury Bixley, Maine. You could keep track of time by counting those falling red petals.

Once inside, Jeanie climbed the stairs cautiously, as if afraid Frances might pop up from behind a lamp or a vase of flowers. She knew her mother-in-law would feel betrayed if she found out about this secret dinner. Frances had now developed a new strategy about Larry: leave him to sit in his room alone and he'll eventually miss the world enough to come back out. But Jeanie doubted this. She envied Larry his solitude behind that bedroom door, a quiet place where he could shape and mold the outer world to his liking. The dinner idea seemed wonderful to her, an invitation to step into that superficial world of the bedroom, the Planet Larry. But what she was remembering now, as she made her way up the stairs, were those times Henry had sneaked her into his and Larry's room, trying to get her past that talking step before Frances rushed out of her downstairs bedroom like a guard dog. Those were the nights that Larry stayed behind, practicing his basketball shots on the court down by the park, only the streetlights to aid him. Some nights he'd be alone, unless a couple of the other guys who had no place special to be were around to shoot baskets with him. When Henry and Jeanie would appear again, an hour or so later as Henry walked Jeanie home, Henry would wave to his brother, a signal that the coast was now clear. Jeanie would pretend she didn't see Larry there, still too embarrassed at what she and Henry had been doing back in the bedroom. But Larry would smile politely as he twirled the basketball on the tip of one finger. Then he'd tuck the ball under his arm and head for home.

At the top of the stairs, the squeaking step alerted Larry, who threw open his door and gestured to her, as if he were some kind of maître d' at a fancy French restaurant.

"Table number one, Madam," Larry said. "Shall I seat you now?" He was dressed in a gray pin-striped suit, necktie and all. Jeanie giggled to see him.

"You look great," she said. And he did. Larry was attractive in a quiet way, unlike Henry's loud and flashy good looks.

"You don't look so bad yourself," said Larry.

"You like it?" Jeanie asked. She twirled around, showing Larry the blue dress she was wearing, a cotton linen, sleeveless and pretty. "I wore this to my wedding reception." She felt a wash of sadness come over her. Maybe this was a mistake, to come here wearing that special blue dress while Frances and Lawrence were planning her husband's memorial service. That's where a good, loyal widow would be, deciding on who speaks first, then second, then third. Deciding who pushes the plaque into the ground, if there will be a flag or not, if the minister should say a prayer before or after the plaque is inserted. All those things that seemed useless to Jeanie since Henry the man, the person it was all about, was gone. Memorial services should be done for the living, let them know while they still can how appreciated they are by friends and family.

But then Jeanie stepped into the old bedroom and, once again, Larry had saved a moment in time. Before her sat a small card table, a white linen tablecloth spread neatly over its top. Two of Frances's crystal candleholders adorned the center, one on each side of a vase filled with what must be flowers from Frances's backyard, a lovely rose among a mixture of mums and tiger lilies. The best china the house had to offer was in place, silverware and plates that Jeanie knew had come from the beloved downstairs china cabinet, the stuff Frances might use if Jesus came to dinner. Two of her preciously guarded crystal wineglasses sat catching reflections from the flickering candles. In the background, a radio was softly playing, an oldies station. At least, the Bee Gees were singing "Too Much Heaven." Jeanie knew that song well. It was all the rage the year before she married Henry, 1979, the year their lives were still heavenly.

"Larry, it's beautiful," Jeanie said, and she meant it.

"Sit, Cinderella." He pulled a chair back from the table. Jeanie watched as he poured them each a glass of wine.

"Did you break the padlock on the liquor cabinet?" she asked. "Or did you actually leave the room and go shopping?" Larry put the wine bottle on the table and then sat in the other chair. He fluffed out his linen napkin.

"Somewhere in between," he said. "I picked the lock and *then* went shopping." He raised his glass. Jeanie did the same with hers, and they clinked them together, gently. Henry had given the toast at Larry's wedding, hitting his champagne glass so hard against the groom's that both glasses had shattered. Everyone had laughed at the time, even Katherine, although champagne had splattered her wedding dress. But thinking back on that day, Jeanie realized that marriages are like that, too. So are lives. They are so fragile they can break if you aren't careful.

"You're thinking of my wedding toast, aren't you?" Larry asked, and Jeanie nodded. Knowing they shared so many memories brought with it a sense of safety, the kind she always felt when Larry was around.

"Tell me again why I married your brother instead of you," Jeanie said.

"Because he was the life of the party," said Larry, "and I was the guy who cleaned up afterward." He lifted the lid of a plate on the table. Jeanie saw almond-stuffed olives, squares of cheese, crackers, a few of the marinated mushrooms Frances loved to buy at the Bixley Deli. The Bee Gees sang on quietly from their corner, as if they were the house band, serenading the diners.

"How could Katherine let you go?" Jeanie asked. "You make what's rotten seem bearable in such a short time." Larry had always had this gift. Maybe it was following in Henry's footsteps that had taught him to put the pieces back together as he went.

"Well, my ex-wife saw it as a nuisance rather than a talent," Larry said. He took another lid off another plate and held it up for her to see. Sliced garden tomatoes, baby cukes, shelled garden peas, fresh garden carrots, all scrubbed clean and presented neatly. Jeanie bit into a carrot.

"I see Frances has a good garden this year," she said, teasing him.

"I'm disappointed in the lettuce," said Larry. "Too much rust on the leaves or we'd be having a Waldorf salad. I saw walnuts down in the fridge. Maybe next time."

A cool breeze pushed through the window Larry had already opened, a book propped beneath it. Wind rippled across the high school banners still pinned like butterflies to the wall, their streamers waving gently as wings. The breeze brought with it the smell of creek, and trees, and grass, and even the aroma of bread baking in some nearby house. Larry sniffed the air.

"Wish I knew who's baking," he said. "Bread would go well with this. Don't gorge on veggies and cheese. I've prepared a culinary delight as our main course." He pointed to a bookshelf over by the window. Books had been piled on the floor so that the top shelf was cleared for a hotplate plugged into a nearby outlet. A covered pan sat on the single burner. Jeanie pushed her chair back so that she could stretch her legs, enjoy her wine, let the evening unroll as if it were some kind of old banner itself, one that's been stored too long in the attic. It had been years, maybe since high school, that she'd felt this free, as if the future were still something far-off and shiny. Leave it to Larry to know just what to do.

Memories came, too, on the wind. For the first time in years Jeanie looked, *really looked*, at the old football picture of the Munroe brothers, still ripe with victory. There was Henry's crooked smile, Larry's polite tilt of head. What a day that had been in all their lives. Larry the captain and Henry the best quarterback in school history. It was that same night, after the big game with Montgomery High, the game where Henry had thrown those seven historic touchdown passes to Larry, that he and Jeanie McPherson first made love. Henry had saved enough money for a motel room. And Jeanie had worn a scarf over her hair, afraid that old Mr. Tyson, who worked the night shift and knew her father, might see her. It was her first time ever with any boy. But there was so much magic that day, talk floating in the air of college scouts in the bleachers with their eyes on Henry, the photographer from the local paper snapping away at the Fabulous Munroe Brothers. Frances and Lawrence beaming from their seats. It was enough to make a girl like Jeanie set her sights on an engagement ring, and that usually meant going all the way, going the distance, just as the team itself had done that year. But that was a long time ago now. Larry had gone on to college and Henry had busted his ankle senior year, a break so bad that he'd never play football again except for a friendly game in the park. That old day of victory was now rolled up like a mat and put aside. A day ambushed by the future.

"Coming into this room is like lifting the cover on our class yearbook and stepping inside for a visit," Jeanie said.

"Not for me," said Larry. He was helping himself to more baby cukes. "For me, it's like *living* in the fucking yearbook."

Jeanie laughed, that out-loud laugh that loosens the stomach muscles and releases the tension. A television show she had once seen claimed that laughing can cure cancer.

The song on the radio was by Rupert Holmes. Jeanie remembered it well, a song about drinking piña coladas and walking in the rain. She wished she were on an island somewhere far away, sun and sand, drinking rum for an entire week. That way, she would have an excuse not to attend the upcoming service.

"Are you going to Henry's memorial service?" she asked. Larry poured more red wine into his glass and beck-oned to Jeanie, who nodded. He filled her glass as well.

"You must be referring to the Frances and Lawrence

Munroe memorial service," said Larry. "Funny how they've given Henry the credit again. Henry couldn't organize an ant fight."

"Are you going?"

"Nope. Are you?"

"I don't want to," said Jeanie.

"Then don't," said Larry.

Jeanie stood and twirled the dress again. She felt like a girl in school, just as she had been when she'd bought the damn dress, she and Mona gliding about the streets of Boston, loaded with shopping bags and having the time of their lives. It was to be their big splurge on life before they both got married later that year and became wives and mothers, which had to come before *friends*. The dress had fitted perfectly then, and while it was snug now, it still fit. Somehow, that's all that mattered. It was another one of those symbolic signs, and Jeanie saw symbols everywhere she looked since the day Henry died. The dress seemed to be telling her that life could be unpacked and put back on, if you wanted it bad enough.

The Eagles were singing now, "Hotel California." The light of day was fading beyond the window, and twilight was bringing a coolness in on the breeze. Jeanie drank more of the wine and felt it warm her, the way just being alive used to do in those old days.

"If 'Disco Duck' comes on, I'm asking you to dance," said Larry. And then they were both laughing, the way they used to laugh at the movie theater, when Larry would come along with Jeanie and Henry, nights he was dateless.

"Dinner is served," he said, and carried Jeanie's plate over to the pan on the bookshelf. With a spoon, he scooped something reddish-orange onto the plate and brought it back to the table. Jeanie saw that it was spaghetti and meatballs, the kind that comes in a can. Jeanie shook her own napkin out and arranged it strategically on the front of her blue dress. There was nothing messier to eat than spaghetti. She waited for Larry to return with his own plate.

"*Bon appétit,*" said Jeanie.

"Sorry about the *bon* part," Larry said, "but this is the best I can do under the circumstances."

"It's all wonderful," said Jeanie.

"We could have eaten downstairs, but what if they forgot something? Or came home early to see if they can catch me washing my underwear in the laundry room?"

"This is better," said Jeanie. "More private."

They ate in silence, savoring private thoughts, peaceful, no need to entertain or be entertained. The way it should be. When they had finished the small piece of carrot cake that Larry produced from the top drawer of his desk, he poured them more wine. Jeanie took her glass and walked over to the bunk beds. She put her hand on the steps leading up to the top bed, Henry's bunk.

"Do you still feel him here?" she asked. Larry didn't answer right away. He stared at the bunks as if he were trying to find the best words.

"Sometimes, it's as if he never left," Larry said. "As if he never grew up, never met you, never got married. Like he's Peter Pan. I wake up nights, and I can almost hear him breathing up there."

Jeanie looked over at him. The wine had made her braver than she'd been in a long time. And besides, this was Larry Munroe, the person more like family to her than her own brother who lived far away in Washington state, a man she barely knew anymore.

"Larry, I know you better than anyone in this family," she said. "You invited me to dinner because you want to talk to me about something. And I came because I promised Frances I'd be her spy." That wasn't true, of course, but Jeanie knew it would make Larry smile, and he did just then.

"If I could pick a sister, it would be you," he said. He had told Jeanie this often over the years, especially at those god-awful tree-decorating parties Frances gave each December, when Henry would always drink too much eggnog and make an ass of himself. And Katherine would go home to correct school papers, always arriving in her own car so that she could escape early. And Jeanie and Larry would sit on the light blue sofa and watch a tipsy Lawrence try to put the aging Christmas star on the top of the tree while Frances held the stepladder and directed from below. It was like watching an old vaudeville act. Laurel and Hardy. Just before the tree came crashing down, or Frances threw up her hands in disgust, or Henry started snoring from the recliner, it had always seemed like a good idea for Larry to thank Jeanie for being the one in the family most like him.

"I know," said Jeanie. "But that's not why you asked me to dinner."

She was right. She did know him better than anyone. What made Larry sad was that it would've been nice to have had Jeanie as his sister in all those growing-up years. He never really got to know Jeanie McPherson until Henry starting dating her. By that time she was an added fixture in front of the television, sitting in their dad's car between

Henry and Larry, sitting between them at the movies, fixing Larry up now and then with a cute girl he happened to notice in chemistry class or at a ball game, something he was often too shy to do for himself. And maybe, just maybe, if his mother had had a daughter to fuss over, it would have made things easier for her sons.

"That woman you mentioned last week," he said, "Evie Cooper?"

Jeanie put her glass of wine down on the table.

"What about her?" She waited.

Larry reached into the pocket of his pin-striped suit and pulled out the envelope he'd put in the *Still to Deliver* pile. He placed it on the table beside Jeanie's plate. She picked it up and read the address. *Ms. Jeanie Munroe, 39 Hurley Avenue.* Larry waited, tense. He felt himself sweating inside his suit. It was the best one he owned, the same he'd worn on every one of those job interviews where he had been turned down, rejected, dismissed. He watched as Jeanie pulled the letter out of the envelope. She read silently, which was fine with Larry since he knew the words by heart.

Dear Jeanie,

I am so very sorry for your sadness. I have seen your car outside my house on many nights. Would you like to come in and talk sometime? I would then have the chance to apologize to you in person, for I owe you that. I realize we will never be friends, but life is too short for us to be enemies.

Evie Cooper

When Jeanie finished, she put the letter back inside the envelope and looked across the table at Larry. She knew this wasn't all. But she had no idea where he was heading, what he was about to tell her. Maybe that Henry had had other affairs? Maybe that Henry, like the race car driver Mona Prescott had seen on television, liked to dress in women's clothing? Who knew what might be coming? The world as Jeanie had known it no longer existed. All the rules had been ripped up and thrown to the winds from the moment she woke up that lovely summer morning a year earlier and realized that her husband was lying dead in the bed beside her. It had all changed, and it would never be safe again, for it was now a world without rules.

"I'm in love with Evie Cooper," Larry said. When Jeanie didn't scream, didn't throw something, didn't run from the room in a burst of tears, Larry reached under the table and grabbed that second bottle of wine he had stolen from the liquor cabinet, just in case there was a *need* for a second bottle. Jeanie said nothing as he uncorked the bottle and poured her glass full. Wind rattled the old banners again, Bixley High school banners. Cars came and went along the street. People were out for their evening walks, their voices drifting up to the window on clouds of excitement. From its corner of the room, the radio was talking.

"Now we're taking you all the way back to 1973, folks," the deejay said. "So come ride that 'Midnight Train to Georgia,' with Gladys Knight and the Pips."

Larry picked up a pretend telephone and put it to his ear. He punched at invisible numbers as he dialed. He waited.

"Request line?" Larry said. "Could you please play 'Disco Duck'?"

Then he hung up the imaginary phone and looked at Jeanie, who still wasn't smiling.

10

Jeanie knocked three times on Chad's bedroom door before she heard him grumble something from the other side. She opened the door and went on in. To hell with privacy. She'd given him far too much *space*, as he called it, and look what he'd done with it. Chad was lying on his back, sheet up to his waist, one arm shading the light of day from his eyes. He lifted his arm and looked at her, his eyes still swollen from sleeping hard and heavy. There were days Jeanie had to knock ten times before the boy even grunted. She grabbed the pillow and pulled it out from under his head.

"Hey!" said Chad. He was waking up now and she could see anger in his eyes. He reached for his pillow, but Jeanie put it behind her back. "What the hell's up with you?"

"I just cooked a great breakfast," said Jeanie. "It's the kind you used to love, before your father died. I want you at the kitchen table in ten minutes, Chad. We're going to sit down and eat as if we're still actually a family, because we are." She threw the pillow onto the end of his bed.

Chad sat up and grabbed it, hugging it against his chest. He was looking up at her face with that same boyish curiosity. This was the kid who asked more *but why?* questions than any child Jeanie had ever known. *But why is the sky blue? But why can birds fly? But why do we need food to live? But why?*

Jeanie turned and left the room, left the boy sitting bewildered on his bed, the pillow cradled in his arms. She took the stairs two steps at a time, an energy and confidence she hadn't felt in many months. It was the first time she mentioned Henry's death. Not even to Mona Prescott had she been able to use any form of the word. Maybe the grief people were right, that if you can survive the first year, you can almost imagine yourself living again.

In the kitchen Jeanie poured herself a cup of coffee. She heard Chad's feet on the floor upstairs as he went into the bathroom and shut the door. Water begun to flush through the pipes. Jeanie dropped four slices of wheat bread into the toaster and watched as the inside coils turned a bright red. She went to the stove and picked up the bowl she'd left there, the eggs already scrambled, with bits of onion and spicy red pepper, the way Chad and Henry liked them. She turned the burner on under the flying pan and poured in the egg mixture. She stirred the yellow mess about with a fork and watched as it began to cook and harden into bite-size chunks.

Upstairs, Chad opened the bathroom door again. Jeanie smiled. Why hadn't she done this months ago? Why hadn't she taken a parental stand? Now, if only Lisa were there to eat breakfast with them. It had been over two months since she'd been home and that was far too long, especially with the baby almost ready to be born. As soon as the memorial service was over, she would pack a suitcase for herself, another one for Chad. They would drive down to Portland and stay with Lisa until the baby arrived. They would be a family unit again, missing one member, yes, but able to function, and with a new member on the way.

Jeanie went to the fridge for the butter dish and a jar of blueberry jam, also Chad's favorite. The toast popped right on cue and she pulled all four slices out, buttered them, and put them on a plate, which she covered with a glass lid. She had already cooked the sausages and now she slid the six little logs off the platter they'd been resting on, into the pan with the scrambled eggs. She nudged the sausages off to one side and turned the burner down to low. They'd be warm again in no time. The timer beeped on the oven. The home fries were ready, nicely baked with slices of mushroom and smothered in freshly grated Parmesan cheese. It had been much longer than a year since she'd made Henry's personal recipe for home fries. Ever since the doctor had told him to watch what he ate, Jeanie had begun serving fresh fruit for breakfast, home-made oatmeal with skim milk, with no attention paid to Henry's constant complaints. And she had set about trying to get Chad accustomed to better eating habits while he was still young. But this was to be a celebration breakfast, one that would speak of those happier times the family had known. Surely this one morning wouldn't hurt. She heard Chad coming down the stairs now, one step at a time, as if he was positive the world would wait for him.

Jeanie filled the cup she'd put by Chad's plate with hot coffee. His juice was already poured, in a small glass with an orange painted on its side. She grabbed his plate off the table and took it to the stove. She spooned out a large helping of the eggs and then rolled three of the link sausages onto one corner. She opened the oven door and scooped up a serving of the home fries, the hot, sticky cheese pulling away in strings. She wanted Chad's plate all ready for him, waiting on the table like a picture out of a magazine. The most wonderful breakfast a boy could imagine. Again, Jeanie scolded herself. Why had she been so tied up with her own problems, her own grief, that she'd let family issues ride this long? Now, with the service just two days away, the best thing she could do to *memorialize* Henry Munroe was to save his son. She put the plate of food back on the table, fitted snugly between a fork and knife. Next to the plate was a freshly ironed linen napkin. The next morning, they would have fresh blueberries, a slice of wheat toast, cereal. And that's when she heard the motorbike start up, out in the front yard. By the time Jeanie got to the kitchen window, all she saw disappearing around the thick bulge of lilac bushes by the mailbox was Henry's orange bonnet.

• • •

It was still early, just four o'clock, when Evie got out of her car in Murphy's parking lot. She looked across the rows of parked cars in time to see Marshall Thompson slide a leg over the seat of his big black Harley. When he saw Evie, he waved a hand that held a beer bottle. Not only was this illegal, it was against Murphy employee rules to let customers leave the establishment with alcohol.

Gail was wiping down the bar as Evie clocked in and started picking up empty glasses, dipping them into the bin of sudsy water. Monique, the new girl, was sweeping the floor over by the jukebox. Evie quickly counted heads seated at the bar and at tables around the room. Only fifteen customers, including Billy Randall, who was at the pinball machine. But happy hour was just beginning, and Fridays were always good nights for the tavern, a kind of early weekend frenzy. Murphy's wasn't fancy enough to beckon to the uptown crowd, the ones with good salaries and retirement plans, the lawyers and computer programmers and college types. They all drove their Beamers and Volvos out to the fancier bars down at the new mall. Murphy's, on the other hand, seemed to call out to anyone who'd had a hard life and little money to spend telling the bartender all about it. Evie always felt good seeing Billy Randall in the place. Shortly after she began working at the bar, Billy had told her that if she ever needed his help, to ask for it. And Evie *had* asked for help on several occasions. And asking was all it took since word was out at Murphy's that "Crazy Billy" had come back from Vietnam with a black belt in karate and jungle skills that even the Viet Cong hadn't learned. If Billy stood up, a troublemaker sat down.

"When's Sheila getting here?" Evie asked. She would need at least two waitresses to handle the tables. And then Sheila would close, allowing Evie to go home early.

"Any time now," said Gail. "Hey, thanks a million for doing this, Evie. I know it's your days off and all, but

Marshall decided spur of the moment that he's just got to see the sun come up over Quebec City."

"It's okay," said Evie. She hadn't wanted to be back at Murphy's so soon, but there were worse ways to kill a few hours. The memorial service was Sunday, and as far as Evie was concerned, she'd prefer to stay in a coma until it was finally over. Then, maybe then, Larry Munroe would find it in his heart to come on back to the tavern, to sit on his favorite bar stool, to go home with her at the end of the night.

She missed him.

Evie looked up to see Andy Southby just coming in for his two beers, those twelve quarters no doubt rattling about in his pocket. She closed her eyes and imagined the face of a clock, the hour hand pointing at the number ten. *Ten o'clock*. In six hours, it would be a reality. The bar would have slowed down by then, and the two waitresses would be able to handle the crowd. Evie would be free to go. Before Monique and Sheila would have washed the glasses, swept the floor, and locked the tavern door just past midnight, Evie would have already smoked a joint on the porch swing, had a midnight snack, and then fallen into bed for a deep sleep.

"Beer," said Andy, as if this were a new revelation. Evie gave him his beer and then noticed that she was out of napkins. Gail was supposed to have stocked the bar before she left. With Andy sitting on his stool like a self-important gargoyle, Evie went back into the small office just behind the bar to get some napkins from the supplies kept there. Gail was standing before the mirror that hung on the wall next to Murphy's computer, brushing out her long hair. Evie had always wondered how so much thick hair could disappear into such a tiny, tight knot, but Gail had a magical way of twisting it. Now, she tossed the dark hair back and fluffed it with her fingers. She pulled a lipstick from her purse and watched as Evie rummaged among the stacked boxes.

"The kids are staying with Ronnie," said Gail. "He's taking them to the fair this weekend."

"Great," said Evie.

"Hey, thanks for talking to Margie yesterday," Gail added. "It meant a lot to her."

"No problem," said Evie.

"Okay, I'll bite," Gail said. "What's bothering you?" She leaned toward the mirror and began to apply the wine-colored lipstick. Evie pulled a large box away from the others, ripped the top open, and took out two bundles of napkins.

"You really wanna know?" she asked.

"Long as it doesn't spoil this night," said Gail. "I got my heart set on cruising along the St. Lawrence, wind in my hair." She smiled then, her best smile, but it had always struck Evie as a sad smile, no matter how hard Gail tried to make it appear otherwise. She'd had a hard life, divorced young, two kids to look after alone, and so Evie found herself wanting to help the younger woman.

"Well, for starters," said Evie, "I just saw Marshall out in the parking lot, waving a bottle of beer around."

"It was almost full and he didn't want to waste it," said Gail.

"Why? Did he pay for it?" Evie asked. Gail got that tight look on her face that she always got when Evie was pushing too far. But Evie no longer cared. "How fast do you think Murphy will fire you if he finds out? How'll you pay the rent then, Gail, when you can hardly do it now?"

"When was the last time you saw Dan Murphy down here?" Gail asked. "We run this dump while he plays golf all day."

Gail flipped up the side flap of her purse and tossed in the tube of lipstick. She went for her jacket on the pegs Murphy had driven into the wall where employees could hang their coats. It was the brown rawhide jacket she'd bought the same week she started dating Marshall Thompson, long rawhide strips hanging down from the arms, strips that grab the wind from the back of a motorcycle.

"I better run," said Gail. "Marshall will think I flew the coop."

"That's what you should do," said Evie. "He's bad news, Gail. You've heard the stories about Paula."

Gail slid both arms into the heavy coat and shook the fringes to get them to fall right. She looked over at Evie.

"Marshall says he never laid a finger on her."

Gail followed Evie back out to the bar. Evie knew she was waiting for a response but decided to say nothing. She watched as Gail grabbed her pack of cigarettes and lighter lying next to the cash register. At the door she turned and looked back at Evie. She blew a quick kiss and then the door closed behind her.

Pop. Pop. Pop. A goddamned triple header. Evie spun around.

"Andy, I'm warning you," she said. "You do that one more fucking time and your ass is out of here."

"Jesus," said Andy. He was putting his first quarter into the poker machine. "Who tied *your* panties in a knot?"

• • •

It was just past nine o'clock when Larry pulled on a pair of jeans and his navy blue sweatshirt. He gathered up the *Still to Deliver* letters and stuffed them all back into the leather mailbag. Then he carried the bag over to his window, which he slid upward until it was wide open. He leaned out and surveyed the drop below. There were a few box elders planted beneath the window, but beyond them was clear and freshly cut green lawn. The Blakely kid, with those crossed eyes of his, had been there early that morning to do the mowing, as he did every Thursday. Larry reached for the mailbag and held it out the window far enough to miss the box elders. He let it drop. He heard it hit with a dull *splat!* on the grass below.

He cracked his bedroom door a few inches and peered down at the living room. He could see his father's legs sticking out from the blue sofa, crossed and dead weight, like two fallen logs. This would have been enough to tell Larry that the old man was asleep, but the soft snores that came rolling out in ripples was full proof. His mother was already brushing her teeth and doing her nightly duties before bed. Larry could hear the rattle of bottles around the tiny sink in her bathroom and the sound of running water. He bypassed the talking step altogether and came quietly down the stairs.

At the bottom he could now see the full living room, his father on the sofa, head back and mouth open, the remote control lying listlessly on the palm of his hand. Now it was a matter of crossing the hardwood floor to the front door and hoping his mother didn't step out of her bedroom and catch him in motion. If she did, Larry would say that he was coming down for a raid of the refrigerator and then do his best to retreat before she could begin her drilling of him. But her bedroom door was closed, a band of yellow light rimming the bottom. He heard the running water stop and the sound of a glass clinking on the sink.

He closed the front door behind him and stood there, staring out at the night that had swept in over Bixley. His neighbor's windows were warm yellow squares. Music wafted in from one yard, the canned laughter of a television sitcom from another. A car sped by, braking for the stop sign at the end of the street. It was the first time in a week that Larry had been out of the house, and now it felt good to have the cool night press itself down on his shoulders. It felt good to open his legs up in an ample stride, something he didn't have space to do within his cramped bedroom. He found the mailbag where it had landed on the grass. He picked it up, checking to see that no letters had fallen out on impact. He shouldered the bag and crept back to the front of the house.

The geranium pot, that cast-iron sentinel, kept watch on the street. Larry had to be certain the house key was beneath it, just in case his mother had *sensed* he would sneak out without her seeing him. She had that talent when it came to her boys, a kind of built-in radar. Once, in the eighth grade, Larry and Henry had slipped out at midnight to meet up with other boys down at the quarry, to throw rocks at the moon and share four cans of beer amongst seven of them, the worst thing they'd done yet in their young lives. But when they'd come home two hours later, they saw that a light was on in the kitchen, a light white with anger. Someone was up, and it had to be their mother. That's when Henry lifted the geranium pot to discover that the house key was gone. After an hour of shivering in the damp night, it was decided that Henry should be the son to knock on the front door. It had opened immediately, and there stood Frances, a dozen pink sponge curlers in her hair, wearing her blue bathrobe and waiting to deliver the little speech she'd had plenty of time to practice. *You are both grounded for three full weeks and that means television too.* For the rest of that night, lying on his top bunk as dawn rimmed the horizon, Henry kept asking Larry, who had no answer himself, *"How the fuck did she know?"*

Larry tilted the heavy pot that held the red geraniums over to one side. There was the silver house key, glittering up at him in a sliver of porch light. He eased the pot back down and then, the mailbag secure on his shoulder, the way a good mailman would be certain it was, he left the light of the porch and headed out into the blue velvet of night.

• • •

Jeanie wasn't sure how long she'd been sitting in the Buick, pulled up to the curb on the opposite side of the street from where Evie's *Spiritual Portraitist* sign was driven into the tiny front lawn. At least, she wasn't sure in the way that time is measured on a clock. But using her new way of telling time, it was easy: she'd been sitting in the Buick at Evie's Cooper's house for two wine coolers and three cigarettes.

She had made a decision just that morning, as the sausages cooked for breakfast, that she was done smoking. And wine would be that lovely glass of white that she ordered over lunch with Mona, now that they'd started their eating ritual again. Or it would be a glass or two of red when she and Larry met up for a visit. That is, if she ever got over her anger at Larry Munroe enough that she cared to visit him again. But it was seeing the orange bonnet spin out of the drive, with no concern whatsoever for her feelings, that prompted Jeanie to put off the no-smoking resolution. And since it wasn't the best day to give up cigarettes, maybe it wasn't wise to give up the wine coolers either. She didn't blame Chad. She understood every move the boy was making. She knew it was his own way of hitting imaginary fists against the world. With all this talk of Henry in the air, all the pain had been brought to the forefront, away from those quiet, private places where people can grieve alone. Jeanie knew because it had happened inside her, as well. After all, when you memorialize someone, you're admitting that he no longer exists. You're putting the idea of his life on a small bronze plaque for passersby to stop and read. The memorial was on Sunday. As Jimmy Buffett once sang, "Come Monday, it'll be all right."

Dear Jeanie,

I am so very sorry for your sadness. I have seen your car outside my house on many nights.

Jeanie got out of the Buick and closed the door softly. There were no lights on inside the house where Evie Cooper lived, and there was no little car sitting in the drive. Jeanie had already spun past Murphy's Tavern and saw the blue Mazda lost in a sea of other cars. Evie was at work, so Jeanie made her way quietly up the walk. *Would you like to come in and talk sometime? I would then have the chance to apologize to you in person, for I owe you that.* Neighbors came out of the house next door, loud voices rushing against the night, a kind of Friday evening excitement. Jeanie stepped back into deeper shadows by the front steps and waited until car doors slammed and an engine roared to life. When the car and its occupants backed out of the drive and sped off down the street, she went up the steps to Evie's door. She lifted the top lid of the wrought iron mailbox and dropped the fisted bits of letter inside. Shards fell upon the porch by Jeanie's feet and she bent to find them, to stuff them into the box as well.

I realize we will never be friends, but life is too short for us to be enemies.

Evie Cooper

"Damn straight we'll never be friends," Jeanie said to the mailbox.

She turned and went back down Evie's walk, crossed the dark street to where the Buick was waiting. She had two wine coolers left. She would save them for the back patio, once she got home. It looked like a full moon night, and there was no better place to sit and watch the moon than out on the little wooden patio, a place that smelled of cedar and phlox. Henry had finally built the patio for her, after years of her nagging, and now she had it covered with flower boxes that brought hummingbirds by day and moths by night. She had her favorite lawn chair out there, the kind you can lie back on, stretch out your full length in order to sunbathe. Or at night, you can just lie still and wait for the moon to inch its way across the sky. She would drink the last two wine coolers out on the dark patio, under the white moonlight, and wait until she heard the whine of the motorbike coming home again. It would mean another day that Chad Henry Munroe was still safe. Another marker in their lives.

On the drive home, Jeanie turned up the oldies station on the radio and smoked another cigarette.

• • •

Evie had unhooked her bra and pulled it off before she lit that lovely joint. With her breasts now free and cool beneath her T-shirt, she kicked off each of the brown leather sandals. With one foot, she gave herself a strong push. Soon the fresh evening air was moving over her as she swung back and forth. Her feet ached in that way only a bartender's feet can. It would kill Murphy to put any kind of thick, protective mat behind the bar. Unless the girls bought it themselves, it was pretty much thin rug over sheer cement, the hardest surface yet for feet and knees.

Evie inhaled the smoke and held it. A mockingbird was singing from a neighbor's tree, singing late to the moon, looking for a mate no doubt. They had moved gradually north, mockingbirds had. Maybe they had come looking for a new life, a chance to start over, just as Evie had done. She took a second long toke. It had been a week since she had seen Larry Munroe. And she hadn't heard from him either, no late-night phone calls as there had been in the past. Evie would be just about to go to bed when the phone would ring its soft bleat and Larry would say, *Hey there, what's going on? Did I wake you? I was just watching this old black-and-white movie and I started thinking about you.* The steady sound of his voice could bring such a calm over her, as if, okay, maybe she was all alone in the world, and maybe she'd made a lot of mistakes, but Larry Munroe was there now and everything would be all right. There had been nothing but silence for a week. So why was Evie still watching the door at Murphy's as if it were the spot where the Second Coming would occur?

On the short drive home from work, she had already decided to forget about Larry Munroe. She had spent too many precious minutes thinking about a man who was treating her as if she didn't exist. Yes, she had a brief affair with his younger brother, Henry. She was far from perfect. Sometimes, she was just lonely. But, realizing the error of her ways, she had ended the affair. She couldn't rewrite history. If Larry didn't accept those facts, so be it. If he couldn't even come back to Murphy's as a client, *c'est la vie.* Evie had been thinking that Bixley really wasn't the best place for her, anyway. And maybe the mockingbird was thinking the same thing, thinking it so much that he'd been singing late into the night, a mournful song. Bixley was a big town that wanted hard to be a small city, a town with an ambitious mayor, an ambitious Chamber of Commerce, an ambitious group of city planners. Maybe what Evie needed was a truly large city, a place that had been ambitious before there ever was an idea called America, a place like Paris, France, maybe. She'd never run out of clients in the City of Lights. If she wanted her spiritual business to thrive so that her feet could have a good rest, maybe she should move, learn to speak French, put the whole damn Munroe family behind her.

That's when Evie saw the white shard of paper lying on her front porch. She put the joint in the ashtray and got up slowly from the swing. Her bare feet felt good on the cool boards of the porch, her toes finally able to breathe after six cramped hours. She picked up the fragment of paper and held it to her parlor window, where the light of the crystal lamp inside offered enough light that she was able to read. There were only four words since the rest were torn away. But four words were enough for Evie to recognize her own handwriting, as well as the piece of linen stationary she used for her important letters. She took the piece of paper back to the ashtray and picked up her lighter. She watched the paper burn, curling slowly at the edges, until it swallowed those four pitiful words: *sorry for your sadness.*

• • •

Larry had resealed the envelopes in the *Still to Deliver* pile as best he could. Three of them had small dabs of folded tape to hold the flaps. It didn't take him more than a few seconds to stuff Andy Southby's two rejection letters into the dented silver mailbox that stood near the street at 566 Gray Lane. The first was from that restaurant management school in Kansas City. *Perhaps your services would be put to better use in some other industry.* And the second was from the world-renowned Howard F. Honig College of Nebraska. *Dear Sir, Fuck off.*

Next, he delivered the wedding invitations from Debbi Sutton, all to their proper addresses. Then the three birthday cards and two sympathy cards, since they were no doubt important to their recipients. The cards would be *late*, of course, but everyone expected that of the post office these days, so why disappoint them? He then dropped off a couple important bank statements and a notice that the electricity would be cut off if Verna Hilton didn't pay up in thirty days. Larry had always liked Verna, who was living now on her social security. He wouldn't want her to end up in darkness one night and not know why, or have the chance to prevent it. He had even left two twenty-dollar bills on top of the envelope. Verna could wonder forever where the money had come from, but at least she could wonder beneath the glare of her sixty-watt bulbs.

From Verna's house, he cut across the back alley where the old drugstore used to stand, and there he dumped all the flyers and ads and wasted paper into the garbage bin that sat there. He hated delivering this junk every day, just as much as people hated getting it. Now, it was a quick jaunt over to Oakwood Street, where Marshall Thompson had rented the upstairs apartment at number 45. The lights were out in the apartment and the big black Harley was gone from its usual spot just beneath the entrance stairs. But it was Friday night. Why would a guy like Marshall squander a Friday night by staying home?

Larry had wondered long and hard if he should deliver Paula's letter.

Dear Marshall,

I think you know by now that this is the end, and I mean it this time. If you bother me again I'll get a court order, so help me god.

Would threatening him only make him worse? Knowing Marshall, Larry figured it would. But what else to do if someone is beating up on you? He dropped the letter into the box marked THOMPSON.

Then, as if savoring this delivery for last, Larry stood on the sidewalk in front of Stella Peabody's tiny bungalow and studied the quaint architecture of the house, its one and a half stories almost hidden in rose brambles. It was a romantic idea in itself, the bungalow, with its broad porch and elephantine columns, its low and overhanging roof, the knee braces under the eaves, the fieldstone foundation, the tiny dormer window. A picture of the house, along with a plea to save it, had appeared a few times in the local paper. Larry knew Stella had been writing to her congressman, to the governor, to anyone who might listen. Her parents had built the bungalow back in the early 1930s, and they had brought their only son to live in it, a boy who went off to World War II and never came home again. Stella had been born in the house, in the winter of 1936. And so the Peabodys set about life without their son by raising their only daughter, a shy and quiet girl who kept her nose in a book and her ideas to herself.

Larry felt a deep respect for the letters addressed to 215 Thorncliffe. In his hand, he could almost feel them beating, the words so heartfelt and filled with love. Stella Peabody had been the same age as Larry's mother and even shared the same classes. She and Frances graduated from high school together, tassel to tassel, one day back in the summer of 1954. Larry wasn't told this information by his mother, since she wasn't the talkative kind who loves the history of towns and old houses. It was Stella Peabody herself who regaled him with stories, sitting out under her low-hanging roof just behind the large, white columns, enjoying a glass of cold lemonade. When she saw Larry come ambling up her walk with the mailbag on his shoulder, Stella would insist on pouring him a glass, too. And he would sit for a while to *rest his feet,* as Stella called it. That's when she would teach him interesting things, like how the word *bungalow* originated in the Bengal region of India, becoming popular first in California as a cottage house. "Where else but California?" Stella would say, with that nice smile of hers. And she'd warn Larry to watch out for heat stroke if it happened to be a sweltering day. Sometimes, she'd make mention of a special occasion, as in how many years her mother had been dead on that day. Or that it was her parents' anniversary. One day, back in June, it was her brother's birthday, George Peabody, who had ended up one of the twenty thousand prisoners who would die, beaten and malnourished, on the horrendous march from Mariveles on the Bataan Peninsula, in April of 1942. "I was only six years old when Georgie left," Stella once noted. "He just went strolling down that front walk right there as if he owned the world. At the corner, he turned and waved good-bye to Father and Mother and me. That was the last time we would ever see him."

Larry needed Stella in his life because of her respect for the past, a place he mourned for daily. He stood now on the street and waited for the small yellow light in the upstairs dormer window to go out. When it finally did, he knew she had turned in for the night. She would have long hours at the library the next day, it being Saturday, and Stella being no spring chicken, as she liked to remind him. Life had been tough on her lately, now that 213 Thorncliffe, the lot next door to her tiny house, had been plowed under and a sign announcing a new McDonald's was standing where once old Mr. Hart's elm tree stood. "Trapped in the path of progress," Stella herself called it, since that older part of town, with ancient buildings better off being torn down than repaired, at least according to the town's ambitious planners, had been designated as commercial zoning.

My own darling. How I have missed the soft velvet of your sweet mouth, the silk of your nape, the tender arch of your back, the hills of your snow-white breasts, which my lips have climbed so many times in the past.

What Larry couldn't figure out, and what he would never ask her, is where and when and how she had met a Sheila Dewberry, from Sioux City, Iowa. Had it been years ago, at some convention for librarians, one so far from Bixley that Stella Peabody felt free of her shyness? Had their hands touched one day, in some library in a large city where they had both gone for a needed vacation? Where they had both ventured in the hopes of finally, *finally*, meeting someone who felt the same desires as they did? Had they both reached for a book on the same shelf at the same time—Jane Austen no doubt—their lives touching, light as butterfly wings, but with enough meaning that from that moment on, they knew: *This is the love of my life*.

Larry lifted the heavy lid of the old-fashioned mailbox that no doubt had been placed there when Stella's parents first moved in. It was dignified, a polished brass, with the name Peabody engraved stylishly across the front. Sturdy, the way lives once were. Dependable, the way people were expected to be. Once.

Please don't keep me from you, nor you from me, for too much longer. My heart, no, my body, needs you and needs you now. I am all fire as I write.

Larry dropped the two letters, resealed and good as new, into the brass box.

He walked down Mason Court and from there, cut over to Dunbar, which led him back to the childhood street where he and Henry had ridden their first bikes. The old neighborhood always seemed to welcome him home, as if the past were a warm blanket you can wrap yourself up in when the present grows bitterly cold. Larry could have gone to Evie Cooper's house, even though it was a half-hour walk. But he didn't know what he'd say to her. Or if he was ready to say anything at all. Or if she would even want to see him now that he'd jumped ship on the world. Some folks saw that as a sign of weakness, and a strong woman like Evie was bound to be among the skeptics. Call him chicken, but he wasn't ready to face her.

When Larry got home, the house key was gone from beneath the cast-iron pot. He had no idea how his mother knew he was going out. Did she have spies everywhere? Did she have large, flylike eyes on the back of her head? He wondered what he would do now, since this time she was not in the kitchen, light burning, practicing her speech. Would he be grounded for a month this time, no television or bathroom privileges? On an impulse, Larry reached out and touched the doorknob. It turned easily in his hand, the door not locked. So what kind of game might this be? Were they waiting inside to spank him? Would the old man take him across his knee, reaching for the silver letter opener, which his mother would produce? He didn't blame them. He didn't blame them for anything they might do to him from here on. They knew now he had tampered with the mail. He was certain of it. And they would come for the mailbag, as they should. He was a failure as a son, and maybe if he could just admit that to himself, he could go on about his life being a failure. He didn't blame *them*, but he did blame *himself*.

At the top of the stairs, Larry heard the step squeak loudly. How could he have forgotten it? He had been thrown off guard by the key incident was how. He froze, waiting for the sound of her door opening, her footfalls, as in all those years gone by. But there was nothing. He could hear the distant rolls of his father's snores, loud now that he was in his own bed and deep into sleep. But that was all. It made sense, once Larry had a moment to think about it. Why should his mother care? Why should she rise in the night from her warm and peaceful blankets if Henry Munroe wasn't standing on the stairs? After all, it was only her oldest son, Larry.

. . .

It was almost midnight when Jeanie woke in her chair on the patio and sat up. The full moon had crested the top of Mrs. Flaver's roof and was now on its way out of sight. At first, she didn't know where she was. The candle she had lit earlier had burned out and now, with all the neighboring porch lights out for the night, the world was too dark. She'd had an awful dream. As usual, she had been looking for Henry. In all those months since he'd been gone, he had not appeared to Jeanie in a single dream. The grief people said it was her own subconscious mind protecting her, that people seem too real and alive in dreams. You wake, reaching for them, still feeling the warmth of their breath, their kiss, their touch. You wake and realize that person is dead. And that there *was* no warm breath, no kiss, no touch. So, it's better not to dream of those you love and miss. Not until you're ready. And so Jeanie assumed that was why she didn't dream of Henry.

But she looked for him. Night after night, she searched for that man the way some people search for lost treasure. She hunted everywhere for Henry Munroe. Sometimes, it was in their own house and Jeanie would go from room to room, calling his name, looking in the basement, the attic, his workshop in the garage. Other times, she would be reaching for the key that Frances kept beneath the pot of red geraniums, and she would take it and open up the house where Henry had grown into a man. She would search each nook, each cranny, lift each dust ball, trying with all her heart to find the man she had married. Other times, Jeanie was just driving, the way she used to on those nights when Henry didn't come home until late. And there had been many of those nights. What she *thought* Larry was going to tell her the night before, as they sat over his spaghetti dinner, was that Evie Cooper was not the only woman Henry had taken the time to know well, after he married Jeanie. But Larry didn't tell her that, and now Jeanie wondered if he even knew that Henry had had affairs with several women *before* Evie Cooper, and even a couple *after* Evie Cooper. Did Larry know that if his brother hadn't died, he'd still be having affairs? Jeanie knew. She had turned in her badge as housewife and put on a new badge: Marriage Detective. She had learned to phone up motel clerks and ask for receipts, to use redial to its max, especially after Henry got his cell phone. She had known every illicit move her husband made, even finding phone numbers from his girlfriends tucked away beneath the velvet padding of the box his electric shaver sat in. Jeanie had become a female Sherlock Holmes, able to sniff the air for a smell of deceit. Evie Cooper was a tiny part of a very big problem. And now, having searched for Henry all these months in her dreams and failing to find him, Jeanie had to admit that maybe it wasn't to tell Henry *off* that she was looking for him. Maybe it was just to tell him *good-bye*.

"Mom?" The voice was so like Henry's that it startled

her. Her foot kicked one of the empty wine coolers and she heard the bottle roll, clinking all the way across the patio. And then she knew. She remembered.

"Chad?" she said. "Is that you, honey?" She reached a hand out in the dark, hoping to touch the boy, his flesh and blood, to touch someone real and not someone dead, not someone from the land of dreams. If she and Chad didn't start touching soon, start living soon, they might as well give up on life altogether.

"I'm right here," said Chad. And she felt his hand take hers and squeeze it. Warmth ran into her from his touch. She could feel it. She could feel herself pulling the sadness out of him and she wanted to do that. She was the older one, the parent. She could handle his share of grief if he'd just give it to her.

"Here are some matches," Jeanie said, her other hand reaching down where she'd left the pack of cigarettes. "Can you light the candle?"

Chad took the matches from her hand, but he kept her other one tight in his.

"I don't want any light," he said. Jeanie understood. She hoped he could tell just by her touch that she understood. "I miss him, Mom."

"I know, son," she answered. "I know."

For a few minutes, there was no talking. There was just the power of their hands, touching in the night. And it was enough. Then Chad pulled his hand away. A car turned the corner of Hurley and its lights cut across his face, his dark good looks, his sad eyes. Her son. Maybe they would be okay after all.

"Guess what?" Chad said.

"What?" asked Jeanie.

"I'm starving," he told her.

. . .

Evie had just stepped naked out of the shower and looked at the clock. Midnight. She was hoping a cool shower might be the best way to help her fall asleep. Her mind was in too much of a mess to do any reading. Not only was there the question of Larry Munroe, but she had found that shard of letter lying on her front porch. Ripped to shreds. This meant Jeanie had done it. And then, it had been a long night at the tavern, with Andy Southby and his knuckles and too many drunks for any sober person to have to listen to in a single night. Evie pulled on the big baggy T-shirt she liked to sleep in and turned back the sheets on her bed. She fluffed the pillow up against the headboard. If she couldn't concentrate long enough to read, or even watch television, she'd smoke the last of the joint. That's when she heard a knock on the door, soft at first and then louder, with sudden urgency.

Evie pulled on her jeans and hurried down the stairs. The small lamp that she left on all night in the front room cast its dull orange glow. Outside, on the porch, she could see the silhouette of what was undoubtedly a woman. She felt her heart beating, a wave of disappointment since she had hoped it was Larry Munroe. He had often caught up with her late, after she'd left the bar and headed home to unwind. A woman. A thought flashed through Evie's mind that it might not be safe to open the door. If Jeanie

Munroe was so angry she had ripped up the letter of apology, what else might she do?

This was when Evie Cooper realized she didn't care. Let it come. Such was fate. Taking a deep breath, she opened the door. Gail Ferguson was sitting on the porch swing, her head down, her arms lifeless on her lap, as if the heavy brown coat with all its long fringes was pulling her down, pulling her under where she would surely drown. Gail's little red car was sitting in the drive, the one she had left at Murphy's for the weekend.

"Gail?" Evie said. She stepped out onto the porch. "Sweetheart, what's wrong?" Gail lifted her head and looked up at Evie. The bruise around her left eye was so violent that already the eye was swelling shut. The skin on the cheekbone, that high and nicely defined area that Gail was so proud of, had been scraped red and was now turning a dark blue. Blood had dried in the corner of her mouth, just below a wide split in her bottom lip.

"I swear to God I didn't do anything wrong," Gail said, a tiny voice.

"The bastard," said Evie. "I'm calling the cops!"

"No!" Gail pleaded. "Evie, I beg you."

"Then I'm taking you to the hospital," said Evie. Again, Gail shook her head. She looked at Evie with that sad, little-girl look. Most days, it was the only look Gail Ferguson had.

"Please," she said. "I can't go to Margie's." Gail didn't have to say why. Evie knew. Margie was awash in her own grief over losing Annie, her little girl. How could a sister who cared about her, as Gail surely did, knock on her door in the heart of night, in this condition?

"Okay," said Evie. If nothing was broken, and that seemed to be the case, she could clean Gail up herself. But she wasn't going to let Marshall Thompson go free. She couldn't. Maybe Gail came from a long line of women who loved men like Marshall. But that was no longer a good enough excuse. Not these days. Besides, the line that wanted to stop men like him was much longer, and that's the line Evie Cooper stood in. She would find a way to deal with Marshall Thompson. She put her arms around Gail and helped her to stand. She grabbed the purse that was lying on the porch and threw the strap around her own shoulder. Then she led Gail into the house, past the singing lead crystals on the lamp shade and out to the kitchen.

"Did I wake you up?" Gail asked, her words thick and heavy, the swollen lips making speech difficult.

"Course not," said Evie. She reached for the brown jacket. Gail had been so proud of that coat. It was the first thing she'd bought for herself in ages, any extra money going for clothing for the kids, for babysitters and school lunches. The jacket was torn at the sleeve joint and its back was covered with ugly grass stains.

"Come to the sink and let me wash you up," Evie said. "I need to get some ice on those bruises." Gail started to cry, the inside crying, the kind that hurts too much to let outside. That's when Evie saw that Gail was holding something in her bruised right hand. She reached for the hand and pulled it up where she could see. It was a long, thick swatch of her own dark hair, a piece of scalp still binding it together. Evie uncurled the fingers and took the hair away. She tossed it into the trash. What was it

Gail had said earlier that evening, her face trying its best to be happy? "As long as it doesn't spoil this night. I got my heart set on cruising along the St. Lawrence, wind in my hair."

"Does Marshall know where you are?" Evie asked. Gail shook her head.

Evie washed the bruised face, using a face cloth and just a bit of soap. All this time she was trying to figure out how to handle the situation. Maybe when she tucked Gail into bed, maybe then she could call the cops, report the assault. Or they could do it first thing in the morning, once the poor girl got some sleep.

"You're gonna be okay, angel," Evie said. And that's when she looked just beyond Gail's shoulder, her eye having caught a slight movement. It was one of the faces of the dead, watching events from beyond that veil, peering into Evie's kitchen at Gail Ferguson's bloody and bruised face. Curious, maybe. But most likely wanting to comfort, as the dead always do. The dead feel sorry for the living, and that's what Evie Cooper had learned most over the years of her spiritual work. The dead wish they could stop our pain. Evie said nothing. She would put Gail to bed, where she would at least be safe. The morning would bring answers. She shook three extra-strength Tylenol from a bottle and laid them in Gail's hand, helped her bring the pills up to her mouth. Evie then poured a glass of water and held it to Gail's lips until she'd drunk enough to wash the pills down.

"I'm putting you in my bed, sweetie," Evie said, and Gail merely nodded. Evie decided then that she'd drive Gail's car into her garage, where she never parked her own. That way, if Marshall came trolling on the big Harley, he wouldn't see it. "I'll be down here on the sofa, all night long, keeping an eye on you." The adrenaline rush had gone out of Gail now. She was ready to fall deep into the safety of sleep.

Evie looked again at the form standing just behind Gail's shoulder, the sweet and loving face, the eyes so full of caring. Sometimes, all the dead want is for the living to know that someone is watching, someone is taking note, someone is nearby, so that the living will never have to hurt alone. And maybe that's why the child had come to pay a visit. But by the time Evie helped Gail to her feet and turned to grab her purse from off the kitchen counter, little Annie Jenkins had already gone.

11

*B*am! *Bam!*

"Larry, open the door, son."

Larry looked at the clock. Seven a.m. The exact time he had predicted the melee would come. It was Saturday, and the old man would have a half day to put in at the post office. He would arrive for work at seven thirty. Since it took him less than fifteen minutes to drive there, Larry assumed they would eat their breakfast first, and then allow fifteen minutes for the confrontation. Sometimes, it almost wasn't fair to know people so well you could predict them that easily. But then, it was this same talent that enabled his mother to rise from her bed the night before and take the house key from beneath the pot of geraniums.

"The door is open," Larry said, and then there they were again, the two of them, standing in his room. They peered at him with eyes that held nothing but disappointment. Larry lifted the mailbag from off the bottom bunk and handed it to his father. It now held all the bills and junk mail he had thrown into the clothes basket, the pile he intended to destroy.

"I delivered the important letters," he said. "I was going to throw these out since all they do is cause people pain. You know, credit card bills for all that useless junk they can't afford, foreclosures, threats from the IRS. But I couldn't do it. So here they are. Gil can glue the envelopes again and then lie about how it happened. Remember how we covered up the time those kids stole his mailbag and ripped open letters while he was getting a coffee and doughnut?"

Larry stopped talking, but all that time he had watched as his father pushed a hand into the precious leather mailbag and riffled a finger among the open letters, lovingly, as if they were children of his that had been abused for too long. Then he watched his mother, watching his father.

"Larry," his father said. "You are *not* post office material." He closed the flap on the mailbag and shouldered the thing expertly, as if it were an extension of his own arm. "You're fired, son. I hope you know I have no choice."

"He has no choice," his mother said. Together, they looked like a plastic couple, the sort you might find standing with white frosting up to their knees, like snow, on the top of an anniversary cake. They had been married far too long to look like the little plastic bride and groom that had stood on the wedding cake Larry had shared with Katherine Grigsby on their own wedding day. If Larry were in charge of manufacturing those plastic ornaments, he would make some changes. The bride would be holding a prenup agreement. The groom would have the name of a good divorce lawyer tucked into the pocket of his plastic tux. Larry realized then that he respected his parents for how they had kept their lives together. It couldn't have been easy, and yet here they were, a responsible pair who raised their family reasonably well, a couple who'd been dragged down the marital highway a few miles. Parents who knew what it was like to have a son predecease them. At least, that was the word obituaries liked to use. Lawrence and Frances Munroe were the last of their kind. No one Larry knew took marriage that seriously. Not anymore.

"You *should* fire me," said Larry. "It's okay, Dad." He breathed out the painful breath he'd been holding. He was just about to resign his job until this revelation came at him. Now, he felt a sure, quick relief. This would make the old man feel better, his mother too. It would be a way of punishing him, and he surely did need a good punishment. If the old man hadn't been the postmaster, Larry could have gone to jail. If he remembered correctly, mail tampering carried a $250,000 fine and a five-year jail sentence. But jail would be another safe square room where he could hide, so long as he wasn't gangbanged and buggered around the clock by the other white-collar inmates.

"We're very disappointed in you, son," said Frances. She seemed even more tired than the day before. Planning the memorial service was draining what energy she had left.

"I know you are, Mom," said Larry. "I know you are, and I don't blame you. To tell you the truth, I'm disappointed too."

"Once the memorial service for your brother is over," said his father, "we'll need to sit down and talk, son."

"We'll talk," said Frances.

"Let's do that," said Larry. "Let's sit down and talk."

Larry was wondering if he should be the one to say, "Well, good to see you then," and close the door. Or if he should wait for one of them to do it. It seemed the big confrontation was already over, with ten minutes left to spare. He supposed that in the early days of their marriage, like most young couples, they might have put those extra minutes to good use. Ten minutes was enough time for a quickie before the mailbag disappeared out the front door.

"Make no mistake about this," said Frances. She followed her husband over to the door and turned to look back at Larry, the knob already in her hand. "You will be at Henry's memorial service." And then she closed the bedroom door.

Larry heard them whispering to each other as they went down the stairs, like swallows trapped in the eaves of a house. A few minutes later, he heard his father's small Toyota back out of the drive and whine down the street, toward the post office, and the tethered pens, and the stack of magazines that recorded the long and prestigious history of stamps and letters.

• • •

Jeanie had just looked in on Chad, making sure he was still there, safe in his bed. They had made a major step toward healing. She would let him sleep awhile longer and then she'd make him the same breakfast she had thrown into the garbage the day before. In her bedroom, she was just pulling on her jeans and a shirt when the phone on her nightstand rang. She was certain it must be

Frances. The memorial service was that next afternoon, a Sunday, which the weatherman had predicted would be sunny and mild, almost like the day Henry died. It would be Frances, talking about who was bringing what casserole and whether Jeanie might speak to Larry, make sure he attended. She hesitated picking up the phone, her hand on the receiver. "Come on," she told herself. "It's just a telephone." It wasn't Frances. It was Lisa.

"Mom, what's up?" In all the years of her growing up, Lisa never used any words but those three. It was never *Hello, Mom.* It was always *Mom, what's up?* And it hadn't changed, even now that she was a grown woman and about to be a mother herself.

"Who is this?" Jeanie asked, and smiled to hear her daughter giggling on the other end of the line. This was the baby that had been the reason she and Henry had married in the first place. And that had made it all worthwhile. And it was Lisa who had come home from a party in tears one night, just two years earlier. She had knocked on Jeanie's bedroom door and then sat on the edge of her bed. Henry wasn't home, and so Lisa had spread out next to her mother in bed, the tears now unstoppable. *What's the matter, baby, what's wrong?* And Lisa had told her. David Carlson was drunk at the party and he'd blurted out that his mother was having an affair with Henry, her father. Was it true? So what did Jeanie do? Did she say *yes, baby, it's true and Wendy Carlson is far from the only one. The last one was Dorinda Freeman, who lives at 910 Hunter's Lane and is always getting packages she has to sign for.* No, she held her daughter in her arms and whispered into her hair that sometimes people say cruel things because they're jealous, or confused, or they need attention. Lisa must promise, promise that very moment, that she would put it out of her mind and never think of it again. Never. And as far as Jeanie knew, Lisa had done that.

Jeanie, on the other hand, had confronted Henry. It wasn't the first time she'd done so, but she assured him it would be the last time, especially since it was now affecting the children. *You do it again, Henry, and I'm filing for divorce*, Jeanie had said. It's what Mona had been urging her to do all along. *Don't let him get away with that crap, Jeanie.* And it seemed as though Henry even heard her that time, as if maybe their marriage was worth saving after all. Henry certainly acted like a different man, coming home to supper on time, taking Jeanie out to a movie now and then. For almost a year. And then she found the receipt to the Days Inn. Room 9. Evie Cooper. No one ever knew, not even Mona, but she had looked in the phone book for a divorce lawyer and kept his number handy. It was a matter of time, of stockpiling evidence, before *Munroe vs. Munroe* became a reality. At least, Jeanie wanted to believe that she would've had the courage to leave Henry. How to tell now?

"Mom, I'm so huge," Lisa said. "I swear I'm about to burst."

"I was huge, too, when I was carrying you," said Jeanie. "I guess it runs in the family." She *had* been huge. And it was at the time when her friends, and Henry's friends, had realized that maybe Jeanie wasn't going to be fun to hang out with anymore. Henry could still be one of the guys as long as he was out fishing, or playing football in someone's yard, or working on his bike. But if he was at home, it meant responsibility. It meant his young wife was about to have a baby and he wasn't ready for it. But hell, neither was Jeanie, and yet she'd gone ahead and handled it. Looking back, Henry had never been a good husband. Not even from the beginning. Not even then.

"Mom, I've got a surprise for you," Lisa said. Jeanie felt a quick beat of her heart.

"Don't tell me the baby came early," she said.

"Nope," said Lisa. "But I'm coming. The doctor says it's okay to travel. Patrick has to work today, but we're getting up early in the morning. We'll be there in plenty of time for Daddy's memorial service."

Jeanie's first thought was to go up and wake Chad. *Lisa's coming home!*

"Your old room will be ready," said Jeanie. And then, "Lisa?"

"What, Mom?"

"I love you, kiddo."

Jeanie put the phone back down on its cradle and stood there by the bed, looking at it. It was the same phone she had picked up the morning Henry died, a year earlier, the one she held to her ear to say the awful words. *My husband's had a heart attack.* It was the same phone that some stranger had used to comfort her long distance, a woman she would never meet. *They'll be there soon, Mrs. Munroe. Stay on the phone with me. Try to be calm now.* A full year, come one more night.

Jeanie lay down on the bed, stretched out full, the way she was that morning twelve months earlier when she had put her head on Henry's chest and waited for the ambulance to come wailing up the street. *He doesn't have a heartbeat, but he's got a sense of humor that won't quit. His favorite food is spaghetti and meatballs. He stills listens to the Beatles, and he loves the Red Sox almost as much as he used to love me.* What had she whispered into his ear before they could rush into the house with their stretcher and carry him away? *Why did you do it, Henry?*

Jeanie said the words again, aloud, hoping that if Henry were hovering somewhere, if there were such a thing as the dead coming back to spy on the living, he might hear her. Maybe he'd send her an answer. Maybe their wedding photo still on her dresser would topple over, the glass shattering into a dozen pieces. Or maybe a bird might fly into the windowpane and drop to the ground outside, its neck broken. She knew these things were called omens, and so Jeanie lay there waiting for her omen from Henry to arrive. She heard wind shake the house. A spring rainstorm was on its way, a heavy one, according to that morning's weather report. It would be a day of thunder and lightning, storm clouds and gray skies. But Sunday would be that sunny and mild day that Frances had been praying for.

Jeanie's question to her husband that morning he died had not been about Evie Cooper. Or any of the other women. It was just the first part of a two-part question that Jeanie didn't finish since it was obvious Henry Munroe was dead. But if she had asked the full question, it would have gone like this: "Why did you do it, Henry? Why did you fall out of love with me?"

What bothered her most about Evie Cooper was the hold she seemed to have over Henry, even when she no longer wanted it. After Evie had ended the affair, Henry was still obsessed with her. Jeanie reached over to the nightstand and pulled open its top drawer. She found the letter and took it out. *Dear Evie, How much longer are you going to keep this up? If I come to the tavern you avoid me. If I wait by your car in the parking lot, you get Gail to drive you home. If I call, you hang up. Come on, girl. You know you can't stay away from me forever. I'll be here, arms open, when you change your mind. Love, Henry.*

Jeanie had found the letter in Henry's Jeep, hidden beneath the coils of the seat. It was lacking a stamp was all, or it would have been ready to mail. It was addressed to Evie Cooper, at 25 Avalon Court. It had the proper zip code, sitting like a small afterthought below the words *Bixley, Maine*. It was everything a letter needed in order to be official. Surely, Henry being a mailman, finding a stamp was not the problem. Maybe it was his pride that had kept him from sending it. Or maybe he planned to mail it on the very day he died. Jeanie's grief counseling class had suggested she write a letter to Henry, a way to tell him how she felt about losing him, a way to come to terms with the anger she was feeling. But Jeanie hadn't been able to do it. It seemed silly, considering Henry had been a mailman and Jeanie didn't know the zip code for heaven. Or whatever the place is where people who die end up going.

Jeanie heard the first pelts of strong rain hitting the bedroom window, and then Chad rising from his bed upstairs, his footfalls heading down the hallway to the bathroom. Lisa's feet used to tread that same hall. It seemed to Jeanie now that you could measure out a family's time together in footfalls, and gallons of water rushing through pipes, tubes of toothpaste, or the moments a refrigerator door opened and closed. The door on a house, too, opening and closing as the kids got older and graduated and then disappeared into the world. Those tiny signs that most people ignore as they live out their days together—maybe they were *omens*—were nothing but markers. They were ways of keeping time, if you had a mind to do so. But Jeanie knew most people didn't.

Thunder boomed now in the distance. In no time, there would be lightning. Jeanie smiled. If this were an omen from Henry, he meant it as a joke, for he was terrified of thunderstorms. How many years had it been since she loved Henry back? Quite a few years. It's a shame when love turns on itself, destroys itself at the roots. But that's what had happened. Jeanie now wondered if she could save Lisa and Patrick from this same fate. Was there advice she might give them so that they could sidestep the omens? But she knew that was impossible. Besides, Jeanie McPherson herself had done nothing wrong but fall in love with Henry Munroe. If she had fallen out of love with him over the years, it was because so many other women he met were standing in her way.

Now that she couldn't vent the anger she felt at Henry, maybe it was time to let him go. Besides, in a few days, she would be a grandmother.

• • •

Evie put a glass of orange juice, two buttered slices of toast, and the bottle of Tylenol onto her painted wooden tray and then carried it upstairs. She figured a light breakfast was better on the stomach, considering the stressful circumstances. Gail was already awake and sitting up in bed. She was staring at the pictures that hung in walnut frames on the bedroom walls. Evie put the tray down on the end of the bed.

"How'd you sleep?" she asked, and Gail shrugged her shoulders.

"How I always sleep," she said. "As if the wolf is not just at my door, but in bed beside me."

"I hope he's good in bed," Evie said, and smiled. Now Gail had to smile, too. Funny how mornings could change a lot of bad things, give them a new spin. For folks like Margie Jenkins, mornings probably didn't change anything at all. But for other people, just a bit of time passing means the wound is starting to heal. Evie had read once that the last stage of healing for an actual wound is called *remodeling*, when the initial scar tissue reconstructs itself. She always thought that sounded like what people do with their lives, too.

Thunder clapped ominously and the rain came fast, striking the tin roof of the house with metallic fists. Evie went over and shut the window. Then she locked it.

"Who are they?" Gail asked. She was staring again at the portraits. They were the proper and dignified kind of photographs, taken in those days when people sat once or twice for a photographer. It was their own statement to the world, proof that they'd once existed, that they had been there on the planet for a time. People did this for the day when they would be gone, so that someone who cared might remember them. But now, with cameras hanging out all over houses, with digital images being rushed through cyberspace, people were getting sick of looking at each other's faces.

"That woman was my mother," said Evie, nodding at the portrait. Helen Cooper was wearing a black tulle cocktail dress. She looked quite regal, and Evie liked to think that her mother *was* regal, once, back in those days when she and her husband went dancing. Back when there was reason to wear a cocktail dress. And what's more, Helen was smiling such a lovely smile. It was a better version of her than the real one Evie had known, the woman who hid from the light, who dissolved in a dark room of grief and sorrow until she disappeared altogether.

"She was very pretty," said Gail. "You look just like her." Evie was told this often, that she looked like her mother, the woman in the lovely black dress, a classic string of white pearls around her neck, posing for some photographer whose name was still printed on the back of the picture. *The Richard Penwick Studio, Philadelphia, PA.* In truth, Evie's mother now looked more like a younger sister. She had died in 1968, the year she turned forty-two and Evie turned sixteen. This was the same year her mother brought Rosemary Ann's portrait down from the attic, dusted it off with a wet cloth, and presented it to Evie as a special gift. Evie was now eight years older than her mother would ever be.

"And that's my father," said Evie, now pointing at the sweet-faced man in the proper, dark gray suit, his hands folded on his lap, the sadness of his life still to happen. "And that's my sister, who died before I was born." Rosemary Ann had the same bow-shaped mouth, the eyebrows that curved like thin rainbows over the dark eyes, the little gold cross hanging down the front of her dress. The dress was pink with a white lace collar. Her two hands, hidden away in white gloves with pink velvet buttons, were clasped together and resting on her lap. "These pictures were all taken the same day, not long before my sister died. A photographer came to the house for a formal sitting."

Gail got out of bed and went over to the portrait of Rosemary Ann. She put a finger up and touched the bow-shaped mouth.

"Can there be anything worse than losing your child?" she asked. Evie knew that Gail was thinking of her sister, Margie, and of her little niece, Annie. "Life sucks," Gail said.

"Yes it does," said Evie. "But it's still the only game in town."

When Gail went back to the bed, Evie noticed that she was limping. She sat down on the edge and reached for her jeans. She pulled them on slowly, as if each movement of her arms and legs caused pain.

"Take a couple Tylenol," said Evie, and Gail did as she was told, washing them down with the juice. She sat in silence, knowing Evie was waiting.

"The weather report said rain, so we had to cancel Quebec City," said Gail. "When we got back to Marshall's place, he found a letter from Paula in his mailbox. He was mad as hell, so I should have let things be. All I did is ask him if it was true, you know, if he beat her like she said."

"I guess he answered your question," said Evie.

"I guess," said Gail. She flopped backward on the bed and began to cry.

"Stop that," said Evie. "For one thing, your two kids aren't hanging in a portrait, never getting any older than six years. And they aren't lying in the Bixley Cemetery, the way Annie is. So sit up and stop whining. For a second thing, you brought every bit of this on yourself. A lot of people warned you."

Gail reached for a Kleenex and blew her nose. Outside the rain was coming down so hard it sounded like nails hitting upon the roof of the house.

"Fuck you, Evie," Gail said.

"Fuck you right back," said Evie. "Now, as far as Ronnie and the kids are concerned, you're away for the weekend. As far as your sister is concerned, same thing. So you can stay here as long as you want."

"If I file charges, he'll probably kill me," Gail said softly.

"Now you know how Paula must feel," said Evie. "So get up and get yourself downstairs. We've got company coming."

"Who?" asked Gail.

"Billy Randall," said Evie. "You know. The Vietnam vet who comes in the bar now and then."

"Crazy Billy?" asked Gail, her eyes growing large with surprise.

"Oh, I don't think he's crazy at all," said Evie. "On the contrary, if Billy Randall ran for president, I'd vote for him."

Outside, above the wind and rain, Evie heard a car pull into her drive. A door slammed. She peered down to see a woman running for the front steps, a plastic shopping bag held above her head to fight off the rain.

"And Paula Thompson is here now."

. . .

Larry was having lunch—pickles, a can of pink salmon, two slices of wheat bread—when he sensed his mother standing outside his door. He stopped chewing the crunchy pickle so he could hear. There was a soft sound, like a grunt, as if she were bending. Larry saw a letter shoot in under his door. He had just watched Santo Jimenez come up the walk a few minutes earlier, carrying his mailbag beneath the sleek raincoat issued to postal carriers. And then he had seen Santo leave again, leaning into the sheets of rain as he made his way to the next mailbox. Larry pushed the can of salmon back on his desk and waited. He must be careful, for there were traps everywhere, he was certain. Was the letter tied to some invisible string, thin and ghostly as a cobweb? If he reached down and picked it up, would she jerk it back under the door, taking him with it, pulling him right through the narrow crack? He had no intentions of going to Henry's memorial service the next day. Larry heard the top step squeak.

He picked up the letter and carried it over to his desk. It was addressed to him, all right. Since he was now living with his parents, it had *c/o Lawrence and Frances Munroe* written beneath his name. It was a sad statement for a grown man's life, but if you're living with your mom and dad, it's a true statement. Santos Jimenez, who was new at the post office, had obviously dropped the letter into the black box at the front door. It had a bluebird painted on its front and hung next to the wooden shingle that said MUNROES. The address in the sender's corner was his former place of employment, Bixley High School. Two weeks earlier, Larry had heard from Maurice Finney that his old position teaching history was open again. Maurice had stopped by the post office and the two had gone out for a social lunch, at the diner where Paula Thompson waited on them. Apparently, or so Maurice revealed between bites of his cheeseburger, Larry's replacement had been a young single woman from Portland who had already grown tired of small-school politics, as well as small-town social life. She had asked for the noose around her neck to be cut, and, according to Maurice, it had been cut with great relish. "She was high maintenance," said Maurice. "The school board members despised her. But they liked you, Larry. I know they hated to see you go. They had no choice, you know, considering the fistfight and all." While Larry sat in the diner's booth, pondering this new event, wondering if he even dared act upon it, Maurice had gone on, between bites of his lemon pie, to reveal that he was hanging on to his own job by the skin of his teeth, considering that the progressive school board didn't applaud his aging hippie look, the longish hair, the corduroy jackets with elbow patches, the matching corduroy slacks. "They're on my ass every chance they get," said Maurice. "But you, Larry, you're the kind of guy that place needs. I think you should come in and talk to Bob. See what he thinks." Bob was Robert Wilcox, the principal and a damn good guy. He had graduated two years ahead of Larry and they had played a lot of football in high school. So Larry had stopped by later that same day and talked to Bob. He had left his résumé. He had even left more copies of his old letter of apology. Let the chips fall where they may. In truth, even with a nice guy like Bob Wilcox on his side, Larry didn't expect much to come of it.

The stamp was a commemorative of Harry Houdini, one that had been issued earlier that year. Larry smiled. It wasn't the kind of stamp to go on a business letter, but he knew Kay Fornsby well. She was secretary to the principal at Bixley High. This would be Kay's idea of a little joke, her own way of telling Larry hello. Kay collected stamps, one of those obsessed people who turn up at the post office on the day of issue, buying up blocks of a new stamp in order to store it in sheets of plastic. For her to use a Houdini commemorative was her way of saying she missed Larry's face in the office. Or maybe she was alluding to his disappearing act. Larry turned the letter over and grabbed a butter knife from the glass jar on his desk. With a quick thrust, he sliced the top of the envelope open in a clean, invisible cut. He had read in one of the magazines that his father kept lovingly stacked in the back room at the post office that the first letter with a date on it was mailed in 1661. This was in England, and the stamp was actually called a *Bishop mark*, after Henry Bishop, the Postmaster General. The idea behind it, according to Bishop, was so that "no letter Carryer may dare to detayne a letter from post to post." What would Henry Bishop think of Larry Munroe, who had not only *detayned* the letters, but had even *redd* them?

Dear Lawrence Munroe IV,

On behalf of the school board of Bixley High, I am pleased to inform you that your application for your former position as history teacher for grades eleven and twelve has been accepted. This reinstatement is accompanied by a period of probation, which will be twelve months and terminate at the end of that time if there have been no unsatisfactory complaints or infractions.

At the bottom of the letter, in bright blue ink, Bob Wilcox had written, *Welcome back, Kotter!*

Below this, Kay Fornsby had written, *And no tricks this time around, Houdini!*

Larry didn't know what to say. He folded the letter carefully and put it back inside the envelope. He now wished that one of those many schools had accepted Andy Southby. He felt a certain measure of sorrow that he had taken such pleasure in the young man's rejections. Surely the Diesel Mechanic School of Nashville would become a better place for allowing the boy to walk among their torn-down engines and carburetors? Rejection hurts, no matter how old you are. From downstairs came the sound of the back door closing. He knew his mother had taken her coffee cup and gone out to the screened-in porch. Saturdays were the days she did the most weeding in her garden, sometimes spending two hours out there, going up and down the rows, talking to herself in hushed tones. But now that the rain was keeping her from it, she would most likely do a crossword puzzle on the porch as she sipped her coffee and watched the storm pass.

Larry sneaked down the stairs and over to the narrow table in the living room where sat a square, old-fashioned phone. Considering it was a Saturday, why would Katherine care if he called out of the blue, for no other reason than to share some good news with his son? She answered on the third ring, sounding sleepy, as if maybe she was still in bed, still curled up close to Ricky Santino, her smooth, white legs entangled in his hairy ones, as if they were two crabs.

"Hello, Katherine," he said. The last thing Larry wanted was to upset her. "Is it possible I might talk to Jonathan? I've had some good news and, well, could I talk to him?" He waited, listened to her even breathing at the other end of the line, knew she was deciding, like she was some kind of fucking god, some divine judge, whether to toss her son's father a bone.

"Okay," she said. He was surprised that she said it almost kindly. Usually, he could feel her hatred coming at him over the miles from Portland, a molten lava, as if he were responsible for all her misfortunes. As if he, Larry Munroe, were an albatross whose only job in life was to fly after Katherine Grigsby's skinny white neck. "Let me see if he's up."

And then she was gone. A couple minutes later, Jonathan was on the phone.

"Dad?" he said. "Is that you, Dad?"

Larry couldn't answer. Katherine could do what she wished and say what she wished, but she could never take that excitement from the boy's voice, the love he felt toward his father. And that's where Larry had excelled, damn it. He'd been a great father. And he'd done nothing wrong that he had to lose Jonathan Munroe from his life. He'd done *nothing* wrong. And now, months later, what he wanted to tell his kid but couldn't was that he would not just be teaching school, he would also get a weekend job. He would save every penny and every dime. He would find a young, hungry lawyer who wouldn't cost him both arms and legs. He would fight for custody of his son. He would do it. And that was the first time Larry Munroe realized *why* he had been holed up in his old bedroom, reading other people's mail, waiting for God knows what to happen. It was because he had broken down after seven months. He had looked up at the top left bedroom window of the house on Pilcher Street. He had looked at the square of glass that used to encircle his son's life. He had looked at the spot by the front steps where Jonathan used to leave his bike. He had looked at the tree in the backyard where he and his son had hung a tire swing. Larry had looked, finally, for a boy who was not there, a boy who had disappeared one day in Ricky Santino's green Jeep. He had looked for his child, and now he wanted him back.

"Dad? You there?"

Now, finally, Larry was slowly rising toward the truth he had known all along but felt powerless to act against. *He* hadn't caused the divorce. He had a *right* to have his son live with him. Just because he was a man didn't mean he couldn't be a great single parent. He knew other men who were doing it, and their kids were not only surviving, but prospering. Larry wanted Jonathan enough to fight for him until he won, or until the day the boy turned eighteen. Yes, that's what it was all about. He finally understood.

"I have some good news, Jon," Larry said. And then he told him. He was to become a teacher of history once more. His eyes blurred with tears. He could almost smell Jonathan's sweet breath as he had gushed those words into the phone. He remembered that breath when it felt warm against his neck.

"Wow, Dad! That's great! When I come for Thanksgiving, we'll celebrate!"

He would fight for this boy until the day he died.

· · ·

Jeanie spent the rest of the day cleaning house. It was one way to keep busy, not to mention the fact that the house really needed cleaning. She began in Lisa's old room, the guest room now, and in no time had polished and vacuumed and straightened until the room looked as welcoming as it had all those years Lisa was still its main occupant. She would buy some flowers at that little shop that just opened next door to Fillmore's Drug, and she would put them on Lisa's nightstand in a ceramic vase. Mums, maybe, since Lisa was about to become one. The thought made Jeanie smile. Funny, but she had dreaded the idea of Henry's memorial service ever since the morning Frances had come by with a chocolate cake and announced her plans. And now, thanks to the service, her daughter would sleep again in her old room, the last time she would do so before the baby came. From that time on, Lisa's life would be different. But for now, she was still Jeanie's daughter, still sounding girlish and even a bit immature. She'd married too young. Jeanie would have preferred Lisa turn thirty before settling down. But Jeanie's own mother couldn't get *her* to wait until she was twenty.

Chad came into his bedroom just as Jeanie finished making the bed. She had done the downstairs already, saving Chad's bedroom until last since it would require the most work. He stopped and looked around the room. Gone were the piles of dirty jeans lying on a chair in the corner. All the magazines had been neatly stacked. All the empty pop cans had been picked up. And so had the candy bar wrappers that seemed to be everywhere, as if Chad shot them about the room after he had scrunched them up in his fist.

"Hey," said Chad. "What's going on?"

Jeanie finished turning down the spread and now the bed was freshly made and ready. The room looked like it used to in those days when Jeanie cleaned it every weekend.

"I know this is your private room," she said. "But I had to clean it. And besides, I got some good news." She was hoping that last part would buffer the first part. She watched as Chad took the orange woolen bonnet off his head and tossed it onto the chair. He flopped down on his bed and put his arms behind his head. Jeanie knew him well enough to know he was feeling threatened again. His body language spoke loud and clear. She wished now she had waited for him to come home, had asked about cleaning the room first. The part of her that wasn't his mother felt a rush of irritation. He should be thanking her for cleaning up after him, the way she never had to do for Lisa. She waited, but Chad said nothing. He closed his eyes. Outside, rain beat heavy against the windows. Wind shook the trees.

"Lisa's coming home for the memorial service," Jeanie said, and the excitement in her voice was so unique after a year of not being there that she noticed it immediately.

Surely, Chad would notice too. He'd be happy that his mother was feeling a jolt of energy again, a taste of life.

"Great," said Chad. Then, "I'm staying at Milos Baxter's house tonight. So don't worry if I don't come home."

Milos Baxter. This was the kid Jeanie had seen give Chad the beer, that day in the parking lot of the 7-Eleven.

"I'd rather you didn't," Jeanie said. "It's such a stormy night." She had picked up the furniture polish and the roll of paper towels from the floor.

"I'd rather I did," said Chad. He rolled over on his side and closed his eyes.

• • •

Rain chased Evie all the way from her car to the front door of Murphy's. It was good to see Billy Randall's truck sitting in the parking lot. Good old Billy. But she hadn't noticed Marshall Thompson's Harley anywhere. Considering the storm, he must have left it under cover somewhere and hitched a ride, for he was sitting at the end of the bar, right at the spot where Gail liked to take her breaks. Billy was at the pinball machine, his usual silence enveloping him, except for the noise of the game. Evie shook rain from her umbrella, folded it, and stood it in the corner. She clocked in and began picking up the bottles. She could feel Marshall's eyes on her as she worked her way down the bar to where he sat. Glancing up, as if just seeing him for the first time, Evie looked surprised.

"What are *you* doing here?" she asked.

Marshall stared at her face, her eyes, trying to read any

signs of whether she was lying. He tipped a bottle of beer up to his lips and drank until it was empty. He put it on the bar for Evie to take.

"Change of plans," he said, that low and deep way of speaking, as if everything was a threat to him.

"So why the hell am I working for Gail if she's not in Quebec City?" Evie wanted to know, hands on her hips, eyes narrow and tense. Seeing this, Marshall seemed to relax.

"Give me another beer," he said. "Bud."

"Where's Gail?" Evie asked. Marshall shrugged.

"That crazy bitch ain't my problem," he said.

Billy had come to the bar for a beer, or so it seemed. But Evie knew he was just checking out the situation. Billy often did that for her and Gail if it seemed a customer was giving them a hard time. But this time it was Marshall Thompson. This time was different.

"You done at the pinball machine?" Marshall asked Billy, who merely nodded. Crazy Billy. The Vietnam vet. The silent one.

As Marshall put his money into the pinball machine, Evie went into the back office and dialed her own number at the house. She let it ring twice and then hung up. She waited to the count of twenty-five and redialed. Gail answered, having recognized the code they'd set earlier.

"He's still in town," Evie whispered. "He's here in the bar. So don't you dare leave the house. And call Paula. Tell her it's still on for tomorrow."

When Evie came back out, Andy Southby had taken his stool in front of the poker machine, and Chad Munroe was standing at the bar next to the cash register. He was wearing the same orange wool bonnet.

"Hey there," said Evie. "Don't you know it's not a nice thing for wool to get wet?" Chad smiled.

"Quarters, please," he said. He gave Evie three dollars and then pocketed the twelve quarters. "And a Megabucks ticket." He pushed another dollar across the bar.

Evie was ahead of him, punching out the numbers even before he said them. *Nine. Eight. One. Twenty-seven. Four. Forty-two.* Henry's same old lucky numbers. Maybe someday someone would win a free ticket with those lucky numbers.

It was almost ten o'clock when Chad finished his pinball games. He came back to the bar and pulled out the stool next to Andy. Marshall Thompson had met up with a buddy of his and had gone off to the pool hall to shoot a few games. Knowing this, Billy Randall had gone home. Evie had thought ahead, to every possibility of what Marshall might do, even instructing Gail to keep the blinds tightly shut and the front door locked. The only lights Evie wanted on at her house were the porch light and the little parlor light, the ones Evie always kept lit when she was working. "You can watch TV, but don't put any upstairs lights on," Evie had warned.

"Hey," said Andy, giving Chad a careful eye.

"Hey," Chad said. He twirled his stool a couple times, complete spins, his whole body going around with it. Evie had watched Henry do that every time his team scored a basket or a home run.

"What's up, Chad?" she said. "You want something?"

"Yeah," said Chad. "You know them sandwiches Uncle Larry likes? The kind with the mushrooms and onions?"

Evie nodded.

"Well, I want two of them," said Chad. "To go. But don't put any onions on mine."

• • •

Larry felt strangely light ever since he had received the letter giving him his job back, as if he were drifting outside his own body. He even considered going down to find his parents and tell them the news. He knew it would mean a lot to them. That's when he decided the best time to do it would be after the memorial service, when his mother's heart would be breaking, feeling she'd lost both sons, one to death and one to life. He would tell her then. "Mom, I got my old job back. I'm going to be teaching history again. So don't worry about me. And I'm going to take Katherine to court over Jonathan. I'm going to get my son back." He would save the good news.

The rain had stopped, so Larry lifted his window again. He decided to turn in early, maybe read a comic book or two. That afternoon, he'd rummaged through the boxes he had stored in the closet when he moved back in, the few things he'd managed to salvage from his marriage on Pilcher Street. He was looking for a photo taken at the lake over a year earlier, the day he and Henry and their sons had gone fishing. That's when he had found the box of old comics, the ones he had read and loved in childhood. He had stored those he knew would be valuable one day in protective covers and there they all were. He'd pulled the box out into the room, the best coming-home present Jonathan could imagine. These guys were all back in style now, thanks to Hollywood. Spider-Man. Wolverine. The X-Men. Hulk. Iron Man. He would give the comics to his boy, a father to his son, passing on a tradition that was far more fun than delivering the mail. But first, Larry had decided to read them again, one by one. In case Jonathan asked questions of him, he would be ready. Traditions must be treated with respect.

He propped himself up with two pillows beneath his head and opened a copy of *Spider-Man*, who had always been Larry's favorite. Spider-Man was like everyone else. He got sick with the flu. He had problems with family, friends, and coworkers. He forgot important appointments and agonized over decisions to the point that the reader wanted to slap him. In the end, a kid could finish a Spider-Man comic and feel almost superior to the hero. A kid could feel great, knowing that Spider-Man was a bit of a fuckup too. Spider-Man was all too human.

Splat against the side of the house. Larry looked up from his comic, waiting, wondering if it had been a misguided June bug, or a moth, or a big drop of rain falling from the downspout. There it was again, a twig or a small rock, hitting the house. He got up from his bunk, the comic book still in his hand, and went to the window. He peered down into the wet night. Chad was standing below, staring up, the orange bonnet on his head and a plastic sack in his arms.

"Hey, Uncle Fuckup," Chad said. "How's it hanging?" Larry smiled.

"You idiot," he said. "What do you want?"

"I want you to throw down your hair, Rapunzel."

Larry knew the boy had been drinking. He had that tipsy flow to his words, and then the words themselves gave him away. He'd never used that kind of language in front of his uncle before.

"If I threw this hair down," said Larry, and pointed to his head, "you wouldn't get up to the first window."

"Where's the key?" said Chad. "All I could find was geraniums."

"Mom took it," said Larry. How do you explain something like this to your teenaged nephew? "Go to the front door and knock. Mom and Dad are still up, watching TV."

"No fucking way," said Chad. "You crazy?" He staggered back a couple feet, the strain of staring upward for so long finally making him dizzy. Larry understood. Of course, he couldn't go knock on the door.

"How many beers have you had?" he asked.

"Two," said Chad.

"That's what everyone tells the cops," said Larry. "Come on, how many?"

"Three," said Chad.

"No lie?"

"No lie."

"Hang on a minute," said Larry. "I'll be right back." He saw Chad give him a thumbs-up from down below.

Larry quietly opened his bedroom door and stood listening for a time to the canned laughter coming from the television set. Then he padded down the hallway in his socks, stopping in front of his mother's linen closet. He found the sheets on a top shelf and pulled three from the stack. They were snow white and folded perfectly. Telling himself he would launder them on Monday, when he knew she'd be doing her grocery shopping, Larry took them back to his room and closed the door. In no time he had twisted the sheets and tied them together to make a perfect rope. He fastened one end to the heavy leg of his desk and threw the other down to Chad.

"You fall and break a leg, Spider-Man, and you're on your own," whispered Larry.

Chad tied the plastic bag around one of the belt hooks on his jeans until it was secure. Then he grabbed the rope and began slowly to climb, one foot ahead of the other, until he crested the windowsill. Larry reached out and helped him inside.

"Man," said Chad. "That would have been easy a year ago." He untied the plastic bag and put it on Larry's desk.

"Wait another fifteen years and then we'll talk," said Larry. "What you got here?" He rummaged in the plastic bag.

"Sandwiches and beer," said Chad. "Thought you might be hungry."

Larry knew they were Murphy sandwiches just by the way they were wrapped, the beige paper taped up like a baby's diaper. He'd seen enough of them disappear out the door as takeout. Those were the nights he sat on his bar stool and watched a game or watched Evie Cooper.

"Man, I've missed these," said Larry. He unwrapped the one that had *Onions* scrawled in blue ink across its paper. He bit into it as Chad popped two beers.

"What would your mother say if she knew I let you drink beer?" Larry asked. Chad shrugged.

"I can drink it in the park with the other guys, or I can drink it here with you. Take your pick. Tomorrow's the old man's service and I figured you'd need company."

This wasn't the night to make a stand, and Larry knew it. And besides, climbing up the side of a house with beer and sandwiches was so like something Henry would do that he was enjoying this visit. It was good to see the boy, to know he was all right on this very important night.

"Hey, wow," said Chad. "Where'd you find this?" He had noticed the framed photograph of the four of them, Chad and Henry, Jonathan and Larry, standing with their fishing poles in their hands and smiling at the camera. Bixley Lake glistened in the background like a blue dream. Mr. Wilkie, who sold bait, was the one who had taken the photo, holding Jonathan's camera up to his eye as if it were some kind of Hubble Telescope and fretting over which button to push. Chad picked up the photograph and stared at it.

"It was in one of my boxes," said Larry. He took a drink of the beer and another bite of sandwich. Liver and onions had been his and Henry's favorite since they were boys. Chad put the photo back on the dresser and turned away. Larry wished now it had stayed in the dark box. But why pretend that Henry and the good old days weren't gone forever? They were gone, at least as they were *back then*. The problem now was to figure out how to create some *new* good old days.

"You going to the memorial service?" Chad asked. He had walked over to the bunks, the can of beer in his hand.

"Nope," said Larry. "I prefer to remember my brother in my own way, quiet and private."

"Me too," said Chad. "This past couple weeks, just waiting for it to come and go, the anniversary, it's like one of them hurricane parties. Know what I mean? It's like waiting out the storm." He tipped back the can and drank. Then, "Which bunk was my old man's?"

Larry pointed to the top bunk and Chad, balancing the beer can in one hand, climbed the little ladder and stretched out on the bed. He stared up at the ceiling, the beer resting now on his chest.

"I graduate from high school in two years," said Chad, "and I have no idea what I'm going to do after that." He turned on his side, a hand beneath his head to prop it up, and peered down at Larry.

Larry had heard this speech before. He was the one who had college in his sights, but Henry had moped and lamented all through high school that he had no plans for the future. So the future came and got him. The future turned him into a mailman and a husband and father. And he was fine with it. Larry, on the other hand, had planned for ages, thought it all out, revised the plan, and then revised it yet again. He had worked it out perfectly and yet the future had kicked his ass.

"When your dad's class voted on a theme for graduation," said Larry, smiling at the memory of it, "Henry suggested *A Hair of the Dog*." Chad smiled instantly. "It was voted on by the whole class, and Henry's motto won. But the teachers and principal didn't think it was so funny, so they chose Felicia Baker's instead. *We Stand on the Threshold* or something corny like that."

"I know that story," Chad said. "We had a keg party last week at Milos Baxter's and I told the guys we should choose *Two Hairs of the Dog* as our class motto. It broke everyone up."

Larry looked at his nephew's face. Like his father, Chad had been born lucky, born with Henry's dark good looks, with the same long, lanky legs. He was Henry in high school, Henry all over again, except that the boy was more serious, having lived in his father's shadow for all of his life, until the last year. But Larry had seen it happening in his nephew, those nights Chad had stopped by Murphy's Tavern to say hello. The boy was slowly becoming the center of attention, almost addicted to the pull of power that comes with such a vocation. But the serious side of Chad seemed to take a step back, as if it recognized early that being the center of attention was a full-time job. He seemed to sense that if he accepted it, he would have to work hard in the years to come. Otherwise, like those kings Larry talked about in his European history class, Chad could be easily dethroned.

Larry took another bite of the sandwich, but this time his teeth hit something that wasn't liver or onions. He lifted the top of the bread and peered down. It was a small piece of cardboard, just big enough to get attention. In blue ink were the quickly scrawled words: I MISS YOU. He glanced quickly up at Chad, but the boy was looking now at the old football picture of the Fabulous Munroe Brothers, their strong arms around each other, their futures still waiting to burst wide open.

"You guys were something, weren't you?" Chad said. He lay back again and stared up at the place on the ceiling where his father had carved "HM" into the wood with his jackknife. Chad touched the letters with his fingers.

"I don't like the sound of that past tense," said Larry. He eased the piece of cardboard out of the sandwich and let it drop into the trash can. He took another bite.

"Can I sleep here tonight?" Chad asked. "Mom already thinks I'm spending the night with Milos."

Larry looked up at his nephew, as old as Jonathan would be in five more years, boys who quit fishing with their dads far sooner than maybe nature had planned it.

"Sure you can," said Larry. Then, "Hey, you wanna try the trout at Bixley Lake next week? We only got a few more weeks until school starts."

• • •

It was already past eleven p.m. when Jeanie turned the Buick right on Market Avenue. Beside her on the front seat was the little overnight bag she had packed in a hurry. Nightgown. Toothbrush. Facial cleansers. Hairbrush. Magazine. Nothing of importance. Just enough stuff to get her through the night. With Chad gone on this eve of the memorial service, she found herself incapable of sleeping alone in the house. There was too much memory in the air of that morning a year earlier. Jeanie thought of calling Mona to come sleep in Lisa's old room. But Mona had her own problems now. She considered sleeping on the sofa, or in Chad's bed, rather than in the marriage bed she and Henry had slept in for so many years. But she couldn't. The quiet of the house itself was talking to her, nudging her, putting her on edge. She knew that after the service she would be all right. She would find a way to cope, especially with Lisa's baby soon to arrive. By the next night, the one-year marker would have come and gone, and with it proof that the universe doesn't keep track of anniversaries the way human beings do. The universe would spin on as if nothing unique was happening at all. And nothing was, except to the handful of people who had known and loved Henry Munroe.

The reception clerk at the Days Inn looked up at Jeanie with sleepy, late-night eyes. The drone of a distant TV came from a room behind the desk, what looked like a small apartment. A cleaning woman, obviously on some late-night shift, was vacuuming in a hallway leading to the first-floor rooms.

"You got any vacancies?" Jeanie asked. The clerk punched out a few computer keys.

"First or second floor?"

"Actually," said Jeanie, "is there any chance that number nine is vacant?"

The clerk stared with tired eyes at the computer screen before Jeanie was given a form to fill out and sign, and keys to the room. Now she was on her way down the narrow hallway toward Henry Munroe's favorite room. *Nine.* The same number Ted Williams had on his uniform before the Red Sox put the number out to pasture. And now, Ted Williams was back in the news, too, dead for just a week himself and already in a cryonic warehouse in Arizona, his son hoping to keep the baseball great suspended in time until he could be brought back. Henry would now have his hero with him on the other side, wherever that might be.

• • •

Evie sat on her front porch swing and smoked the joint slowly, letting loose the tension of the past week. She had checked in on Gail, who was sound asleep, just her sad face peering from beneath the fluffy bedspread. Soon, Evie would know one way or another if Larry Munroe was able to rise above the past, to take a new run at the future. Otherwise, she had decided it was time to move on. Since she was without family, maybe the best thing for her to do was to create roots for herself. Maybe she would move back to Temple City, Pennsylvania, to the place where she had been born, the place she had lived until her parents died. It was the same place where Rosemary Ann had died, too, and where Evie had first discovered she could see the faces of the dead. She would take the big portraits in their heavy walnut frames and she would put them up on a wall in some house in Temple City. If it wasn't roots as some people know it, at least it would be as close as she could get. She would build her own foundation. She would create a kind of museum for the people she had known and loved and now missed dearly.

Across town the church bells struck the hour by ringing twelve times. This was Evie's favorite time of night. The town had wound down, like the mechanism of some great clock. Now it was almost motionless. Quiet. That's when the night creatures took up the job, the crickets and bats and owls, the things that wait for the humans to give the night up to them. In the spray of light that fell from her porch and out onto the lawn, Evie could see the sign she'd driven into the earth there, just a year and a half earlier, hoping maybe like the pioneers of old she'd stake a claim. *Evie Cooper, Spiritual Portraitist.* She'd leave Bixley if the memorial service came and went and still no sign of Larry. She'd move on, like those pioneers did when they were looking for water, or trying to escape locusts, or hoping for more fertile soil to plant their crops. Evie would find a tiny piece of land to call her own and she would settle down to plant roses, to trim roses, to water roses, and then to die with a sense of roots beneath her. But wasn't this the very dream that had brought her to Bixley, Maine? She took another long drag off the joint and drew it far down into her lungs. She needed to give the shit up. As she let the smoke spool back out in a gray stream, she kept her eyes on the sign in her yard, on that silhouette of a woman, standing beneath that silhouette of a star.

• • •

A few hours before dawn, the rain returned for one last barrage so that the mild Sunday predicted by local weathermen could follow. A loud crack of thunder woke Larry instantly. He lay on his bottom bunk, his eyes adjusting to the room and its items, especially the glowing numbers on the clock. *Three thirty.* Rain came at the window now in long and angry threads. Lightning broke ragged against the sky. In the dim light Larry could see an arm dangling down from the top bunk. Before his mind was fully awake, in those first confusing seconds, he was certain it belonged to Henry. How many times had he seen that arm during the years they spent together in that room?

On those nights of thunder and lightning, he knew his little brother was afraid. Larry would often reach out and touch the hand, just a quick brush to let the younger boy know he wasn't alone, enough touch that a boy wouldn't have to be embarrassed the next morning about being afraid of a silly rainstorm. Then Larry remembered that it was not Henry sleeping above him, but his son. He knew this, and yet he couldn't help himself. With thunder now rumbling in the distance, moving on to the next town, Larry reached up and touched the hand at the wrist, felt the warmth of it. He heard Chad mutter in his sleep.

"It's just a storm, Henry," Larry whispered. "It's just a storm."

• • •

The last thunder that the storm could muster woke Jeanie as it passed over the Days Inn, on its way out of Bixley. She sat up in the middle of that strange bed, in the middle of that symbolic night, in room 9, and reached a hand out into the darkness, certain that Henry Munroe was standing there by her bed. She could almost smell his cologne and the sweat of his body after a long day.

"Henry?" she whispered. Then she felt silly. She snapped on the bedside light and looked about the room. Nothing. She went into the narrow bathroom and turned on the tap. She scooped cold water into her hands and patted it about her flushed face and neck. In the mirror she could see the room behind her, the shower curtain, and the bath towel folded and hanging from its rod. Was

Henry hiding in the shower? Would he jump out of the tub and go *boo*? He did that sometimes, hiding in the kitchen or his workshop, when he was horsing around with the kids. Had Henry come back to check out room 9? Was there really such a thing as the departed coming back for another peek at the living? Jeanie doubted it, as much as she wanted to believe. It would be nice to think her mother and father were keeping tabs on her, as they had done all through high school. They had begged her not to date Henry Munroe, much less marry him. But once she and Henry had gone all the way, Jeanie felt it was the right thing to do. Henry had laughed when she insisted on wearing a scarf over her hair, disguising herself so that she could slip past Mr. Tyson's reception desk. It was that adrenaline-filled night of the big football game. The Munroe brothers had reigned supreme. Henry had rented a motel room so that he and the captain of the cheerleaders could finally make love. Now and then, over the years, Jeanie wished Mr. Tyson had spotted her sneaking into the motel and called her father. Maybe they could have stopped her from being so much in love with that wild Munroe boy.

There was nothing but the empty shower behind her. As was typical in their last years of marriage, Henry must have made other plans. Jeanie got into bed and snapped out the light. The room fell back into darkness. But what if Henry *had* come? She couldn't help asking herself the question that had been on her mind all evening. Would he have been disappointed to find *her* there, and not Evie Cooper, or Wendy Carlson, or Annette Page, or Marla Benson? Would he be heartbroken to learn that it was just his plain old wife, Jeanie McPherson Munroe, waiting for him between the cool white sheets, as she had that night of the big game? And that's when a weight had rolled away from Jeanie's heart, a stone lifting itself from the rest of her lifetime, there in the darkness of that god-awful room at the Days Inn. She felt it go, just as she had felt Henry's soul float up and into eternity the morning he died. Jeanie knew then that she was free.

12

When Jeanie pulled into her drive, Frances was already there, standing by the side of her car. Jeanie quickly pushed the overnight bag onto the floor by the front seat. The last thing she wanted that morning was to explain to Henry's mother why she had spent the night in Henry's favorite motel room. Jeanie grabbed her purse and summer jacket and got out of the Buick.

"Look who's up early," said Frances. "I figured you'd still be in your jammies, the coffee just making."

"I couldn't sleep," said Jeanie. She looked up at the blue sky and took a deep breath. Sunshine was everywhere. A soft breeze rippled through the elm tree on the lawn. "What a great day for the memorial." It was hard to explain what was happening inside her at that moment, but Jeanie sensed a new beginning just ahead. She had even rolled down the windows of the car as she drove over from the Days Inn, letting the air stir up the old particles of dust. She'd take the car in next week and have one of those professional places clean it from top to bottom, get rid of the cigarette stench, wash out the cobwebs, vacuum up the human hairs, clean out all the old memories. And she knew, too, that this was what she must do to her own life. She was just wondering if she should insist on Grandma or Gran. Grannie was out. Too old. Too *Beverly Hillbillies*. Nana was nice. Nana sounded young and vibrant. She liked Nana.

"What brings you over so early?" Jeanie asked. She put her arms around Frances and gave her a sincere hug. Frances hugged back, and this time she didn't cry.

"I just wanted to be sure that you're okay," said Frances. "That you can get through this day. If you can't, well, I want you to know I understand. This memorial service wasn't your idea. It was mine." These were the times when Jeanie felt a true love for her mother-in-law. These were the times when she forgave Frances Munroe for spoiling the devil out of Henry.

"I'm fine with this day," said Jeanie. "We're all gonna be fine, Mom. Come on, I'll make us some coffee."

Jeanie put her arm around France's shoulder, urging her toward the house.

"I don't want to intrude," said Frances. "I just had this strange feeling."

Jeanie knew what the feeling was. Several times when Frances had come to visit, bringing those countless casseroles and desserts, she would often find some excuse to leave the kitchen. Maybe she was just going out to the patio to see how Jeanie's plants were faring. Or maybe she was on a quick trip to the bathroom. Or maybe she was just looking for that book on gardening that Jeanie kept on a shelf in the living room. Whatever excuse it was, Jeanie knew that Frances went into the room where

Henry had died and just stood there, immobile, as if there were one of those cold spots you read about in ghost stories, a portal out that Henry had taken. Maybe Frances felt she could be closer to her son in the place he'd last been alive. Jeanie knew, and now she no longer minded.

"Let's go in," Jeanie said. "I made a cake yesterday. It's that same recipe you gave me back when Henry and I first got married."

"Chocolate Devil's cake," said Frances. And this time she smiled. But Jeanie saw the tears there, a wet glistening. She tried to imagine losing Chad or Lisa. Do spouses and lovers learn, after so much pain, to let go more easily than mothers and fathers?

"Guess who's coming to the service," Jeanie said then. "Lisa and Patrick. The doctor says she can make the trip. They'll get here just in time for four o'clock."

Jeanie would put some coffee on and ask Frances if she'd mind going to the bedroom to fetch Jeanie's reading glasses, on the table by the bed. Jeanie knew they were there since she'd forgotten to take them to the motel the night before. And that would give Frances her time alone, her chance to say good-bye, maybe for the last time, to the son she loved so well. Saying good-bye for the final time in one's life was important. Jeanie knew.

· · ·

Larry opened his eyes to sunshine and the sound of the patio door opening and closing downstairs. His mother or his father, one or both. He threw the blanket back and got out of bed. Chad was sound asleep on his bunk, mouth open, little snores popping softly, as if he were blowing invisible bubbles. Larry used to put stuff in Henry's open mouth to get him to wake up, sometimes a browned apple core, or maybe pizza crusts from the night before. And once, even the tip of one of Henry's dirty socks. Most times, Henry would just spit out whatever it was and keep on snoring.

Larry could smell the fresh coffee before he even got to the kitchen. He poured himself a cup, found milk in the fridge, and the sugar bowl in the cupboard, where his mother had kept it for as long as he could remember. It felt strange to be just standing there in the middle of the room, calmly, no longer sneaking in for supplies. Before, coming to the kitchen was like walking out into an open field where a sniper might see him. But he was past all that now. He had his breakdown moment and he was over it. He even felt ashamed, considering the stress it had put on his parents at such an emotional time, a year after losing Henry. They would never get their son back. But Larry still had Jonathan.

Larry took a drink of his coffee before he opened the back door. His father was sitting alone on the patio, a cup on the table in front of him. He was staring straight ahead at the maples in the backyard. They had been planted years earlier as a privacy border along the fence. Birds were now busy at the hanging feeders tied to branches of the two largest trees. Butterflies and bumblebees hovered about the many planted flowers and above the neat rows of the vegetable garden. It had been one of the family stories the Munroe boys had grown up hearing, how their mother agreed to marry the senior Lawrence Munroe provided the couple always had trees, flowers, and vegetables growing in the backyard of any house they might live in. Lawrence had not broken that promise to his wife, and now he sat staring into the backyard, that wedding gift to his bride.

"Dad?" Larry let the screen door close behind him. Lawrence looked up, surprise on his face, as if he'd been told once, years ago, to never be caught daydreaming. He looked at Larry with weary eyes. He had aged in just the past year, more whitish-gray hairs, even more lines around his mouth. He had aged from losing Henry, but so had they all.

"Son?" Lawrence said, as if to ask *how* and *why*. Then, as if it didn't really matter what decision had brought Larry back to the land of the living, "This will make your mother happy."

"Dad, I have a lot of things to apologize for," said Larry. "So many things, I don't know where to start."

His father looked away from the backyard maples, the pansies and hollyhocks, the green onion stalks and the trellis of sweet peas. He reached for his cup of coffee and motioned for Larry to sit. Larry pulled out a chair and sat across the table. They weren't known for father-son talks. He waited.

"I never had a good relationship with my father," Lawrence said. Larry felt his stomach cramp. He didn't want this, didn't need an apology of any kind. He was the one who should apologize.

"Dad, I got my old job back," Larry said. "I'm waiting until after the service to tell Mom. This is all my fault, not yours." But his father held up a hand.

"Let me speak, son, please," he said.

Larry looked out at the brick walkway that led over to his mother's cucumber beds. Maybe he could count the bricks to help ease the anxiety he was now feeling. There were positive points for never leaving one's room. How had he forgotten that so quickly?

"I never had a father I could talk to, and neither did you boys. Henry, well, he lived his life the way he wanted, not the way he should. And that hurt Jeanie. It hurt a lot of folks. I heard the gossip down at the post office. I knew. I never told your mother, of course. Why hurt more people? But you, you're more like me than Henry ever was, and yet we hardly know each other."

"Henry was Henry," said Larry. And he knew that the reason Henry could be king was because his servants wanted him to be. They demanded it, especially his mother, in those formative years that are supposed to be so important in shaping character. This meant that everyone around Henry Munroe, his *satellites* as Jeanie now saw them, they were all what the talk shows call codependents. They had built the man themselves.

"I never wanted to be a mailman," his father said then, and this took Larry by surprise. He looked down at his hands as if he held something important in them. He couldn't look at his father. Even the air around the table was becoming static with this revelation. "But I had that tradition stuck on me, like a tail on a dog. My father and grandfather pretty much built the post office. Christ, I can still smell them down there, as if they're standing in the corners, watching every move I make. But sometimes, the only thing a man can do is to take tradition and wag it around. You pretend it's not really a dog's tail. Instead, it's a flag or a banner, and you're proud to carry it."

"You're a good mailman, one of the best," said Larry, forcing himself to look up at his father's face.

"I do what I can," said the older man. "And you should too. So lead the life you want to lead, son. And remember that no matter what she does, your mother wants the best for you, just as she did for Henry."

Wind rattled the chimes hanging from the post with the hummingbird feeder. From off in the trees, sparrows and warblers sang with that after-the-storm excitement. The grass smelled fresh, still wet at its roots, the whole day alive with sound and color. After a couple minutes of silence, Larry realized that this was all his father had intended to say. It was all, and it was enough. He knew what the older man meant. He knew the book that lay behind those few words. It was another reason that Larry wanted to be a good father to Jonathan.

"I'm sorry about the mail," Larry said. But his father had returned to the man his son had always known him to be.

"All that rain last night," he said. "It's good for your mother's garden."

• • •

When Evie opened her eyes, she heard Gail out in the kitchen, the rattle of cups, water running in the sink. She wished she could sleep forever. But regardless of what Larry Munroe might and might not do after the memorial service, Evie had a busy day planned. She sat up on the sofa and arched her back. Two nights away from her bed and already her body was complaining. Gail came into the parlor carrying the painted wooden tray. On it were two mugs of coffee, two bagels, and the butter dish.

"Wow," said Evie. "How long has it been since someone brought me breakfast in bed?"

Gail put the tray on the coffee table and handed Evie one of the mugs.

"It's not breakfast in bed," she said. "It's breakfast on the sofa. And that's another reason why I'm going home today, once this is over. You deserve your bed back."

Evie felt the instant caffeine rush from that first coffee of the day. She watched as Gail buttered them each a bagel.

"Are you positive you're done with Marshall?"

"I had a couple days to think," Gail said. She sat on the sofa next to Evie and reached for the other coffee mug. "While I was lying up there in bed feeling sorry for myself, I thought of Margie and how she's living without Annie, just as you said. And I looked at the little girl on your wall, your sister. You're right, Evie. I need to go to plan B, because plan A ain't working."

Evie held up her mug so that Gail could click hers against it. And in that second Evie knew what she was going to do in her own life. She was going to stick to plan A. There would be no more running, no more searching for roots. This is where she wanted to be, to live and die, this sweet house with the calming porch swing, with the roses in her backyard, this town of Bixley, where people saw her at the bank and said hello. Where cars sometimes tooted in recognition as she sped to the grocery store or out to the mall. Where some of the customers at the bar now seemed like caring friends. Gail was one of them. Regardless of what Larry Munroe did, Evie Cooper was already home.

"I have something to tell you," said Evie. "Murphy asked me last week if I wanted to buy the tavern."

Gail looked surprised at first, and then she smiled.

"I don't know which is more amazing," she said. "That Dan Murphy actually showed up at his own place of business, or that you're gonna be my boss."

"Well, for one thing," said Evie, "Murph didn't stop by. He called me on his cell phone from the golf course. And for another thing, what makes you think you'll be working for me?"

Gail studied Evie's face, as if not sure if this were a joke.

"We'll go over to the bank on Monday and talk to Elmer Fisk," said Evie. "The way I see it, I can't imagine a better business partner than you."

• • •

By the time people were done filing into the massive back room at the restaurant, Jeanie counted over seventy faces. Frances had done well in tracking down people who wanted to say a final farewell to Henry Munroe. The plan for the memorial service had changed again, and Jeanie felt nothing but relief to learn of it. Frances decided it was better for everyone to stay at the restaurant and not visit the grave. A string of cars inching out to the cemetery, bumper to bumper, would be too much like a funeral and not a celebration of Henry's life. The family could put the marker from the postal service on Henry's grave at some later and more private time.

Jeanie looked past the tables loaded with cheeses and crackers, salads and casseroles, cupcakes and cookies, and there stood Chad. He was tall and handsome in the suit she had bought for him just two weeks before. The one he had worn for his father's funeral no longer fit. He'd grown taller in the past year, his chest expanding, his arms stronger. But looks were deceiving for he was still a teenager. Maybe this was the mistake Frances had made with Henry, maybe she had let the boy strive to become the man too quickly. It was a mistake Jeanie would not make with her own son. She had already begun making calls, asking questions, inquiring about groups who counsel teenagers with drinking problems. Maybe Chad needed some of that grief counseling that Jeanie had already outgrown. And Jeanie herself would make some new plans. Even if the job at Fillmore's Drugstore did become available, it was only part-time. And it was part of her old life. Maybe it was time to take those real estate classes that Mona was enrolled in. It was time to find a new vocation, other than that of Henry Munroe's widow.

"Mom?" It was Lisa. Jeanie took her daughter into her arms and held her so tightly she could feel the enormous belly against her body. Lisa's face was alive with the rush that comes from pending motherhood, a freshness in her eyes, her skin radiant. She had her long brown hair pinned up in a neat sweep off her neck. She was wearing a lavender maternity dress, tiny white flowers around the neck. She looked beautiful, and Jeanie told her so, kissing her face several times.

"You angel," said Jeanie. "I didn't want to pressure you, but I'm so glad you're here."

"I knew you wanted me to come," said Lisa. "Just because I don't live with you anymore, Mom, doesn't mean I can't pick up your little hints. Patrick's parking the car."

Jeanie pushed some of Lisa's brown hair, hair with blond highlights like Jeanie herself used to have, back from the side of her face. Patrick came into the restaurant then. Jeanie watched the expression on Lisa's face when she saw her husband. She knew that look. She had felt it herself once, for Lisa's father.

"There's Chad!" said Lisa. "And Uncle Larry!" And Lisa was gone again.

Jeanie saw her brother-in-law across the room. Larry had on the same gray suit he had worn for their little dinner on Thursday night, and now, with his shoulders back straight, he looked like the teacher he was. Why had they all dreaded this gathering for weeks? It was coming together nicely. It was now more like a birthday party than a commemoration to someone dead and gone from them. The memorial service was joining them again, reminding them that they needed each other more than ever. Maybe Frances was wiser than they had realized, maybe the matriarch in her knew some tricks. As if on cue, Frances appeared out of the crowd, wearing her dark green skirt and jacket, a white silk blouse. Jeanie had expected her mother-in-law to be teary-eyed and mournful. But Frances was smiling. She pulled Jeanie aside to whisper in her ear.

"I invited Katherine," said Frances, "and she's here."

"What?" Jeanie asked, astonished. "Does Larry know this?"

Frances shook her head.

"He knows I asked her to bring Jonathan," she said, "but he doesn't know she actually did. They just arrived. She's leaving right after the service. She's in the ladies' room now." Jeanie knew her face must have shown the amazement she felt.

"I think you should tell Larry," she said. Frances nodded across the room.

"Someone already is," she said.

Jeanie looked over to see Jonathan, very proper in a blue suit, standing just behind Larry, waiting to be noticed. His dark hair had grown longer since she saw him last. The boy himself seemed to have grown taller in the past few months. Chad had been like that, too, sprouting up past the other boys his age. Larry was talking to Leeann Boyle, the real estate agent who had sold the house on Pilcher Street when he and Katherine divorced. Leeann noticed Jonathan first, and smiled. That's when Larry turned to see who was standing next to him. There is something in how a parent looks at a child that gives proof of why it is we live, and love, and die. It's those single moments of elation that make up for the hours and days of madness. Jeanie watched as Larry pulled Jonathan into his arms, holding him close, in that way his own father had never been able to do.

• • •

By the time Marshall Thompson roared into the parking lot at Murphy's Tavern, the only car he would see parked outside would be Gail's little red Chevy. Inside the bar, they heard the noise of the big bike, and then silence as the engine died. Evie motioned to Gail, who went to the back door and stood there, waiting to unlock it. Sundays, the tavern was always closed. Evie looked over at Billy Randall and Paula Thompson. They had already left their stools at the bar and were disappearing into the back office. She glanced over at Gail, who had now unlocked the door but not yet slid back the bolt. Evie held up one finger. *Give me a second,* the finger said. And then she joined Billy and Paula in Murphy's office.

Evie put a finger to her lips, but by the look on Paula's face, it was obvious she didn't have to tell Marshall's ex-wife to be quiet. The fear Paula still felt was in her eyes, in the fidgety way she twirled a lock of her hair, in the fading bruises still marking her slender arms. Evie glanced over at Billy Randall. Tall and intense, gray among the thick, dark hair, he stood motionless, his ears tuned to the noises in the front room, his eyes narrowed as he listened. Evie wondered if this was how Billy had stood in Vietnam, under the wet and dripping leaves of the jungle, waiting for the enemy, watching, hearing everything that walked or crawled. Billy had won the Medal of Honor before he left that country for good. He had brought his entire platoon out of an ambush alive. Sometimes, seeing him play pinball at the tavern, Evie wondered why his wife had left him as she did. He had come home a hero, to an empty house. Billy was a good man, and anyone who met him knew it. That he was silent much of the time, so deep in thought he might be thousands of miles away, well, why not? It had gone all around the bar how

Billy caught up with the man who beat his sister Amy so horribly she was in the hospital for two weeks. This was Pete Fuller, who ran with Marshall's crowd. No one ever knew what Billy did or said, but his sister wasn't afraid to live anymore. It was Pete Fuller, her ex-boyfriend, who started the nickname *Crazy Billy*.

"Hey, girl, how you doin'? I'm glad you called."

It was Marshall's voice. Evie heard the back door close and the sound of the bolt as Gail locked it. She saw a slight tremor in the muscle near Billy's mouth, but the look in his eyes didn't change. He didn't even blink. Evie wondered what it was like to be in war, to have bombs falling, to have the enemy trying to kill you at every turn in the road. And yet there was such a gentleness in Billy Randall. He was only eighteen when a helicopter dropped him off on that hilltop in a foreign country, a machine gun in his hands and pure fear in his heart. Billy never talked about it, but his sister did when she stopped by the bar for a glass of beer.

"Want something to drink?" Gail now asked. Evie heard the bar stool scraping back, its legs against the wooden floor. Marshall would be just sitting down on his favorite stool. She heard the sound of a cap being twisted from the top of a beer bottle.

"Come on, what's wrong? I just wanna kiss you." Marshall's voice. Sometimes, Evie wanted to look back into the childhood of anyone who was fucked up. She wanted to find reasons and clues and answers. But just now, looking at the terror on Paula's face, reasons didn't matter. Would Peter Fuller finally have killed Amy if matters had been left alone? Maybe. And *maybe* means the odds are far too high. She saw Billy straighten, his head cocked back, one ear pointed to the front room. Paula was trembling. Evie reached over and put a hand on her shoulder, hoping to calm her.

"We're not alone," Gail said. "Got someone in the back, fixing the air conditioner." That was the cue. In three seconds, Billy Randall had left the back room and gone out to the bar.

When Evie stepped out of the office, Marshall's face was already shocked enough, seeing Billy appear. He sat motionless as Billy went down the bar toward his stool.

"Hey, Marshall," Billy said.

"Hey," said Marshall, still trying to assess what was happening.

"You carrying anything?"

"None of your business," said Marshall. Billy grabbed Marshall from off his stool, flipped him onto his stomach on the floor, and pinned him there. It had happened so fast, no one had seen it coming, especially Marshall.

"That wasn't polite," said Billy, pressing the man beneath him even harder into the wooden floor. "Evie, come see if he's got anything on him."

Evie knelt and patted Marshall's pocket, then ran her hands down his legs. It was apparent he had nothing under the tight T-shirt he was wearing. Evie stood up.

"Nothing," she said. Paula had come out of the back room and now she stood, frightened, watching from behind the bar. Billy pushed Marshall down deeper into the floor. Evie heard him grunt as he struggled to get free. Billy twisted the arm back more and Marshall finally lay still.

"Now you listen to me," Billy said. "I'm obligated by law to let you know I have a black belt in karate. That way, you see, I can't be sued for not disclosing that fact. But you personally won't have to worry about legal stuff like that. If I'm sued, it'll be by one of your surviving family members, if you got anyone left who gives a shit about you."

"Let me up!" Marshall shouted. He squirmed again, trying to wrest free, but Billy applied more pressure by pulling Marshall's arm up higher onto his back. Marshall cried out in pain. Again, he quit struggling.

"According to legend, karate began more than a thousand years ago," Billy said, as calmly as giving a lesson, "when a Buddhist priest named Bodhidharma arrived in Shàolín Sì, a forest temple in China. He taught Zen Buddhism in that temple and exercises to strengthen the mind as well as the body."

"You fucker!" said Marshall.

"Karate is an interesting art," Billy said. "It even includes a kind of aerodynamics. For instance, by the time you find your balls, you'll have already found your dick, since balls fly farther than dicks, given that they're round."

Billy pulled Marshall up off the floor and pushed him into a chair near one of the front tables. That's when Marshall saw his ex-wife, Paula, standing at the bar. He looked from her face, back to Gail's, over to Evie's, and he understood. He'd walked into an ambush. And Billy Randall knew all about ambushes.

"You might call this an intervention," said Billy. "The way I hear it, Paula here has tried a lot of times to get you to go on about your life and leave hers alone.

Instead, you been beating the crap out of her every chance you get."

Paula started to cry. Marshall looked as if he might bolt from the chair at any second. Billy walked around behind him and put a hand on his shoulder, forceful enough that Marshall seemed to change his mind.

"You're a pretty big fucker, ain't you?" Billy asked. "How tall are you? Must be at least six feet. So why not pick on someone like me, instead of the women you happen to know? I'm standing here unarmed, except, you know, for those little tips I picked up from that old Buddhist priest."

Marshall sat motionless, his eyes on the floor in front of him. Billy looked over at Gail and Paula.

"Either one of you ladies care to have a turn with him?" Billy asked. "He won't fight back with me here, will you, Marshall?" Marshall said nothing. Both Gail and Paula shook their heads.

"See?" said Billy. "The violence is all one-sided."

"You'll notice he didn't ask *me*," said Evie. Billy smiled at this.

"You know how your pal Pete Fuller says I beat the crap out of him?" Billy said to Marshall. "Well, I didn't touch him. It was my little sister Amy who beat him. All I did was watch. Kind of like a referee."

"What the hell do you want from me?" Marshall said. Gone was the big, baritone voice that boomed out to the world to beware.

"I want you to stay away from these girls," said Billy. "Now, I don't think all women are perfect. I know there's some who will beat on a man until he lifts a hand to protect himself and the next thing he knows, he's in jail for assault and battery. But that's not the way it is in your case, is it, Marshall? See, what happened with my sister Amy is that she did just what Paula did. She followed the law and got herself a restraining order. And when your friend Pete Fuller beat the daylights out of her, that restraining order was lying on the kitchen table the whole time. Gail over there, she's scared to death to press charges for what you just did to her, afraid you might come looking for her one dark night as she leaves the bar. But you're not gonna do that, are you, Marshall?"

Marshall looked over at Gail, who stared back.

"You need to make a decision for yourself right now," said Billy. "I can beat the crap out of you before you crawl out of here, just like you did to these two women, if that'll make you feel better. Or you can leave here as if nothing ever happened. No one will know but the four people in this room. Ain't that right, ladies?" All three women nodded. "But if you should get all mad and liquored up some night and come looking for one of these girls, let me give you some valuable advice. I'm gonna teach each one of them karate. And I'm gonna take them out to the firing range, show them how to use a gun. What's more, they each have my phone number memorized. I want them to call *me* long before they dial 911, or the cops. See, you might have heard how I don't sleep much anymore. Well, that's true. I see Viet Cong in the strangest places. So, what's it gonna be?"

Marshall seemed to let out air, as if he were a large balloon. He was growing smaller, sitting there in the chair. Evie noticed that Paula seemed less afraid, as if now that she saw how much of a coward the man really was, it made her stronger.

"Get out of here," said Billy, "before I change my mind and spread you all around this bar."

Marshall stood. On his way past Paula, he stopped. She had a confidence about her now, it was true. Evie could only hope it would be there when Billy wasn't.

"I want my right to see the boy," said Marshall.

"I have no problem with that," said Paula. "So long as you follow the rules about visitations."

Gail unlocked the door and let him out. They all stood quietly in the bar, as they had just twenty minutes earlier, and listened as the engine of the big Harley roared to life. Pebbles spit as the bike lurched from the gravel parking lot and whined off down the street. In no time the sound had died away and Marshall was gone. Gail looked over at Billy Randall, who had reached for the untouched beer Marshall left sitting on the bar. He tilted the bottle and drank.

"You think it'll work?" asked Evie.

"It probably won't stop him from beating up the next woman in his life," said Billy, "but he's lost face in front of these two. You break a man's pride, you pretty much stripped him naked."

"Guns?" Evie said.

"Naw," said Billy. "Guns make me nervous. I just threw that in for effect."

"You really gonna teach us karate?" asked Gail. Billy finished off the beer and put the bottle back onto the bar. He looked over at Gail, surprised. And then he seemed to remember. He grinned.

"I never did find the time to learn karate," said Billy Randall.

. . .

Larry saw Katherine for the first time as he rose to read the speech he hadn't planned to give. Two hours earlier, he had come down the stairs wearing his gray suit, and when he saw his mother's face, he knew that he would do everything she asked him to on that day. And she had asked him to say a few words. "No one was closer to him than you were," Frances said, and that had been true. "So I'd like for you to speak after the minister. I want your words, Larry, to be the last we hear as we say good-bye to your brother." So Larry had told her early about getting his job back, about how he was going to fight for his son. And then, he'd spent a half hour sitting at his desk, waiting for his mother to dress in her green suit, and his father to put on the black trousers and jacket. And he had found something to read that would say what he felt in his own heart.

"I have been asked to say a few words," said Larry. She had grown thinner, Katherine had, but she was still in her perfect mode, every blond hair in place, her eyebrows drawn neatly above her eyes, her rigid skirt and suit jacket, all stylish and starched and frozen. She was sitting in the back row, as if ready to sprint when the last speech was read. Larry didn't blame her. She never liked his mother, or his father, or Jeanie. She had never liked Henry. Hell, if the truth were known, she had never even liked Larry. But she had brought the boy all the way from Portland, and for that he would be eternally grateful to her. When the service was over, he intended to tell her. *I'm going to fight you, Katherine. I don't want to but I have no choice.* He knew he would do it, too. Just looking at Jonathan's face was incentive enough. He was sitting in the front row, next to Chad, and with his grandparents to his right, sitting up straight, respectful of the moment since his father was speaking. Larry saw on the boy's face a kind of peace. He was right where he wanted to be, with his family. *My mom says I can go home for Thanksgiving.*

"This is something I first read in college," said Larry. "It's a poem, even though Henry wasn't keen on poetry." A sea of smiles came at him, people thinking of Henry and his macho ways. Jeanie smiled too, and that meant more to Larry than anything. "It was written a long time ago by the Roman poet Catullus. It's called '*Atque in perpetuum, Frater, ave atque vale.*' Since Henry knew more about the Red Sox than he knew Latin, I'll say it now in English, in case he's listening." Even Frances smiled now. There was a time, Larry knew too well, that just the mention of his brother's name could make her cry. And so, for a lot of months now, no one had spoken Henry's name in her presence. She'd come a long way. They all had in the year since they'd lost him. "It means 'for an eternity, Brother, hello and farewell.'"

The room was silent. He saw Frances take a tissue and dab at her eyes, saw his father put an arm around his wife, soothing her. Larry felt his own eyes grow moist, but he refused to cry. He wanted to do this for Henry, yes, but he also wanted to be strong for Chad and Jonathan. They both looked at him now, from their chairs in the front row, as if he held the only answers the family had left. He saw Jeanie reach for Chad's hand, and then Lisa's. How had they done it? How had they managed for a full year? Larry looked back down at the poem he held in his hand.

"From far away and over many a wave, I come my brother to your early grave, to bring you one last offering in death, and o'er your final rest, expend this idle breath, for Fate has turned your living mind to dust, and snatched you, cruelly, Brother, from us. Yet take this gift, brought as a brother bade, in sorrow, to your passing shade. A brother's tears has wet them o'er and o'er. And so, for an eternity, Brother, hello and farewell."

Larry folded the sheet of paper. He could never explain to anyone why he did it, but he looked at his mother's face, and then at his father's. He could never explain it, but he knew. We are always children to our parents. When we are gray-haired and worn from the years, we still need that pat on the back. We still want someone to look up to. Larry knew, and he would remember it when his own son was grown into an adult. He looked again at his mother's face, their eyes locking for the first time in a long time, because Henry's death had brought with it a kind of embarrassment. All deaths do. Larry didn't know why this was. Maybe it was the kind of stuff that Evie Cooper knew. Maybe death strips us all naked before each other. It separates the strong from the weak, lays bare the vindictiveness in some souls, the divine integrity in others. It's the great revealer, death is.

Larry put the poem back into his jacket pocket. Frances

rose from her chair, her husband letting go of her hand, helping her up. He had always loved her, beginning with the promise of flowers and trees and a garden in the backyard, and for this Larry felt a deep respect for his father. For all of his life, Lawrence had loved the woman he married. Frances came toward him, into the circle of his arms. Larry held her tightly. She felt like a girl, small and fragile.

"I love you, son," she whispered. Larry rocked with her now, noticing that people were looking down at the memorial cards they held in their hands. Or they picked pretend lint from sweaters or stared at their shoes. They were allowing a private moment to pass between mother and son. Sometimes, love is just as embarrassing as death.

"I love you too, Mama." He hadn't called her that since high school. Frances wiped her eyes with the tissue. She was from that generation of women who never forgot to put a few tissues in their purses, for weddings *and* funerals. She turned and looked back at the faces in the room.

"Folks," she said. "My husband and I would like to thank you for coming to our son Henry's memorial service." Larry reached down and took his mother's hand. He squeezed it and felt her squeeze back. "We thank you on behalf of Jeanie, and Chad, and Lisa Munroe. And our son, Larry. And our grandson, Jonathan. And now, shall we eat all that food that's waiting for us?"

The tension in the room broke to smiles. Larry knew that once the salads, and the casseroles, and the cakes were consumed, everyone could go back about their lives without Henry Munroe in them. They would mourn him forever. But they would live. And then Jeanie, his favorite sister, was standing in front of him.

"I'm proud of you," she said. Larry kissed her forehead.

"I'm proud of you, too."

Jeanie leaned in closer to him, close enough to his ear that her words were a whisper.

"This will be our secret," she said. She straightened Larry's tie. He knew exactly what she was saying. What had happened between Evie and Henry would go no farther than the few people who knew about it. It would be a way for Larry to start his life over with someone new. He hoped one day Jeanie would be able to do the same.

"Let's go eat," Jeanie said. "It looks better than spaghetti and meatballs."

"In a minute," said Larry. "But first, I need to meet and greet the former Mrs. Larry Munroe."

"Be gentle," Jeanie said, and then she was gone.

Katherine was standing with her back to the room of guests, looking at a poster that hung on the restaurant wall. She didn't turn when Larry first approached. She kept her eyes on the poster, a Norman Rockwell scene of old-fashioned people in old-fashioned clothing, full of old-fashioned values. Larry thought of Stella Dewberry. He would start a petition. He would help her save the little bungalow with the spreading rose brambles and the white elephantine columns. Katherine turned and looked at him.

"I want to thank you for bringing him," said Larry. "I know you didn't have to."

"I did it for him," said Katherine, "not for you." She had

always been brutally honest. And maybe, in some other dimension, that was a good thing. "We had a long talk, Jon and I, on the drive up. He's very unhappy in Portland. He and Ricky, well, they don't get along. Ricky never wanted children and so it's difficult for both of them."

Larry nodded politely, sensing that this was going to be his victory and so he needed to play it safe. Shouting at her just then, which was what he wanted to do, wouldn't help his cause. So what if the son of a bitch didn't want his kid? So what if the bastard had only wanted his wife? What he really wanted to shout at this woman he'd married was the truth. *You didn't want children either, Katherine Grigsby!*

"What are you saying?" Larry asked calmly.

"I'm saying that I'll take Jonathan back to Portland with me today. He'll need to get packed, say good-bye to his new friends. There's still time to get him enrolled for fall at his old school. I'm saying I want him for summer vacation, every other Christmas, every other birthday. Jeanie told me you got your job back. Maybe now you're ready to be a father."

Larry felt his heart beating so hard and fast in his chest he was sure she must have seen it. And it wouldn't be wise to let Katherine know he was feeling pure joy. How had it gotten so good so fast? How had life spun itself around for him in a matter of hours? No long months of lawyers and courtrooms and finances being sucked away forever?

"Thank you, Katherine," said Larry. "I'll do the best job I can. And I'll see that he calls you as often as you want. You can visit him any time you wish."

Katherine had that tight little smile on her face, the one that always made him feel like he'd lost the argument, even when he'd won. The smile that said she wanted to tear his heart out every time she looked at him.

"We have a long drive," she said. "Will you tell Jon I'm ready?"

As Larry turned to find the boy, to tell him the good news, to tell his mother and family the good news, Katherine put her hand on his arm. He looked back at her, hoping the joy in his face wasn't too obvious. She could take it all back in an instant if she wanted.

"I never loved you, Larry," she said. "And I want you to know that."

Larry said nothing for a few seconds. He realized he'd been nodding his head and so he stopped.

"I *did* love you, Katherine," he said.

And then he went to find Jonathan, to tell him that his father, his cousin, and his grandfather would delay their fishing trip in order to wait for him. There was enough room for four in that big canoe they rented from Mr. Wilkie, all well-meaning Munroe men, even if only one of them was a mailman.

• • •

It was just eight o'clock when Jeanie stood in the doorway of Lisa's old bedroom. There was something perfect about the sight of that small suitcase opened on the bed. Jeanie heard Lisa brushing her teeth in the narrow bathroom. When she came back into the room, she was wearing maternity pajamas with yellow teddy bears in the pattern.

No matter how many children Lisa might bear, how many grandbabies she would bring into Jeanie's life, she would always be a little girl to her mother.

"You're early to bed," said Jeanie. Lisa was pulling back her long hair now, slipping it into a ponytail.

"Patrick and Chad are watching some stupid show on TV," she said. "So why don't we play a game of Monopoly like we used to do nights when Daddy wasn't home?" She was already digging into the closet for the game, pushing past Clue, and Risk, and all the others she and Jeanie had played dozens of times over the years.

"I got an idea," said Jeanie. "Let me get in my pajamas too, and then I'll make us popcorn. No butter."

"And those chocolate kisses you keep in that jar on the kitchen counter," said Lisa. "What Dr. Simon doesn't know won't hurt him. Besides, the baby loves chocolate."

Down in her own bedroom, Jeanie stood for some time before she opened her dresser drawer and found clean cotton pajamas. Chad and Patrick were out in the den, shouting at the television screen. The Red Sox were most likely playing. On this night of all nights there was life again in the house. There was the sound of a suitcase being opened, of water running in the guest bathroom, of feet padding around in the upper rooms, of sweet and innocent laughter. There was the sound of popcorn popping, and a bat cracking against a ball, the way the house used to sound when Henry and Chad watched a game together. So it could be done. They could learn to live again.

Jeanie sat on the bed and pulled on her cotton pajamas. She found her slippers, their toes pointing out from under the bed. She looked over at the pillow where Henry used to put his head. "Henry?" Jeanie had asked his lifeless body a year ago to the day. "You okay?" And she realized now, twelve months later, that she had to ask herself that same question. *Jeanie, you okay?* The answer was yes. Lisa appeared in the door, both hands resting on her belly, as if she were already holding a baby.

"Chad and Patrick say they'll play Monopoly too, if we wait until the ball game is over."

"Good," said Jeanie. "I like beating Chad."

"He wants the race car and Patrick wants the cannon," said Lisa, "but I get the hat."

"Deal," said Jeanie, "so long as I don't get stuck with the iron or the thimble."

"I'll go get the popcorn," said Lisa. And she was gone.

Jeanie reached for her reading glasses on the bedside table. She would need them for the game. She turned out the bedside light and the room fell into darkness. She could hear the voices of her children floating in from the den, filled with energy, their lives still mostly ahead of them. She and Henry had created this family. Jeanie wasn't sure if there were such a thing as an afterlife. She knew only about *this* life, the life she and her kids still had left. And that was enough.

• • •

It was still early, just eight thirty, when Evie stepped out of the shower and toweled herself dry. But it had been a long and exhausting day. She pulled on a clean pair of jeans and her faded denim shirt. This was usually the time of day when she would reach for a soothing joint, something to make her mellow enough to take on the rest of the night. But now, looking at the joint in her hand, she decided against it. Instead, she tossed it into the commode and flushed, watched it whirl around like a small white fish until it disappeared. She was fifty years old. It was time to rethink her recreations. And then, nothing but time on her hands, she decided maybe a walk would be a good way to wear off some of the day's tension. That's when her doorbell rang. Almost no one used the bell and that was because it was so hard to find under all the wind chimes Evie had hanging near the door. Larry Munroe was always teasing her about that. *I'm the only one who can find your damn doorbell, Evie.*

Behind him, parked close to the curb, was Henry's black Jeep. Evie just stared at him. In the past two weeks she'd almost forgotten why she liked his face so much. It was a face that tried not to draw attention to itself, like Henry's face had always done. It was a quiet face that most people would never tire of seeing.

"Hello, stranger," Evie said.

"How've you been?" he asked.

"Same old, same old," she said.

Larry reached out and pushed some hair back from her face. She'd been looking for the elastic band she often wore, the one that held her hair back in a ponytail, when the doorbell rang.

"I like your hair down, did I ever tell you that?"

"I don't think so," said Evie, "but I'll keep it in mind. You wanna come in?"

"Not tonight," said Larry. "I thought I'd spend this

night with Mom and Dad. I thought maybe they'd like that." He knew they would. He was the only son they had left. Evie understood.

"Sure," she said. She stepped out onto the porch and heard the crystals on the lamp shade jingle as the door closed behind her. Larry put his arms around her and Evie lay her head on his chest. She could hear his heart, a tiny *thump, thump, thump.* Larry's good heart. She lifted her face and let him kiss her.

"I have missed you so much," he said. Evie couldn't stop the tears that came into her eyes. But she didn't cry. It had been a rush of love that she felt, a statement she had been trying hard to deny, that she loved this man too much to imagine life without him.

"I've missed you too," she said.

"How about dinner tomorrow night?" Larry asked. "I got a lot of stuff to tell you, such as how I think you should plant flowers and a garden in the backyard."

"I got a few things to tell you, too." She would call Elmer Fisk, over at the bank, first thing in the morning. She and Gail still hadn't decided on a new name for the tavern. They might just let it stay Murphy's. After all, people are creatures of habit. A new name might make everyone nervous, everyone except Andy Southby. But Evie had already decided. Once she and Gail owned the place, a new sign was going up: *No Knuckles Popped On These Premises!*

Evie waited until the Jeep had pulled away from the curb before she went down the steps and out to where the sign stood on her lawn. *Evie Cooper, Spiritual Portraitist.* Beneath the words was that same silhouette of a lone woman standing beneath a guiding star. She used both hands, one on each side of the sign, and quickly pulled it from the earth. There are many ways to stake a claim, ways to put down roots, nurse a dream. She carried the sign back to the front porch and into the house where she leaned it against the parlor wall. She knew Larry thought the faces of the dead came out of her own imagination. He had said so, once, and never mentioned it again. But Evie knew better. She knew the faces come from a long way *beyond* her imagination. They travel from a very great distance. She was certain of this. And being certain of it, maybe it was time to study the faces of the living.

Evie flicked out the porch light and closed the front door. It was just as she turned back into the little parlor, with its potted palms and Boston ferns and incense bowls, that she noticed a movement in the mirror, the one she had put on the wall behind the sofa where her clients always sat. She had put the mirror there when she'd read in a magazine that it was a perfect way to make a tiny room look larger. A mirror would "open it up," the article said, would reflect hanging plants and paintings and lamps as if "another whole room existed." Evie liked that notion. And it must have opened the room up more than she ever dreamed, for there was Henry, standing behind her left shoulder. Of course Henry would appear on the night of his memorial service. As Evie had always said, the subject had to be about *him* or Henry just wasn't interested. *Henry.* He looked younger, more rested than she'd ever known him to be in life. And that was one thing Evie always liked for her clients to know about their loved ones, that heaven seemed to be a place where they could get a good, long rest from the weary blues of earth. Heaven might even be a great big Days Inn, with all the soft beds you could ever ask for, and pillows stuffed with angel feathers. *Henry Munroe!*

Evie reached for her sketch pad and pencil and then, seeing something in Henry's eyes, knew that this was not to be recorded. This was private, between just the two of them, as it had been those steamy nights at the motel. And besides, Henry looked different now. There was something in his eyes as he stared at Evie from his reflection in the mirror. She knew that look well, had seen it many times. But it was only when Henry was sound asleep, his head resting on the pillow, that he was at peace. Being the center of attention is a long, hard job. Evie smiled, for it was good to see Henry again. He leaned forward, in that same way they all do, all the faces of the dead who come to visit Evie Cooper. He leaned forward as if looking into the mirror at his own reflection.

"I don't pretend to have any answers to any big questions about life and death," Evie said aloud. She knew Henry couldn't hear her, and that was fine. She'd been giving this warm-up speech to her clients for a lot of years, and now, for the first time in her life, she was saying the words for her own benefit. "I just believe that when we die we do not cease to exist. I believe we live again. As a matter of fact, I know it, for I have seen the faces of the dead since I've been a very little girl. For some reason, God—or whatever power may be—has seen fit to give me this talent. I do not ask the dead questions. Instead, I study their faces, their eyes, and in this way, they are able to tell me what is still in their hearts."

Henry's heart was talking all right. So were his eyes. If

Evie had wanted to sketch him, it would be her master-piece. It would be the crowning point to a long career, a rare talent that she would never use again. *Can I go now?* the eyes were asking Evie. *Is everybody fine?*

"Sure, Henry," Evie whispered. "Everyone you love is doing just fine."

Evie put her pad back down on the sofa, then lay the pencil on the table, causing the little crystals to jingle again. She would tell no one about this visit, not even Larry. But she knew what it was that had given Henry the strength to do such a remarkable thing, and it is *remarkable* for the dead to come this far, to make this journey. It's love that brings them, a love so pure and fine that even they don't understand its pull. There will never be anything man-made, there will never be a rope, or a net, or a wire cable invented by the best minds that will ever be stronger than love.

And now that Henry Munroe had appeared, now that he had traveled that great distance, it was Evie Cooper's last job to tell him he could *stop* being remarkable. He could go in peace, for the earth would spin on without him. He would exist now only in flashes of memory, just sparks and electricity. His old life was nothing but a field of fireflies. And Henry seemed to understand this, for when Evie looked again he was gone.

About the Author

Author photo by Doug Burns

Cathie Pelletier was born and raised on the banks of the St. John River, at the end of the road in northern Maine. She is the author of eleven other novels, including *The Funeral Makers* (NYTBR Notable Book), *The Weight of Winter* (winner of the New England Book Award), and *Running the Bulls* (winner of the Paterson Prize for Fiction). As K. C. McKinnon, she has written two novels, both of which became television films. After years of living in Nashville, Tennessee; Toronto, Canada; and Eastman, Quebec, she has returned to Allagash, Maine, and the family homestead where she was born.